THE SEVEN

Society for the Eradication of Vampiric ENemies

MATT USEY

For Carrie *

* not a Vampire

TABLE OF CONTENTS

They watched him.

As he drove to work, they watched. As he hocked perfume, they watched. As he went to the bathroom, they didn't watch because that would be disgusting. But when he returned, they watched.

They didn't really know why they watched. Their boss had said, "Watch him!" and so they watched. Did anyone care that they had other work to do? Of course not. If they had been allowed to watch him and then kill him, or maybe just maim his chunky friend, that would have been cool. But no.

They watched him.

CHAPTER 1: LIKE IT OR NOT

Jackson Krol left a swirling scent of women's perfume in his wake as he plodded through a mall with his friend Chester.

"So I take it you're surprised you got fired?" Chester asked.

"Not really. What does surprise me is that the flamethrower actually worked." He ran his hands through his unruly brown hair. His dark eyes were almost the exact same shade, as though God had only one crayon when he colored him.

"A perfume tester bottle and a lighter is not much of a flamethrower."

"Tell that to the old lady. I didn't see her coming. I just hope her eyebrows grow back." He eyed the selection behind the glass at China Chen's Super Wok as they crossed the food court.

A bored employee stirred the Orange Chicken as a fly buzzed above it, trying to escape but bouncing off of the protective glass meant to keep flies and phlegm on the other side. The employee swiped at it with the spoon, trapping it in the sticky orange glaze. He stirred it back into the chicken.

"All hollow point rounds are on sale now in the Ammo Shack, in the kiosk in front of Massive Mike MacCutlery's Mini Muffins," a seductive female voice announced over the overhead PA. *"Half off."*

Chester said, "On the plus side, we can talk about that job again."

"The Vampire one? You were kidding about that part, right?"

"No, not really."

"So no Vampires?"

"No, I mean 'not really kidding.' They do relatively... somewhat like... partially kind of Vampire stuff. Like research. Academic."

"No way."

The mall announcer interrupted again. *"Tired of looking tired? Head to Celebrity Secrets for a tub of Roxy's Stem Cell Facial Rejuvenator. It's 100% pure embryonic, 40 babies in every ounce!"*

"Come on, man," Chester said. "Don't you want to be successful, like me? I'm wearing a vest!" He tugged at the lapels of his cheap gray suit. Like most of his clothes, the suit didn't fit right on his pudgy frame, always appearing twisted or bunched. Unlike Jackson, Chester's build seemed slapdash, created with spare, ill-fitting parts, and any ball tossed in his vicinity would be in little danger of being caught.

"You call yourself successful?"

"At least I can hold down a job for more than a month."

Ouch. "You sound like my dad." He didn't need this. Well, he *did* need a job. Just not with institutionalizables.

"That is low. At least—" Chester stopped in mid-sentence as a young woman with pink and purple hair walked past them. He smiled at her.

"How might you be, my young lass?"

Chester's attempts at sophistication and charm were as unsuccessful as his efforts to resuscitate his British accent after the whipping it had experienced from the barrage of Texan over his years as a British expat. In this case, he shot just wide of "charming" and hit "lecherous" dead center.

The woman spat at Chester's feet as she passed.

Jackson knew that beneath all Chester Bittlestone's clueless lewdness lay an actual decent individual. Like a coconut dropped into a sewage tank — it was probably quite sweet inside, but most people wouldn't notice.

"Listen," Chester said, returning to business. "That lady friend of mine said it was a good company, and that they really needed a graphics guy. Like you. That's what you do, right? I mean what you were *trained* to do. What you *really* do is get fired from crappy jobs."

Ah, friends. "But they have a website about hunting Vampires," Jackson said. "That rates the job pretty high on the 'crappy' meter." He pushed open the outside door, feeling the refreshing blast of Texas heat hit him. The deep cold of the mall had somehow penetrated his pores, making him feel artificial, like a wax statue, or maybe an embalmed corpse.

Chester's eyes shot to one side. "They're just, uhh, a little eccentric, or so I hear." He looked back at Jackson. "It sounds like a place where you could really make your mark."

"No thanks." He appraised the sky. One of the clouds had the copper tinge that sometimes preceded a sudden cloud drop, but he hadn't heard anything about it in the forecast. He'd try to avoid it just in case. He was in no mood for another concussion.

"They're going to call you. I gave her your number."

"What!?"

Chester held up his hands defensively. "Calm down. Just talk to them. They may be weird, but they pay with normal money."

Jackson considered this. He'd known a few artists who didn't exactly roll down the same tracks as the rest of society. And money was money, and his was almost out.

As they crossed the parking lot, Jackson had to raise his voice to be heard over a cop practicing wheelies on his police motorcycle a few aisles away. "So your lady friend just happened to mention — ahh!" He jumped back as a teen girl in her grandma's Lincoln boatmobile narrowly missed them, her concentration focused on the cell phone that she held in both hands just above the steering wheel. Something clicked ominously from under the hood, shifting downward in pitch as the car sped away.

"How did you know that she was coming?" Chester asked. "Your back was turned to her."

"Who?"

"The stupid driver who was texting."

Jackson looked back in the direction of the incident as though the girl was still there. "Err, I don't know. Maybe I just heard her coming."

"Yeah, maybe." Chester sounded skeptical, then brightened. "Listen, the whole thing might be tongue in cheek. Really bad website design too. Come on, it could be fun. You could meet a Goth chick."

"I don't think—"

"Their money is still green."

Jackson imagined what his dad would say about it. "Take the damn job, you idiot," he'd say. "They haven't been exactly banging down your door." Plus he'd top it off with something obscene like, "You turning down a job is like a 16-year-old virgin turning down a hand job from Farrah Fawcett because he prefers brunettes." A lot of his dad's analogies involved sex acts with Farrah Fawcett.

"I need to think about it…" Jackson said.

"Think all you want. They're going to call you anyway."

And that was that.

CHAPTER 2: BAGELS, GARLIC, AND VIOLENCE

"You got fired. That's a big steamin' dump of a surprise," Jackson's dad Victor said. He dropped a packet of Ramen noodles into a pot of cold water and twisted the knob on the stove.

"It works better if you heat the water first," Jackson said, trying to steer the conversation away from its current course.

"Oh!" Victor said, turning around and gesturing with the empty noodle wrapper, dusting the kitchen with dried noodle fragments. "Maybe you could get a job with Frachel freaking Fray. You could be her noodle bitch." He turned back to the kitchen, and Jackson knew that the conversation was over. At least for now.

Jackson had anticipated this exact conversation with the exception of being called a "noodle bitch." He looked at the refrigerator. "What do we have?"

Victor thumped Jackson in the forehead then pointed at the stove. "That's what *I* have. God gave you two lazy ass hands. Use them."

As Jackson pulled open the fridge, his cell phone rang. Nervousness seized him as he remembered his conversation with Chester. *Don't sound stupid.*

"New job," he said to his dad, pointing at the phone.

"Hello, this is Jackson." Absentmindedly rubbing his forehead, he walked into his bedroom and closed the door, not wanting any (off) color commentary from his dad.

"Jackson Krol?" said a man's voice. He sounded older than him, perhaps in his 50s.

"Yes." Then he quickly added, "Sir. Yessir, this is Jackson."

"I'm Talbot. So I hear you're a graphics designer." His distant drawl sounded West Texan.

Jackson nodded. "Yes. Yes sir. Graphics design." He sat at his small desk and immediately stood back up. "I'm a graphics designer."

"I got a website devoted to one of my passions, and we need us a new designer. Are ya any good?"

"Awesome. I amaze myself all the time." Jackson laughed.

Talbot did not. "So I'll want to check out yer portfolio, but I want to also ask you a few questions first."

"Sure. Shoot." That word was appropriate because he felt like he was looking down a barrel. Here it comes.

"What are some of your design principles? I mean, what do you like to see in a design?"

"Clean function. Simplicity. An elegant design works well but is also attractive." He believed it, but it still sounded like BS when it came out of his mouth.

"Hmm. What are your weaknesses?"

"I'm gassier than most people, probably because I love pinto beans so much. Oh! And I also tend to make jokes at inappropriate times."

I am an idiot who can't carry on an adult conversation. How's that for a weakness?

"Yeah, I think I got that one."

Silence. Jackson wanted to fill the awful void but figured anything he said would make it worse. Just as the silence reached peak awkwardness, Talbot continued, asking him several other design-related and employment type questions, though he skipped the "if you were a flower, what type would you be?" After the rough start, Jackson felt like he was doing a decent job knocking the ball back over the net, though some of his responses dragged on for too long.

"So," Talbot said, "how do you feel about garlic?"

"Err, like do I like eating it?"

"It's an open question."

Jackson tried to figure out how this could apply to the position. "Garlic is good. It tastes good. It smells bad on my breath." He then added, "That's why I don't eat it much." Remembering the Vampire conversation with Chester, he also added, "But I'm not afraid of it or anything."

"Why would you be afraid of it?"

"Like, you know…" Maybe Chester had been pulling his leg. "Like maybe someone might throw it at you." *Please let it drop.*

"Why would they do that?"

"You know. Like if they were mad and that's all they had lying around."

"That has happened to you before?"

"Oh, no! Never. Though someone once threw…" He shouldn't have started that sentence. His mouth had just grabbed it from the brain without giving it a chance to proofread it first. But he had to finish. "… a cream cheese bagel at me. It was a girl. You know." He paused. "It stuck to the glass window."

Talbot said, "Okay," with a heavy emphasis on the "o."

"How about danger?" Talbot asked. "How do you deal with dangerous situations?"

Jackson was too relieved that the conversation hadn't abruptly ended with his previous answer to focus on the implications of that question. He knew that he should probably respond in "interviewee mode" by describing how he faced issues head-first, adding little anecdotes describing his awesome performance. But his brain was on auto-pilot.

"I typically avoid them."

"Me too."

Jackson laughed.

Talbot once again did not. "Are you against drawing scenes of violence?"

"Not at all. In fact I enjoy…" Again, the brain veering off the road toward the cliff. "… drawing challenging scenes. And violent scenes probably include people with strong emotions, and I'm an expressive artist."

"Can you keep a secret?"

"Of course. Zip, zip, no words. Key over there." He paused. "This is me not blabbing." He listened, waiting for the secret that inevitably follows that question.

It never came. "Okay, Mr. Krol. We'll be in touch."

Click.

CHAPTER 3: VAMPIRES VS. MONEY

A couple of days after the call, Jackson received a terse text message saying he had been approved for an in-person interview and cleared for entry into the Tovac Zone.

Oh no.

Situated outside of the city, the Tovac Zone was one of the most notorious Free Reign zones (or "evolutionary open market municipalities," according to those who promoted the zones but rarely lived there). Ergo no police. Keep the pedal firmly planted. Leave the safety off and a round chambered. Roll 'em up.

He had no desire to even pass through a Free Reign zone, but on the day of his appointment, he found himself standing before their office building wondering why he had come. After pushing through a bashed metal door, he realized that the office was consistent with the insane mentality of the people he was here to meet. The conversion from an old factory complex to an office campus seemed to have started and ended with dragging desks into one of the factory buildings, scattering them amongst massive monstrosities of metal rising from the floor. It would have made an awesome loft apartment had its location not been smack dab in the middle of a region known for daily mayhem and terror. Just a tiny downside.

The factory interior had bare brick walls, a two-story ceiling, and hardwood floors that looked "hand-scraped," though the scrapes were likely accidental, and likely caused by big-ass pieces of machinery getting dragged around. Those Industrial Revolution guys really knew how to jazz up flooring with some old-fashioned distressing. He smelled oil mostly, with an undertone of old wood. Overall, the place smelled like work, real work — not the tip-tapping of fingers on keyboards that was occurring now; rather, sweaty men climbing on hulking beasts of metal and steam, monsters with gears for mouths that could pull a man to his death one cog at a time. The smell of the place breathed life into the ghosts of the building.

Currently, only about half of the area was used as office space, a lit island of cubicle walls and wires in the center of a vast space populated by the retired metal machinery, now silent but no less imposing. They stood like soldiers in the room, towering over the office workers who flitted from cubicle to cubicle, like rats running under a protective canopy of trees. On all sides of the space, windows looked out onto the razor-wire encircled "green zone" that enclosed the office staff's cars and a few paid grunts with itchy trigger fingers. He shuddered to think what it must be like around the place at night.

The acoustics were odd in the open space. He heard sporadic mumbling from all around him as soon as he had entered, even though he wasn't near the cubicles. It reminded him of the otherworldly murmuring sounds that came from the vents in his house when the heater was on.

When they frisked him, the guards found the small wooden level he always kept on his person and, after subjecting him to a thorough eyeballing, returned it. He breathed a sigh of relief when they gave it back. They then led him to a small office off the back of the main room, and he sat in front of a wooden desk with amazing clawed feet, waiting for Talbot. The tan walls were bare except for a framed portrait of an ornate crest behind the desk. In some ways it was a typical crest, shaped like a shield and adorned with leaves that were probably symbolic of something like peace or integrity or itchy rashes, perhaps. The rest was more in the atypical camp, however. For one, all of the figures were stick figures. Second, these stick figures were apparently denizens of a land of horrible violence.

Two squatted like gargoyles on ledges on the outer edges, watching the carnage on the rest of the crest. These two had slanted slits for eyes as their only facial feature. The others each had a single line for a mouth and two long triangular teeth extending below it — obviously these were the Vampires. A Vampire on the lower right was being dragged out of the crest by a huge hook firmly engaged in one of his ears, while one on the lower left was in a similarly dire situation, with a short spear extended from his stomach out his back, the spear containing a barb at the end and a metal chain attached at the base of the hilt. A vertical spear in the dead center of the crest impaled three Vampires, each angled in different directions and in various degrees of agony, insomuch as a stick figure can display pain.

He had never seen such violence inflicted on stick people. It didn't seem right somehow. It was like a picture drawn by a child who had taken the life aptitude test at school, and whose counselor had delivered the news that he was most suited to a life of serial killing, or perhaps politics.

He turned his attention back to the desk which was covered with disorganized stacks of papers. He knew that someone could be watching him, but he couldn't help it. He pulled out his level and placed it on the edge of the desk, sliding a few pages back in the process. Perfectly level. In order to forestall an urge to shove the papers onto the floor and check the levelness on other parts of the desk, as well as to distract himself from his creeping nervousness, he dropped to his hands and knees to examine the woodwork of the desk's feet. Just as he got down, a pair of shiny black shoes walked up and stopped beside him. A slight man with crisply parted black hair and a black mustache, both oiled, stood beside the desk, staring as though Jackson had just rolled in something dead. In his charcoal suit and white gloves, he looked like a butler.

"Please stand," he said.

Jackson did so, asking, "Are you Talbot?" He didn't sound like Talbot; this guy sounded like he looked, not like a country boy.

"Don't move," the man said, removing one of his white gloves. A buzz-cut Hispanic guard toting a machine gun drifted in, not exactly doing his best to appear inconspicuous. Mustache Man pointed his ungloved index finger at Jackson's face, then moved it forward until it touched his forehead.

Jackson crossed his eyes to look at it, then refocused on the man's face. He appeared to be concentrating.

"What—?" Jackson started.

Mustache Man said, "Quiet!" and the guard flinched, his gun coming up.

"Okay. We're clear," Mustache Man said. He pulled his finger away, threw the removed glove into a trashcan, then sprayed his exposed hand with a small bottle, rubbing it in with a tissue. As he turned and walked away, he pulled on a new glove, saying over his shoulder, "Talbot will be here shortly."

Jackson had expected weird, but these guys really knew how to kick things up.

The guard's excited face drooped into boredom as he lowered the gun barrel.

Jackson started to ask a question, but as he opened his mouth and sucked in a breath to speak, the gun barrel quivered again. For a brief insane moment, he considered making another sound to see if the barrel would pop up again. That might be fun until he got shot in the face. He sat in the chair, his back to the guard. He wanted to get the hell out of there, but it seemed like the safest bet was to slog through the interview, then proceed with the hell-getting.

The perfume counter hadn't been so bad after all, he decided.

"I am Talbot," a voice exploded behind him. Jackson was airborne by mid-sentence, too startled to cry out. The man had crept up behind him and smacked him with a sonic bitch slap.

"Hi!" Jackson screamed just as he landed back on his seat. He stood and turned in time to offer his hand to Talbot's back as the man moved around his desk.

After he got to the other side of his desk, Talbot shook Jackson's hand. Firm grip, thick rough hand, like a farmer's. The man was, in a word, intense. On the phone, he'd sounded a bit like a bumpkin. In person though, he looked like a military man, with short gray hair, round glasses that made Jackson think of Germans, and gray eyes that seemed capable of disemboweling a man.

Look him in the eye, Jackson told himself. To look confident at an interview, you had to do that. Shake hard and hold a stare.

The gray eyes drilled him.

Jackson decided it would be rude to stare. "Nice to meet you," he said, passing his eyes over the trim man's white pressed shirt and gray slacks. His gaze snagged on the holstered pistol under Talbot's right arm, and his eyes bounced back up.

"You too," the man said, though his razor-edged eyes continued to say, "I'm going to tear one of your limbs off." He gestured to Jackson's chair. "Please sit."

Jackson threw his portfolio onto Talbot's desk as he sat. The stack of paper on which it landed shifted. "Portfolio," he said. He wanted to say more but couldn't.

Talbot stared at him a moment longer as he reached out and pulled the bound portfolio across the desk to him, the hiss of the sliding papers the only sound in the room.

Jackson took in a slow breath and let it out. He could do this.

Talbot's head twitched in a movement that could have been interpreted as a slight nod, and then he turned his attention to the portfolio, flipping through it in silence. At one point he looked up, and Jackson leaned forward to respond to whatever Talbot was about to say. But the older man just stared at him for a bit, then returned to the portfolio.

"Vampires, what do you think about them?" he asked after reaching the last page.

"Uh, I think anything that wants to rip my neck out should have a stake driven through its heart."

Talbot nodded. "Good answer. That's what we do here, but that doesn't leave this office, you understand? As far as anyone else is concerned, we are the Suttle Group, a boring internet firm which needs rough concept art for our private unspecified clients. Got it?"

"Got it." That was the only possible response. Jackson wondered about Talbot's "that's what we do here." Did he mean "general study-type stuff involving the supernatural" or did he mean "jam sticks of wood into Vampires"?

Talbot grabbed a shiny black pen off of his desk and wrote something on the front page of the portfolio, then slid it to Jackson.

"That is your salary," he said. "You start tomorrow."

Jackson forgot his nervousness and looked at the number. It was higher than his perfume gig. "Monthly?" he asked, just to be sure he was understanding the number right.

"Weekly," Talbot said. "Unless you want it monthly."

Jackson felt his mouth pop open, and he quickly shut it. Then he reopened it. "Weekly is good." He had an urge to gush about what a great job he would do and how excited he was, but he checked himself, knowing that he could only screw things up at this point. This was not a high-five moment, though it certainly felt like it. "See you tomorrow," he said.

Talbot nodded once to Jackson and again at the guard.

Jackson hopped up and offered his hand.

Talbot took it without standing. "Don't let me down," he said.

"No," Jackson said with conviction. "I won't." And this time, he meant it.

He wasn't sure which was the stronger motivation: the salary or the fear.

CHAPTER 4: REALLY GOOD OR REALLY BAD

Simpson re-entered Talbot's office and waited just inside the door, interlocking his white gloved fingers.

"Whatcha think?" Talbot asked.

"The same, or perhaps even more so."

"Hmm. There's something about that kid, that's for sure." They were both wary of him, even though one of their trusted civilian consultants had discovered him. They both found it odd that she found an apparent "Latent" with graphics arts skills – and good ones at that – at the exact time that they happened to need a graphics artist. On top of this, his bloodline came through his mother, a person who had been missing since the kid was just an infant. So they couldn't check her out. His father was nobody. Despite all these warning signs, Talbot liked the kid for some reason, and his gut was usually right. "Why more suspicious?"

"His aura is off." Simpson paced, his voice pained.

"'Off' strange or 'off' none?"

"'Off' none. Blank." Simpson made a move like a sophisticated umpire calling "safe" at home plate, though Talbot doubted that Simpson had ever watched a baseball game. "I am not sure if it is I or this individual. But definitely not right."

Talbot nodded. "Hmm. I've got a feeling about this one." That feeling could mean something really good or something really bad. "Watch him. Close."

Simpson eased his head forward in a half nod – half bow, his mouth twitching almost imperceptibly. A smile.

CHAPTER 5: A VISION IN BLACK

The next day, a minor earth-cloud inversion storm wound down outside the warehouse windows, the black rain slowly clearing.

"What happened to the last guy?" Jackson asked, popping his head over the five-foot-high cubicle wall that separated him from Archer, an accountant. Archer was trying and failing at a comb-over, his gray hair long enough but too sparse. His gaunt face seemed to have been flash-frozen at a moment of extreme despondency.

Archer flinched so hard that he dropped his pen. "Don't do that!" he yelled, looking at Jackson over the top of his now-crooked glasses. "Don't pop your head up over the wall. Walk around." He pointed at the opening to his cubicle with one hand and did finger walking with his other hand.

Chastised, Jackson slid his head down and, still crouched, shuffled around a rusty metal gear that rose four feet from the floor at the edge of his cubicle, then around to the opening of Archer's.

"Don't forget to knock," Archer said.

Jackson knocked on the cube wall, creating approximately zero sound.

"Can I help you?" Archer asked.

Jackson blinked. "What happened to the last guy who did the graphics?"

"He, uh, had to go away."

"Huh? You mean, like he got fired?"

"Yeah, fired. Something like that. Oh, that reminds me, don't post your home address online."

Jackson wished he'd never started this conversation. He was struggling to convince himself that this job would work out. For that salary, he could overlook a lot. Plus if he bailed, his dad would ride him even worse than usual, if that were even possible. Jackson could tell his dad was proud of him by the way he had said, "Don't 'F' this up" that morning. He didn't — *couldn't* — tell his dad about the kind of work The Seven did. Who would believe him? He didn't want to let him down, but dang, this was a freaky place.

"Don't post my address online?" Jackson asked. "Why is that bad?"

Archer cut his eyes to the side like someone was watching. "Oh, no reason. Accidents happen." He picked his pen up off the floor and returned to his notebook, turning his back.

Jackson was about to press him further when he saw the machine-gun toting guard walk down the aisle that ran beside his cubicle. Jackson retreated back to his desk. As he sat to review the new employee paperwork, a voice behind him said, "So you're the new guy?"

He turned around. A tall man of about 35 leaned against the edge of his cubicle, mug in hand, smug on face. His light brown wavy hair fell over his ears, smugly.

"Yeah. I'm Jackson." He stood, intending to offer his hand, but something held him back.

The guy just nodded and took a sip of his coffee. "They probably told you about me. I'm Gary." He waited.

Jackson sat back down.

Gary continued, "I'm one of the project managers around here." He cut his eyes back toward Archer's cube and then added in a low voice, "The main one, really." He nodded, took another sip of his coffee, and raised his eyebrows.

"No, you're not the main one," Archer said from the other side of the cubicle.

"Shut up, Archie," Gary said, anger making a dash across his face before smug chased it down and swallowed it.

Though Jackson really wanted this guy to just go away, his fist felt an immediate and unexpected attraction toward the man's face.

"So," Jackson started, "you –"

"It'll take you a while to learn the ropes here," Gary interrupted. "Just do your job and keep your head down and you'll be okay. Probably."

"Keep my head down?"

Gary nodded and pointed at him with the index finger of the hand holding his coffee mug, then spun away without responding.

Jackson stared at the empty space that Gary had just vacated. The first few weeks of a new job is the worst part, he told himself. Things will get better. Assuming of course he could get past the first few weeks.

As he stared out of his cubicle, a short creature of a man darted past, mumbling to himself something about "alternating current" and "partially hydrogenated byproducts." The man's incoherent speech faded.

Jackson realized with a start that, for the first time in his life, he might be the most normal guy on the job. His dad would be so proud.

He returned to the stack of employee paperwork on his mostly level desk — it was fine left to right but it slanted a bit toward the back in the center. His eye caught on a form that basically said, "If anything bad, even something really freaking horrible, happens to you, you can't sue. Even if you're dead. And don't tell anyone about anything, or perhaps something really freaking horrible will happen to you on purpose." It went into disturbing detail about all the possible ways he might die, including getting run over by a train, getting hit by a thrown pipe, and catching a bullet in the head, execution-style.

That last one did it. He stood and headed for the door. His dad could jump on his balls with spiked cleats for all he cared; he had to get out of there.

Then he saw her. Glossy black hair, straight, long, almost iridescent. This and her pale skin screamed Goth, but she had no black lipstick, no black fingernails, and no chunks of metal in her face. So maybe just a lazy Goth.

Just before she walked past him, her downcast eyes flicked up to his face. They were as dark as her hair, so black that he couldn't see her pupils. When those eyes locked into his, he felt like someone kicked him in the chest. She hesitated, her expression wary, then dropped her gaze and continued around the corner. One strip of hair on the back right of her head was pure white from root to tip. He watched her drop out of view in a cubicle on the other side of the room.

"Hi," he said to no one in particular.

Maybe he could give this job another few days.

CHAPTER 6: GARGOYLES AND GOOD GOALS

The next morning, Jackson walked into a small break room behind a copse of peeling black and rust-colored pipes that ran from the floor to ceiling near the back of the office. He staggered back in surprise. A man with cropped red prematurely receding hair was sitting on his haunches on the counter next to the sink — just sitting there staring out like a buzz-cut gargoyle on the corner of a building. The guy was approximately the width of a side by side refrigerator-freezer combo — one of the good ones, not those little cheap jack ones that you found at Wally's Appliance Emporium. His limbs were as thick as rolled up sleeping bags.

"What? Whoa. Hey," Jackson said, struggling to regain his mental and physical balance. He tried to say something unrelated to the pink striped eight-legged elephant in the room. "Weather," was all he could get out.

The guy didn't respond, just staring out. Maybe this was a hidden camera comedy show or something.

Jackson followed the man's stare to the opposite wall. Nothing there. He didn't want to just stand in the doorway in shock, and he refused to retreat despite the thick stench of lunacy in the room, so he instead walked over to the coffee pot. He had no cup. They had told him where the coffee mugs were. Ah yes, of course, in the cabinet next to the hypnotized psychopathic linebacker taking an imaginary dump on the counter.

When Jackson shot past him and opened the cabinet, he felt his skin nearest the man cramping, trying to squeeze all the pores shut lest something drift in uninvited. At the same time, he had a strong urge to climb up on the counter next to the guy and to mimic his pose so he could watch the reaction of the next person to enter the room. Then again, the size of the lump of muscle on the counter and the size of the number that Talbot wrote on his portfolio put the "almost" into that almost uncontrollable urge.

"I'm Jackson," he said, his head hidden behind the open cabinet door. He grabbed the first mug he saw; it said, "Bite Me!" in red dripping letters. The man neither talked nor moved as Jackson returned to the coffee pot. He yanked the pot out, causing the machine to hiss and steam. A stream of coffee poured out of the machine, passing through the space formerly occupied by the pot in Jackson's hand, and splattered into the hot metal plate.

Jackson slammed the pot back into the machine and feigned intense interest in a Girl Sprouts cookie pamphlet on the counter as the spilled coffee between the pot and hot plate crackled in the heat. The smell of burnt coffee wafted past.

"Hi, my name is Susie," the flyer said. "My dad is a big shot at the office, and I'm selling Girl Sprout cookies. I'm very cute and pitiful. Please buy these energy-rich cookies. Their artificial flavors and colors and preservatives ensure that they will arrive in a fresh condition, as nasty bacteria could never grow in such a hostile environment. Girl Sprouts have taught me valuable life lessons, such as how to sell cookies. If you don't buy these cookies, you probably don't like children and people will think you are a horrible person. Buy some cookies! Sincerely, (insert your name here)"

A glossy picture of a cute girl was taped at the bottom of the flyer, though whoever had attached it had failed to cut out all of the advertising text at the photo's edge. It said, "Sale on—" at the top right and, "Limited ti—" at the bottom right.

The coffee maker was almost finished, at the final dripping stage. He pulled the pot out, poured his coffee, and slid the pot back in with a clank.

"Huh?" the man on the counter said.

"Oh!" Jackson said, coming very close to spilling his coffee. "Jackson," he said. "That's my name."

The man said something that might have been Buck or maybe Bill, but Jackson didn't want to ask for clarification. Jackson headed out but stopped at the doorway.

"Uh, do you know the woman with the straight black hair who's about 30? I can't remember her name." He had actually never heard her name.

"You mean Sy?" Buck-Bill said.

"Yeah, I guess." He rolled the name around in his head and decided that he liked it.

Out in the main office room, a woman burst out laughing.

"That's not her, is it?" Jackson asked, trying to picture the calm Goth Sy laughing so hard.

"Who?" Buck-Bill asked.

"Sy."

"No, that sounds like Mandy. You'll get used to Mandy. Sometimes I'm not used to Mandy and I want to jam clay into her mouth but I don't ever do that. What do you need with her?"

"Mandy?"

"No, Sy. What do you want with Sy?" Buck-Bill slid off the counter onto his feet, menacingly. Well, it might not have been intentionally menacing, but when a massively built gargoyle drops from his perch and approaches, menace kind of tags along for the ride.

Jackson's head filled with an image of Buck-Bill and Sy in an intimate embrace while Jackson lay alongside, unconscious with a Buck-Bill fist-shaped imprint on his face.

"Uh, nothing. Just wondering if she handled, you know, payroll."

Buck-Bill looked at him blankly.

"Or something," Jackson continued.

Buck-Bill's eyes popped into focus, as though he just noticed him. He hadn't been staring him down, but rather just in a daze.

"Huh?" Buck-Bill said.

"Oh, nothing," Jackson said, backing out. "See you later." He would just sit at his desk and keep his head down. Don't get fired; don't get killed; talk to Sy. Those goals weren't exactly in order of importance, but they'd do for now.

CHAPTER 7: A MOTHER'S HAND

Sylvia Goji (Sy) waded through the flowing stream of shoppers at the mall, somehow always against the current. They all seemed to move in private bubbles, isolated from the throngs surging through the mall like white blood cells prowling for something to attack.

Earlier, Sy had sat alone on a mall bench, unnoticed, unnoticeable, figuratively encased in a sort of social camouflage. She watched and wondered about the passing people – where they were going, why they were there, who loved them. She searched for someone to pique her interest, someone she could study. After a time, a mother and her two daughters had walked by, the harried woman dragging a girl of around five by the hand while lecturing her other daughter of perhaps ten, the latter weaving annoyance into her look of boredom while crossing her arms in an obvious indication that hand-holding was out of the question.

Sy had chosen them.

There was nothing creepy about her following them — no more unusual than tagging a penguin's ankle and then tracking its progress across the ocean using a laptop with GPS software. Sy was just like a curious scientist, a detached observer, separate.

The mother took the girls into a department store, and the older child perked up. Even at her tender age, clothes seemed to hold power over her. Her excitement deflated as the mother passed the young adult section and headed into the men's.

Sy turned into the adjacent women's section and pretended to look at a blouse that she would never wear, even to a costume party. It was a poofy off-the-shoulder glittery sparkly number, so bright that it seemed battery-powered.

The mother released her younger daughter's hand and rifled through spiked leather belts. That daughter promptly dove into a freestanding rack of men's shirts, disappearing except for her tiny legs and pink shoes. The older daughter sat on the floor in disgust.

"That would look lovely on you," said a clerk at Sy's side. The middle-aged woman sounded pleasant and seemed to be making a valiant effort to appear that way too. Her nose was wrinkled as though detecting something repugnant, and she wore a misaligned smile that looked foreign on her face, like she got it at a yard sale. Sy could see the muscles quivering. She smelled of artificial flowers, or rather the scent was an artificially fabricated one intended to mimic a flower — not the scent of artificial flowers, which typically smell somewhere between dust and plastic. The odor matched the smile.

"No thanks." *Please go away.*

"But it would look lovely," the saleslady repeated, her smile failing.

"No thank you."

In the men's section, the mother now held up two belts, comparing them. The older daughter, apparently trying to express her displeasure in a more obvious fashion, rolled back from her sitting position and lay spread eagle on the floor. Half of her body extended into the aisle, and shoppers veered around her.

"Lovely," the saleslady said in a hoarse whisper to Sy, her face veering toward a more natural expression of revulsion and anger. "Lovely!"

"I can't afford it."

That did it. The woman's shoulders dropped along with her face, as though a string connected them. She stomped off, mumbling something that included the phrase, "total waste of my time."

A scream rang out. The older daughter was sitting upright and cradling her hand, her pained face flushed. With tears in her eyes, she glared at a laughing young man walking away. He must have stepped on her hand. The mother kneeled to console her, her face flipping between concern for her daughter and fury at the young punk.

Sy watched the young man walk toward her. Something burned inside her.

"Psst!" she said to him. She bent her face into a smile.

Still grinning broadly, he ogled her before approaching. She leaned toward his ear as though to whisper something. He also leaned in, turning his head to hear what she was going to say. Instead of an erotic whisper, he possibly heard the dull smack of Sy's karate chop to the side of a neck just a few inches down from his ear, though he definitely did not hear his body hit the floor with a thud between the racks of women's clothes.

A moment later, the man's body made another thud. The saleslady, now smoking a cigarette in her red lips, pulled her foot back from the unconscious man's ribs. "Now that felt good," she said. "Thanks for teeing him up for me, sister." She winked at Sy, tapped the ashes off her cigarette above the man's face, then walked off, throwing her head back as she took a deep drag, blowing the smoke toward the high ceiling. She must have been smoking one of the new "black tar" cigarettes because the column of black smoke looked like it could have come out of a coal train's chimney.

Sy moved away from the unconscious man at her feet to another vantage point to watch the woman and her daughters. The older girl, now standing, buried her face into her mother. The mother stroked her gently while the younger daughter hugged her big sister from the side. The woman whispered to both girls, and they nodded. Sy wished she could hear what was said. They walked past her out of the store, the older daughter still sniffling and leaning into her mother.

Sy didn't want to be in the mall anymore. She didn't want to be around people anymore. She left the store and drove home, lost in her thoughts, thinking about a girl's delicate fingers encased in the warm and protective grip of her mother's hand.

CHAPTER 8: FIRST BLOOD

A week passed before Jackson saw blood at the office.

As directed by head-poking mustache man Simpson, Jackson had started the day sketching up images for the website at his desk. No one had specified who was his immediate supervisor, though Simpson directed his assignments for the most part. Talbot occasionally materialized behind him in order to scare the crap out and then back inside him. On top of that, Gary seemed to feel he needed to monitor his progress and micromanage him though he probably had no idea what Jackson was supposed to be doing.

"Simpson shifted my priorities," Jackson lied, enacting his plan to get Gary out of his hair by jacking with him. "He said that Talbot's boss wanted me to work on a secret project."

"Talbot's boss? Wait. Secret project? I didn't hear about a secret project," Gary said, a pained look passing over his face. After a moment of silent pouting and deep thinking, he seemed to recover. "Well, I've heard about several of them, but I'm not sure which one they want you to do."

"I see," Jackson said, returning to his latest sketch. He didn't bother to put the pen to paper yet.

"But," Gary started, then faltered. "So tell me which one you're working on." He stepped into Jackson' cubicle and crouched.

Jackson covered his work by flipping the top page over on the others. "Oh, no," he said, "I'm not authorized to share that information with anyone who's not authorized." A mental image of Gary repeatedly popping his head over Jackson's cubicle or shoulder slid through his mind, and he wondered if he might have just shifted the problem from micromanaging interruptions to "trying to sneak a peek" interruptions. "And I have to report any intelligence violations to Simpson immediately, so I hope you didn't see anything. You didn't see anything, did you?"

Gary straightened and put his hands up in a defensive position. "No, no, I didn't see anything."

"It looked to me like maybe you caught a glimpse. Maybe I should just call Simpson over here just in case." He stood and looked over his cubicle wall as though searching for Simpson.

"Ah, no! Don't do that!" Gary said over his shoulder as he bolted around the corner heading for the safety of his own cubicle. "I didn't see anything!" He was moving away so fast that the sentence almost doppler-shifted.

Jackson sat and turned the top page back over. At the top of the blank page, he wrote, "Secret Project." He scribbled out some quick notes about using trained owls to stab Vampires with needles dipped in sleeping poison developed by Transylvanian-educated Indian medicine men. He also wrote this: "Per Simpson's orders, collect data on potential bio-agent by adding three drops of mind-altering hypno-juice to Gary's coffee each day. Report the resultant behavior and any subsequent mortality." He slid the paper to the edge of his desk nearest the cubicle doorway.

Back to it.

For his professional work, he liked to work with pen and paper first, then redraw them on-screen using a pen-tablet system. All of his work at the moment focused on creating coarse images of Vampires attacking humans. Hoping to get further inspiration (and to take a break), he clicked around the company's current website again, avoiding the "professional but ridiculous" sections that made up the majority of the site and instead focusing on the "purely ridiculous" sections, such as the blogs and forums. A new short article had been posted on the "Blogs by the Big Man" page. It described how Vampires hypnotized people into thinking that they were handsome, when really they were quite ugly, stupid, and poorly endowed. In the Q and A section called, "What's up wit dat?", the Big Man of blogger fame answered questions submitted via email.

The latest question said, "I think I have a Vampire living in the crawl space under my house. What can I do? Sincerely, Scared-Because-A-Vampire-Lives-In-The-Crawl-Space-Under-My-House, Cleveland, OH."

The reply: "Dear Wussy Pants, Vampires don't live under houses, unless it's a Vampire raccoon. Animals typically don't get vampirism, in fact never, unless of course a Vampire mates with a raccoon and passes on its bestial seed. I wouldn't put that past them. Therefore, I would recommend getting the family out of the house, then burning the house down to the ground. That's the only way to be safe. Have a great day. Sincerely, Big Man"

He clicked into the forums, hoping that there would be a few more interesting posts since the last time he looked. One thread that got a lot of traffic was "Vampire anal probing." He couldn't bring himself to venture into that thread, though he was curious to know which group was the prober and which the probee. Another hot thread covered Vampire sightings. A few of the members must have had perfectly tuned Vampire-finding eyes, lived in popular Vampire breeding grounds, and had horrible-tasting blood because this small group of three or four made up for about 80% or more of all the postings. The Breaux's Best Bingo Parlor in Port Neches, Texas, was apparently a hot bed, according to one Ingrid Aschoff.

He thought about the people that he'd met at the company. As hard as he looked, he never saw a single tongue in a single cheek, so he was forced to conclude that these people believed this crap. Where they got their money, he had no idea. Maybe a rich paranoid delusional funded the operation.

He grabbed his "Bite Me" mug and headed toward the small break area. After two steps, he froze because he saw Gary telling Mandy a story. The young woman in her mid-twenties — whom Jackson had named "The Blue Streaked Jumper" because of the blue highlights in her dirty blond hair and her habit of jumping into the air and stomping both of her feet when laughing — was bouncing on the balls of her feet, causing the single pigtail on the right side of her head to flap like a wing. When she spoke, Gary's face contorted, obviously upset that someone would involuntarily dare to convert his monologue into a dialogue.

Jackson backed into his cubicle, not wanting to get ensnared by the conversation. He reviewed his latest sketch. While he admired the way his drawn "defender" was defensively ramming a spear into the eye socket of an attacking Vampire, a commotion exploded outside his cubicle. He looked over his short wall. A red light strobed the room. Away from the isolated oasis of cubicles in the center of the warehouse, a door on the back wall had been flung open. A tall thin man in a black hat and a floor-length black overcoat ran into the room carrying another man in his arms. The other man's long blond hair was matted in blood, the blood dripping from his limp head onto the scarred wood floor. Another black-clad bald man followed, hovering over the unconscious (or dead?) man in the tall man's arms. Several guards were close behind, their faces set and their weapons at the ready.

Big red-headed Buck-Bill ran from the cubicles toward the group. He held a vicious spear in his hand, one eerily familiar. Talbot had shown Jackson a picture of just such a spear, and Jackson had recently finished drawing it half-embedded in a Vampire skull. So they were real. But where the heck had Buck-Bill kept it in his cubicle? Why was he running over there with it? And why hadn't they given Jackson one? Maybe you got one after a year of service.

Buck-Bill conferred a moment with one of the guards at the door and then ran out. Further down the wall, Talbot's door opened and the procession ran inside. The white-gloved Mustache Man Simpson jumped out of the door and glared at Jackson.

"Down!" Simpson yelled.

Jackson pointed at himself and raised his eyebrows.

"Yes, you!" Simpson screamed. "Sit back down!"

Jackson eased down and then popped his head back up, unable to follow the order without at least a cursory salvo of feigned ignorance. "You were looking at me, right?" Before Simpson could unleash vicious butler fury on him, Jackson's self-preservation circuit kicked in and slackened his leg muscles, lowering him like a hydraulic jack back into his seat. He turned, planning to ask Archer through the cubicle wall what the heck was going on.

Sy crouched at his doorway, keeping her head lower than the top of the cubicle. Her eyes were fixed on his.

"Oh!" he said. His mind screeched around a corner, lost a hubcap, and crashed into a concrete barrier, ejecting its contents through the windshield. "I mean, oh! It's you."

"No, not really," she said, her voice a smooth drawl, either East Texan or just relaxed. Probably both. She dropped her gaze.

"Oh," was all he could muster, not really sure how to take that. This was their first official conversation, and there was nothing swimming about it.

"I'm not here on purpose." She glanced over her shoulder, then turned back to him, her eyes down. "I didn't want Simpson to yell at me." The red flashing light illuminated the half of her pale face that wasn't covered by her hanging black hair. She was not beautiful in a classic sense, but striking nonetheless. He guessed that perhaps she had an Asian grandparent or great grandparent. The dark hair and pale skin... he wasn't really sure what made her seem so alluring.

Her dark eyes met his and darted away. She turned, about to leave.

"Yeah," Jackson said, grasping for a coherent thought. "I was too slow. Simpson yelled at me."

She faced him and flicked her eyes up again. "He does that." Again she turned.

"Wait!" he said in a panic. "I mean, what was that all about?"

She just shook her head and then crept out. On the way, she did something strange, like a little dance move, but not quite. She stepped out, stepped back in, and stepped back out again. Then she was gone.

CHAPTER 9: GRAB THE CABOOSE

"Like, did that mean, 'I don't know' or 'Don't ask'?" Jackson's friend Chester asked. He put down his game controller after pausing the game. They were sitting on Chester's couch playing School Rampage on his Z-Box console. Onscreen, a grenade froze inches above a table full of academically-gifted students enjoying their lunch pizza.

"I don't know," Jackson replied. "I mean, I don't know what it meant, not that that's what she meant, you know?"

Chester picked up a plate from the coffee table and took a bite of his hamburger. A mushroom slid out the back and plopped onto the edge of his plate. He nodded and gestured as though about to speak but instead chewed for another 30 seconds while Jackson waited for the response.

"Are you kidding me?" Jackson said.

"Nice work on the job. I think the dog poop gig was a better choice."

"Why does this always happen to me?" Jackson gestured with a French fry. "I just want a regular job. No punk teenage managers, no mall, and no blood! I mean, if you bleed on the job, you're probably in the wrong job. You should only bleed if you're having fun."

Chester considered this. "I'd say not even then. So, before we get into what to do about this, you need to tell me more about the girl you mentioned. Is she smokin'?"

Jackson nodded. "Black dress. Narrow delicate face. Moved like a dancer." At least that's how she moved in his mind. He didn't actually remember anything remarkable about her walk, though it was possible she was a dancer, so technically it wasn't a lie. "Mysterious."

Jackson regretted telling him about her. Who knew what degradations his friend now mentally inflicted on her in his twisted mind? Best not to know.

"How old?" Chester asked.

"Our age. Maybe a bit older. Early 30s."

"Single?"

"I think so." That was wishful thinking because he had no idea. After the blood and siren and "get your head down Jackson!" incident, he had tried to walk over to her end of the cubicle farm, though one of the guards had stopped him, asking him where he was going. He had said, "To hell if I don't change my ways." The guard had remained as stationary and jovial as a telephone pole, and Jackson returned to his desk.

"You need to do a little reconnaissance," Chester said. "Figure out what's going on."

"With Sy?"

"No." Chester paused before continuing, apparently concentrating on something. "Well, I suppose you could reconnoiter her too, but first things first. The office. You need to figure out what you've gotten yourself into."

Jackson considered reminding Chester who'd gotten him mixed up in this mess to start with. "They catch me snooping and I'll be into something a lot deeper. I'll be the one bleeding this time. You're crazy."

"Crazy like a foxtail! Which are actually quite dangerous to dogs."

"Maybe I'll just quit, and she could leave with me."

"Oh, yeah. Since you made such an impression on her, I'm sure she'd leave her job to run away with you."

Jackson feigned the feigned part of a feigned hurt expression, which was a bit confusing. It was true though — she probably wouldn't even leave a root canal to go anywhere with him. She didn't even really know who he was. "She might…" he said, trying to think of a snappy retort.

"Listen, I've got some surveillance equipment that you can borrow. I got it to… uh… never mind. I just have it. Don't ask."

"They'll kill me, you know. I mean, like seriously totally dead. They're not stable. Plus it's in a Tovac Clan Open Market Zone. Murder's probably allowed there. As long as you know the right people. Or kill the right people."

Chester made a dismissive gesture. "My lady friend who told me about the job and set this up said that they were a little eccentric, but you just needed to ride it out."

"But—"

"Just spy on them a little and you'll probably learn that it's nothing. Then you won't have to worry, you'll get to keep an interesting if somewhat unusual job, and you'll win the girl of your dreams. Fairy tale. Like my life." He picked up a glass, tipped it to his lips, and then set it down, seemingly hurt at the empty glass's betrayal.

Jackson stared at his own plate and decided that he wasn't really hungry anymore.

Life had pulled away from the station, and he still stood on the platform. He needed to grab the caboose railing before it was gone. Even if it ripped his arm off.

CHAPTER 10: GRANDMA, GAZPACHO, AND

FLYING POODLES

Sy stepped into her apartment. She didn't think she'd been followed, though she wasn't too worried about that. There was a decoy office in a different free reign zone, and The Seven's true headquarters location wasn't public. On top of that, no one could get into and out of the Tovac Zone without a clearance from the Tovac clan, so any casual kooks would never even get close. Just the same, as directed, she always varied her exit out of the Zone heading home, and she kept an eye on her rear-view mirror.

Her apartment was small because that's the way she liked it – bigger just meant more empty. She had enough furniture to be functional, though if she threw a party, most guests would have to stand. Not too likely, there. A simple vase of peach tulips topped the kitchen table.

"Work went pretty well today, Grandma," she called out. "I met a new friend." She thought about this. "Well, I met a nice man who could be a friend. Some day." The thought lingered.

The kitchen was typical for a tiny apartment, with off-white poorly maintained appliances. However, the cabinets were filled with high end equipment that would be at home in any upscale restaurant, as long as it had at least two stars and three dollar signs.

She set her bag of fresh produce on the counter and grabbed a butcher knife, her favorite – perfectly weighted. She always wondered how it would throw, though she would never dream of throwing that one. It would be like..., like maybe throwing your prize poodle off the high dive to see how good a swimmer he was. She pictured a groomed poodle tumbling through the air, his shiny blue bow catching the light as it spun, his legs kicking at the air. She smiled then, just a little.

"Grandma. How about gazpacho tonight? I won't have time to chill it much, but it will still be good."

Grandma didn't reply. Grandma never replied any more.

CHAPTER 11: AWAITING THE KNIFE

"Come in," Talbot yelled through the door.

Jackson pushed the solid door and stepped in, his first time in the office since he'd been hired. A strong antiseptic smell hit him, and his memory flashed an image of the bleeding man who'd been carried in there the day before. He flicked his eyes downward but saw no bloody drag trail.

He held a tiny radio microphone and transmitter unit in the palm of his left hand, pressed into some adhesive putty. The plan was to stick it under Talbot's desk. His hand was so sweaty that he worried that the putty wouldn't stick.

From his seated position behind the desk, Talbot stared at Jackson over the top of his glasses, his eyes the color of a honed knife blade poised to plunge between a man's ribs. He wore a long sleeve shirt, a tie, and an expression that would make a Spartan whimper.

Jackson was frozen. What was he doing? How did he let that jackass Chester talk him into this?

"Yes?" Talbot said, sounding impatient.

"Oh! I just wanted to come by and show you the latest set." He dropped his most recent sketches onto Talbot's desk. With his other hand, he stuck the transmitter under its rim. He didn't want to do it; he knew he shouldn't do it; but he did it. He'd planned to do it so he did it. Now he just had to haul himself out of there.

"What is that?" Talbot asked, and Jackson's hammering heart rolled over and played dead.

"I don't, I mean I wasn't … oh, you mean that figure?" Talbot concentrated on one of the sketches, not on Jackson. He felt the constriction in his chest twitch, then loosen a notch. "Yes. That's just—"

Jackson stopped when he felt something plop onto the top of his shoe, directly below the place where he'd just placed the microphone.

Oshitoshitoshitoshitoshit!

"What is that?" This time it wasn't Talbot; it was someone behind Jackson. He knew who it was without turning. Mustache Man — Simpson.

Jackson bent down and picked up the putty and microphone unit. "Oh, like I was about to tell Mr. Talbot, that is the Gouging the Socket maneuver," his voice about an octave higher than usual. He pointed at the paper on Talbot's desk, "And this guy here—"

"No," Simpson said, taking a step closer, pointing to Jackson's closed fist. "That thing in your hand. Let me see that."

Jackson's heart had an explosive bowel movement in his chest. His instinct was to haul ass, but sudden movements in this place might activate a bullet magnet on his forehead. Or a spear-wielding Buck-Bill. His "fight or flight" instinct short-circuited, freezing him in place.

Simpson leaned close, moving his gloved finger closer to Jackson's hand.

"That?" Jackson said. "Oh that. Yeah...." His brain flickered on like an old fluorescent bulb. "That! That's my chewed gum. I was about to throw it out. Do you want to see it?" He squeezed the putty over the top of the microphone unit to cover it and then held it putty-side-out toward Simpson's face. It got within a foot of his nose when Simpson suddenly blurred and Jackson's hand erupted in pain. The putty flew across the room.

"Ah!" Jackson yelled in shock and pain. Simpson had just whacked him in the hand with a short stick that had somehow materialized as Simpson had spun. *What the hell?* He had moved so fast that Jackson didn't even perceive the blur.

"Pick that up," Simpson said, sliding the stick back into the sleeve of his blue sports coat. "And never put things in my face."

"Yes, okay, yes, sir. I mean Damn!" Jackson, still rubbing his hand and recovering from the shock, picked up the putty with the embedded microphone and threw it in the trash by Talbot's desk. He considered reaching down to push it deeper into the trash so no one would see the microphone sticking out of it, but that would be even more obvious than just leaving it there. Besides, he was ready to get the double dog hell out of there.

"I'll talk to you about those later," Jackson said to Talbot, pointing toward the papers on the desk but not looking at him. "I've... I've got to take a dump." He walked to the door without waiting for a reply. "A big one. Mexican food." And he was out.

Please oh please don't let them find it! During the entire walk to the restroom, he tensed for the inevitable, for someone to yell at him or grab him or smack him with a crazy spinning cane in the back of the head. His neck muscles were locked in a double knot. After waiting in a bathroom stall for the approximate duration of a Mexican food-induced diarrhea session, he returned to his desk, watching for the telltale red laser dot that tended to precede the catastrophic formation of sniper holes. Maybe Buck-Bill would instead hop over the cubicle wall and harpoon him. But he saw no one, only hearing the soft clicking of keyboards. He reached into his backpack, flicked on the recorder, and slipped it into a drawer in his desk, wiping off his fingerprints, just in case. He could claim someone put it in there. He would just leave it in there for a few days where it would only record when sound was detected. Once he was sure Talbot's trash had been taken out, he'd bring it home to examine. Until then, he would put it out of his mind lest Simpson somehow pick it up from Jackson's brainwaves.

The next few days were agony. He slid his drawer open a hundred times, each time considering moving the recorder and each time deciding against it. He tried to free his mind from images of his own possibly impending violent death by drawing scenes of others experiencing their own violent deaths.

Once or twice a day, Jackson felt the pressure of someone's gaze and turned to find Simpson standing there like a butler-shaped mustachioed zombie with white gloves, just watching him. No doubt itching to repeat his special spin pipe smack maneuver, this time to Jackson's head. The first time, Jackson said, "Hi," but Simpson had only slid from view — not turning away and walking, but rather sliding out of frame while keeping his eye on Jackson. After that first time, Jackson just ignored him. Well, he tried to give the appearance of ignoring him. Actually he just said nothing while his guts did the hokey pokey.

Finally, he could take it no more. At quitting time, he slid a notebook into the drawer, wedging the recorder between the pages. He then pulled out the notebook with its embedded cargo and shoved it into his backpack. He bolted to the door.

Just as he reached it, Simpson called his name.

Jackson turned around, expecting to see guards with raised guns or Simpson brandishing a samurai sword, maybe with a bandana around his head. Instead, Simpson just waved. "Have a pleasant evening," Simpson said, not even trying to mean it.

That was bad. Simpson never did that, so it must mean something horrific was about to happen. "Yes," Jackson said. "Yes, I will. At least I hope so. I'll try anyway. To have a great night, that is." He left without another word, wondering how tight he'd have to flex his back and shoulder muscles to deflect a thrown knife.

Miraculously, he arrived at his car intact. Somehow, he even made it out of the parking lot and free reign zone without getting shot. He drove home watching the rearview mirror more than the road in front.

Within minutes, Chester was sitting on the couch next to him, rewinding the audio surveillance recording. "You didn't even listen to any of it?" Chester asked.

"No. I was too scared. I thought it best to just wait for you."

Chester pushed play.

CHAPTER 12: STAY, QUIT, OR GET MURDERED

"… trust the guy ."

The muffled voice on the recording sounded like Simpson's. The majority of the tape was music. Talbot apparently liked Baroque music at a volume just above the minimum to start the recording. 90% of the tape was filled with harpsichords and opera singers in various stages of agony, 9% was unintelligible conversation, and they were listening again to the 1% remaining.

"But you didn't get a negative read," Talbot said on the tape.

"That's just the thing. I didn't get anything at all. Again."

"But that's good. That's what we want."

A rustling noise. "Not exactly—" A few muffled words. "—explaining myself. I normally get a blank read for sheep. But with this guy I still get no read at all. Nothing. Silence."

The audio degraded. Simpson said a few muffled sentences. "… a latent … kill … option to consider… time."

Jackson stood up; he had no plans to go anywhere but felt he really needed to rush somewhere right away.

"We're out of time," Talbot said. He said more, but that's all they could understand.

Jackson and Chester stared at the silent recorder on the table.

"Did he say, 'kill'?" Jackson asked.

"Uh…"

"I picked the wrong time to stick with a job." He sat back down. "But now I *can't* leave."

"Why not?"

"Because what if they were planning to kill me for some reason? What do you think they'd do if I left? Say, 'Oh, we were going to kill him, but he didn't show up today. So let's just forget it.'"

"Maybe." Chester opened his mouth, paused, and then said, "Maybe… uh… no. I'm sure that's not what he meant. Besides, that recording could be from days ago."

"Why don't you call your friend who helped get me the job there? Maybe she could help us."

Chester's face paled. "I haven't been able to get a hold of her for over a week. It's like she just disappeared."

Jackson felt like a balloon with a hole in it, zipping around out of control, deflating the entire time.

"What the hell are you two Nancy boys doing?" yelled a voice. Both men turned just as Jackson's father Victor stormed into the room, chewing on a drinking straw. At 5'7, he was several inches shorter than Jackson, with cropped gray hair. He wore gray shorts and a v-neck t-shirt, his unofficial house uniform — which meant he wore it 99% of the time. "I didn't bust in on you two fellers as you were a-courtin', did I?"

"We're just talking about work, Dad."

"You gonna quit again?"

"I never quit."

"No, you never quit. You just get your ass fired, which is quittin' in my book. I'm getting a sandwich. You want one? Good, get your ass up and make it yourself. And stop sitting so close together. You look like a couple of mustache-munchers."

"Thanks Mr. Krol," Chester said, smiling.

Victor pulled the straw out of his mouth and whipped it toward the floor, slinging out a stream of drool. He then returned it to his mouth and pointed a gnarled finger at Chester. "If you weren't my boy's friend, I'd put a pot knot on top of your head the size of my last dump, and that thing would've taken down the Titanic, I tell you. There was villagers living on it." He left for the kitchen.

"Your dad's such a sweetheart. I can see why you stayed."

Jackson nodded, thinking about what his dad had said about his work history. Maybe he had been right. After a minute of silence, he said, "Nothing happened."

"Huh?"

"Ignore it. Run right through it. It didn't happen."

"You can't just… I mean… what do you mean?"

"What can I do? Nothing. So I do it hard."

"I don't even know what that means. But it sounds dirty."

"Everything sounds dirty to you. I mean, I stay there. I work hard. I pretend nothing happened. I don't quit." And he meant it. Mostly. He wasn't going to leave.

Unless of course they stuck a spear through him.

CHAPTER 13: THE RESEARCHER

The Tovac Clan Open Market was the one of the newest free market zones in the area. It hadn't so much been incorporated as it had simply imploded, with the governments of the surrounding areas ceding control over to the Tovac Clan. Those in the bordering regions were glad to be rid of the burden of keeping order in the Zone and hoped that maybe the Tovac security personnel, or "SecForce," would grind down the rougher edges of the populace. Or at least keep some of the burs from escaping out into the general public.

The State still had overall jurisdiction, as it did for all free market regions, but they too seemed content to let the Tovacs handle security for the Zone. Most in the Zone were so worn down by the previous near-anarchy that they gladly traded a little freedom for some semblance of security.

On Thursday morning, Jackson passed through the security checkpoint at the entrance to the region in a priority lane, as Tovac credentials had been added to his car's electronic identification beacon. The Zone didn't look so different from a regular slum to the naked eye — which his eyes in fact were — but he knew that despite the swift Tovac justice meted out to wrong-doers, those wrong-doers were just swift enough themselves to find some wrong-do-ees on which to do the doing.

With this thought in mind, Jackson looked upon the guards waving him into "The Seven" factory office compound with gratitude.

"Good morning, fellas!" he called out as he rolled past the gate, trying to exude some friendly warmness.

"Keep moving!" a helmeted guard screamed, throwing ice water on the warm greeting while gesturing with his automatic rifle.

Jackson switched from friendliness to mocking, one of his core competencies. "Okay!" he said, his car not moving. "I'll just pull on through then?"

The barrel of the gun turned toward him, the aim drifting close to his head. That and a feral grunt from the guard nudged Jackson back from his standard mode into something approaching seriousness, or at least toward life-preservation. Threats of impending violence have that effect.

"Okay, I'll catch you boys later!" he called as he drove off. "Let's go grab some lunch sometime!"

In his cubicle, he felt eyes on him though he was alone. The wind was building outside the straw house of denial that he'd constructed around the potential danger of The Seven. Crazy is one thing, but crazy plus guns is, well, two things. Like twice as many. An old saying warped in his mind: "Give a lunatic a gun, and he'll kill someone. Teach a lunatic to shoot a gun, and he'll kill lots of people for a lifetime, especially idiots who bug the office."

He thought of his dad, of Sy, of Buck-Bill with his spear, and of Talbot and Simpson. The images fought in his head, none the victor. Maybe Talbot had been talking about some other guy instead of Jackson. But what did they mean by getting a "read" on the guy? It could have been a figure of speech, but it sounded more specific than that. Plus something about "kill." Perhaps "kill some time." Sure.

On autopilot, he stepped into Gary's empty cubicle and moved his coffee cup to the opposite side of his desk. Back in his own workspace, someone had deposited a new stack of instructions for him, and he hid from his anxiety in his artwork. After a couple of hours of work, he finally stopped flinching at every sound.

Later in the day, he heard footsteps and turned in time to see Buck-Bill run past, hole-puncher in hand. That's all he really seemed to do: punch holes and hoist a spear. And squat on counters — can't forget that. It probably made for an interesting resume. Small circles of cut paper lay at the entrance of the cubicle, with one tumbling softly down to join them.

He heard a crash, and his body seized in anticipation. No one came for him. He stood.

Several employees' heads peeked over their walls, searching for the source of the ruckus. His eyes remained focused on the place where Sy's head should pop up.

"Hello," a woman's voice said, close to his ear. He jumped.

Before he could see who had just snuck up on him, a door burst open behind him, and all the other heads dropped out of view like invisible Whack-A-Mole hammers had just descended. He turned in time to see the door shut. Much closer, Sy stood crouched at his own doorway, holding a piece of paper. She looked at him out of the corner of her eye, then dropped her gaze.

His brain shrieked as the gears struggled to reverse directions and crank out some clever witticism. His mouth opened and waited for instructions from his brain, but nothing came. "Hi," he finally said. "I mean, hi." What was wrong with him?

She stepped in.

"Oh! Come in," he continued. He kicked his rolling chair towards her so she could sit, but a wheel caught the edge of the gear that rose from the floor, and the chair tipped and landed on her foot. "Ah!" He lunged for it but missed. For a brief horrible moment, he thought she was about to leave.

She bent and righted the chair. "I really like this picture." She turned the page so he could see it. It was one of his images. "But I wanted to … point something out to you that might help."

"Oh, thanks." His mind seized the topic of the artwork like a raft in the sea of frothing idiocy that churned in his head.

She set the paper on his desk. He could feel her closeness, like a buildup of static electricity soon to arc. "The face doesn't look quite right." She pointed to the simple cross that Jackson used to represent the Vampires' faces.

Was she serious? Didn't she know that he was drawing their faces in abstract? He hesitated, not sure how he should proceed.

"That was a joke," she said without smiling. "This," she pointed again at the Vampire, "is almost perfect. But this ear is a bit off. It needs to look like this." She drew a small ear on the pad. It was a bit larger than what he drew, and quite a bit more pointy. It was true that he had taken some poetic license with their appearance. The rough sketches that they'd originally shown him were a bit different, but what did it matter? It was all made up anyway.

"And this," she continued, pointing at the Vampire's forearms. "They're a little too short. They grow in attack mode."

Crap. She's as crazy as the rest of them.

Then it hit him. She was describing the exact areas in which he'd altered the Vampire's appearance from the sketches. How did she know that it was different? A tiny voice in his mind said, "She's seen a Vampire!" but a louder one said, "She's seen the original sketches! And why am I yelling?!" That latter voice was more obvious, but for some reason he still doubted it. He had made the subtle changes because he thought the original sketch artist must have made a few minor mistakes, though his own changes had felt somehow wrong to him too, though he didn't know why. His changes had made them look more human.

She turned to leave, and he realized that he'd been silent as he had considered what she'd said. Had his lips been moving as he talked to himself? "Wait!" he said. "I … I mean. What do you do here?"

"Research."

"What do you research?" he asked, but he knew the answer already.

He thought her mouth might have curled in a slight smile, though it was so subtle that it might have been something else, like an involuntary facial twitch while passing gas. Without another word, she left the cubicle, pausing at the doorway only long enough to repeat the odd feet-shuffling maneuver that she'd done the last time. That time, he'd explained it away, like maybe he hadn't really seen her step out and back in and back out again, or maybe she just forgot something and had planned to come back in before reconsidering. This time, though, she'd done the exact same move.

He felt marginally better about the level he carried around in his pocket.

He was still staring at the doorway of his cubicle where he'd last seen her when a screeching siren wrenched him into focus. The sound made him want to dig out his eardrums with a screwdriver — it sounded like a robot opera soprano shrieking a vibrato death cry, overlaid with rending metal, with some fingernails on a chalkboard to boot. Spinning red lights in the high ceiling bathed the entire factory floor.

"Alpha Team mobilize," a pleasant female voice announced over loudspeakers that he had never seen or heard, her voice somehow rising above the shrill alarm. Everyone was in motion. Buck-Bill vaulted over his cubicle wall and ran with his spear toward a door along the back wall of the factory. That door had always been locked when Jackson had tried it, but he had seen people go through there into a dark hallway. It must lead somewhere forbidden, like the teachers' lounge. Several others followed Buck-Bill.

"You should go," Sy said behind him. He spun. Red lights played across her face as she peered at him through those depthless eyes. She was more animated than he'd ever seen her, rocking on her toes.

"Down that hall? Am I part of Alpha Team?"

Her face twitched. "Alpha Team? No, I mean you should go home." She looked as though she wanted to say something more, opening then closing her mouth.

"But ..." he saw several others, including Gary, heading for the door that led to the parking lot outside. He looked from there to the others charging toward the hallway.

"Go now!" she yelled, her black hair whipping as she spun away.

Screw that!

He followed and nearly ran into her when she paused at the doorway of his cubicle, repeating her little dance maneuver, though much faster, like a tap dance. She headed toward the hallway door. He'd stuck with this for this long — might as well follow it through to the end. Just as she passed into the hallway, with him on her heel, he was yanked backward. He turned to see who had grabbed his collar.

Talbot released him, his face hard. He scrutinized Jackson. "That is not your path."

"But I want to see what's going on!"

"Go home," Talbot said, pushing past him. "Don't follow us."

Now *that* was an idea.

CHAPTER 14: A NEW FRIEND

Jackson sat in "The Vomit," his aptly named car, parked near the back entrance to the factory office complex. He guessed that the Alpha Team would "mobilize" out of this exit rather than through the main gates. Though it was bolted shut and appeared unused, Jackson had discovered it in his first week of work, his curiosity outweighing his instinct for self-preservation.

He waited behind the solid walls. Eventually, several engines started and tires crunched on gravel beyond the gate. In seconds, the gate swung outward and vehicles rolled into the street, charging past him. He slid down until he heard the last one pass and then shifted the car into gear and pulled out.

The final vehicle in the convoy was an old conversion van, complete with running boards, curtains on the windows, and a colorful sunset painted on its side. He wondered if Sy was in there, perhaps taking notes for her "research" while luxuriating in the shag carpet interior.

After proceeding quickly but not recklessly for ten minutes, they entered a region that the Tovac Clan must have placed at the bottom of their "to-do" list, as the road became progressively more rough, the buildings more dilapidated, and the inhabitants more... freaky. A middle-aged man with ragged red and gray streaked hair and beard sat on an upturned bucket on a street corner with a sign that said, "Feed me or I will gnaw the flesh of your children's feet." A block down the road, a woman strolled in an old flowery summer dress while wearing a white football helmet with a skull and crossbones on its side. A child behind her dragged a limp cat by its tail across the crumbling sidewalk.

Jackson was just glad that it was still daylight.

In direct response to this thought, the sky darkened as though God had thrown a celestial switch with one hand while flipping Jackson off with the other.

"Crap!" This was not the time for an earth cloud inversion. He flicked his headlights on and looked skyward as though he'd see something other than blackness. He returned his gaze to the van. Earth cloud inversions made him claustrophobic, as though he were in a coffin.

The weather phenomenon was a misnomer, as there was no real inversion, else he'd be driving on clouds. Rather, the theory was that the massive airborne particulate matter (or "air dirt" for the lower of brow) coalesced in the clouds, unseen until a solar flare shifted their chemistry and they became opaque. They weren't necessarily black — they just appeared that way because they blocked out the sun. Fortunately, Jackson was not in the direct center of the inversion because he could see light coming from off to his right. Not so fortunately, they were all still under it and, depending on the air dirt's consistency and the sun's mood, the dark blanket might harden, abruptly dropping from the sky in a hail of black rocks.

He could turn right and get out from under the storm in just a few minutes. This thought crossed his mind and kept going. Instead, he continued to follow the caravan, trying to stay far enough back to avoid detection. He could just make out the final van's red tail lights in the gloom.

The front cars of the caravan turned a corner to the right. As he approached, the cars that had completed the turn hit their brakes and moved toward the curb. He didn't dare turn behind them, as there were almost no other cars on the dark road. Instead, he drove past the corner and pulled to the curb as soon as he was out of eyesight. After a nervous look at the black sky, he ran back to the corner, arriving just as the last of the Alpha Team jogged out of sight a block away. When he followed and peeked around that corner, he saw the team turn into a side alley at the other corner of the same building. He crept forward and stopped close to the entrance into the alley. Whispers reached him from just around that corner; they must have stopped.

If anyone from the Alpha Team turned back, Jackson would be caught. He needed to get off the street and find a vantage point.

The five-story corner building appeared to be an apartment block. Making as little noise as possible, he ran back to the front door. Wires from its ruined intercom panel reached out from the wall by the door like the fingers of zombies emerging from cemetery mounds. Tentatively, he pushed the door with his fingertips, and it swung inward in spite of the deadbolt protruding from its edge. The blasted and fragmented doorframe had apparently retired long ago and could barely hold itself onto the wall, much less restrain a deadbolt.

The dark interior of the building beckoned him like a meat-grinder might call out to a choice cut. Feeling his fear rearing up, he plunged inside before he had a chance to think too deeply about what he was doing.

A sweet smell of rot hit him as soon as he crossed the threshold. Ahead, he heard a man's muffled voice shouting through a wall. Trash filled the dim entrance hallway, concentrated by an ajar door to his right. He pushed it open and could just make out a stairwell in the gloom. He waded through knee-high trash as he climbed, the trash gradually thinning into occasional islands of filth. These islands kept the needle in the red zone at the far boundary of his nose's stench gauge. Though his eyes were adjusting to the dim conditions, the darkness made a valiant effort to keep up, growing thicker the higher he climbed. Eventually, he climbed in total darkness, stumbling over things that best remained unseen and unknown, the sticky railing his only guide. Unintelligible excited voices drifted from the distance over the sound of his rustling feet.

"Hey!" a voice burst from his right on one landing.

Jackson screamed in fright and kicked out. His foot made contact with someone who grunted as the kick smashed him into the wall. Jackson ran as fast as he could up the stairs until he face-planted into a rudely placed door. He shoved at it in panic, feeling his unknown assailant close behind him. The door flew open to reveal a dim rooftop, lit only by sunlight off in the distance, like a hallway light spilling into a dark room from under the door. He slammed the rooftop door behind him and backed away, waiting. No one came. He leaned his head close to the door and listened. Realizing that anyone shoving the door open would also slam it into his head, he pulled his head back and stepped to the side.

He picked up a broken brick and wedged it against the door. It wouldn't keep it closed, but it might make enough sound that he would hear anyone coming through. There were no other doors on the roof; his pursuer only need wait just inside the door. Great. He picked up another fragment of brick, planning his next move. When it was time to head back down, he would yank the door open, heave the brick through the opening, and then smile as he heard the satisfying thud of brick-on-face and the diminishing clamor caused by an assailant tumbling down a trash-strewn stairway. That was his three-step plan, and it seemed pretty solid. In the meantime, he needed to see what was going on with the Alpha Team from the office; those guys were way scarier than some drunk guy loitering in a stairwell.

He got his bearings and ran toward the edge of the rooftop that overlooked the alley. The wall along the rooftop was only about two feet high, and he kneeled to peer over the edge at the figures below, just hazy smudges in the darkness. Some members of the Alpha Team had fanned out with a small contingent staying in the rear in a tight group. Two members stood a distance behind them, likely the rear guard. He prayed Sy was in the small group in the protected center.

What the hell were they doing?

From his vantage point, he could make out movement ahead of the group further down the alley. Shapes darted amongst trash dumpsters and shells of cars. He couldn't make out any details. Were these the "Vampires" that The Seven claimed to stalk? Or, more likely, was the team about to attack a bunch of drunk alley bums?

The Alpha Team apparently hadn't seen the others yet, and as the team grew closer to them, the movement of the other shapes stopped, either hiding or setting an ambush. What if they were dangerous? Vampire or not, these guys might hurt Sy. He looked around and found another brick, surprisingly already in his own hand. He heaved it at one of the cars. It struck with a thunderous crash, and the Alpha Team rushed forward with a deep roar. As it did so, the other dark shapes launched themselves at them, shrieking in a pitch several octaves higher, sounding almost like squeaking bats.

He leaned further out from the edge, pushing his face downward as though the extra few inches would allow him to see what was happening in the gloom. The flurry of movement and screams signaled a vicious battle, but he couldn't tell who was winning. He remained frozen, straining to make out details below.

"That wasn't very nice," a voice said at his ear.

Jackson almost pitched himself off of the building but managed to roll away from the voice. A shadowed man in a ragged coat hunched over him, holding a pipe.

"I just said, 'Hey,'" the man said, his face hidden in darkness. He took a step toward Jackson. "Then you hit me. That wasn't very nice." Another step.

Jackson crab-crawled back. "Sorry! You just startled me." He kept his eyes on the pipe in the man's hand.

"Sorry? I guess I could accept that."

Jackson moved sideways toward the stair doorway.

The man continued, "But you hurt my feelings."

The doorway was the same distance from each man, but Jackson was still on the ground. He slid toward the door. "Yeah. Sorry again about that. Maybe I could buy you a drink some time."

The sounds of the raging battle echoed up from the alley before ending with a man's horrible shriek.

"Okay," the man said, apparently deaf to mayhem. "I could use a drink. Someone just punched me in the chest." He gestured with his pipe toward the door. "You first."

Jackson didn't like the idea of a crazy dude with a metal pipe standing behind him, but he figured that once he made it through the doorway, that guy would never catch him.

"Okay," Jackson said. "Me first. Here I go." He scrambled to his feet and walked toward the door, not moving his eyes from the man until crossing the threshold. Once through, he bounded as fast as he could down the stairs, stumbling but never quite falling. Almost never. He made so much noise that he had no idea if pipe man was in hot pursuit. Nearing the bottom floor, he risked a look over his shoulder. A misplaced foot sent him crash landing in the sea of trash, disappearing beneath the surface, his fall broken by a nice soft layer of filth. Before he could stand, a hand grabbed his shirt front and yanked him upward.

"Boy, you're eager for that drink," the man said, putting his arm around him and walking him out of the stairwell and into the street. His powerful grip said, *"Don't bother trying to wiggle free."* The smell from the building did not end when they exited, as the man seemed to be a concentrated mobile form of the odor.

"How about I meet you there?" Jackson asked.

"But we already met!" the man said. "And the bar is right there." He pointed across the street. Off to Jackson's right, a convoy of vehicles screeched around the corner, heading away, the conversion van at the end of the convoy. So much for following them back to the office complex. He had no idea where he was, but looking at the man next to him, he realized that might be moot.

In the dim light, the man looked at least sixty years old, with black streaks in his long straight gray hair and beard — either black hair or globs of goo. His beard was twisted into a braid that fell to the middle of his chest.

I'm about to be murdered.

They crossed the street toward a dilapidated bar, the man still holding him fast. Seeing the broken neon sign of the bar, Jackson wondered if he was safer with this insane man or with a group of both insane *and* drunk men who would inhabit a bar in this part of town. On the positive side, he wasn't likely to get nailed by a black chunk of particulate matter falling from thousands of feet in the air if he were in a bar.

"Wait," the man said, releasing Jackson. He wedged his pipe between his thighs and grabbed his long gray hair. "This is a classy joint." He tied his hair into a knot on top of his head. "There."

At first, Jackson considered grabbing the pipe and giving the old man a refreshing whack in the knee, but he instead just watched him fix his hair up. Really, was this guy any scarier than the folks at the office? He had just followed his office-mates on a Vampire search-and-destroy mission deep in the bowels of the bowels of the city's bowels. A crazy old man, he could handle. Probably. Maybe. Plus he could use a drink. He might even learn something from this guy.

"You bringing that pipe in there?" Jackson asked.

"You want it?" the man said, handing it to him. "I've got a backup." He patted his thigh.

"Err, thanks," Jackson said, eying it as he turned it in his hand. It was a good pipe, he decided.

CHAPTER 15: CHILLIN' WITH THE TOVACS

The bar was dark, but compared to the black blanket outside, it seemed almost festive. Well, perhaps that was a little generous. The place was only about twenty feet wide by approximately forty feet deep with the bar running along most of the length of the left wall. The right half of the room held tables populated by a Thursday night crowd of grubby figures hunched over their drinks. A bald bartender leaned against the other side of the bar, talking to two women drinking out of jars. He wasn't wearing a shirt. He should've been wearing a shirt.

When Jackson and the old man entered, every face turned in their direction. Several hands darted into jackets and under tables. One man stopped stabbing a bloody knife blade into a tabletop between the bloody fingers of his outstretched hand and froze, a single drop of blood falling from the knife tip to the table.

Jackson thought about the rolly polly that had wandered into the ant pile near his house a while back. The ants had enjoyed quite a feast of the little guy before Jackson had discovered it. He felt distinctly rolly pollyish at the moment. He gripped the pipe and took a step backward, bumping into the door.

He leaned to the old man, keeping his eyes on the hostiles, "Perhaps we should find another—"

"Abner!" the entire bar called in unison. Each raised their drinks, their mouths splitting into cracked grins of mangled and missing teeth. Most kept their eyes firmly fixed on Jackson.

Abner danced over to the edge of the bar and hopped onto an empty stool, patting the one next to him while inclining his head to Jackson. "Two of the usuals for me and my new friend here," he said to the barman.

The barman gave Jackson a skeptical glance, then looked at the old man and said, "You got it, Abner."

The smell in the place was warm and thick, though not overpowering. It was close to the smell of sautéing onions, but far enough from that to be vaguely disturbing, like something extra had been thrown into the pan. He had a flash memory of his old coworker Naral, whose skin seemed to exude garlic oil. Odd how the smell of garlic from a pan is so inviting while that same smell from a body is quite repugnant. He took another sniff and detected something sweet intermingled with the odor before deciding to stop thinking about it altogether.

The barman dropped two jars on the bar in front of them, then dug in his deep belly button while giving Jackson the eye. He could only give him one eye because the other was milky white and pointed in the wrong direction.

"Thanks," Jackson said.

"Drink it," the barman said.

Jackson looked at the jar. It wasn't the ironically cool jar of a swanky restaurant, but rather a plain jar that was probably once used to preserve peaches. The drink inside it looked like a beer, but with a pale white sphere like an eyeball floating in it. He looked at Abner.

"Drink it," Abner said, reaching for his own jar.

Jackson pointed at the floating eyeball. "What's the—?" he started.

"Drink it!" the entire bar yelled.

Jackson looked at them, at Abner, at the barman, at the drink, then at the door. He grabbed the drink and downed it in a huge open-throat gulp, though he managed to catch the eyeball in his mouth. The drink tasted like a cross between a martini and a beer, and the eyeball tasted like an onion in his mouth. The drink was odd, but surprisingly non-revolting. He spit the pearl onion back into the jar.

The bar patrons returned to their unintelligible mumblings. Abner gave him a toothy grin, his mouth alone holding more solid white teeth than the entire bar population. The barman gave him a curt nod and took the empty glass, put it to his own mouth, and ate the onion.

Abner sipped his drink and then loudly smacked his lips for ten seconds. The barman watched him. Abner repeated the sequence. The barman leaned close, eyebrows raised. Abner nodded and smiled, and the barman relaxed.

"So," Abner said, turning to Jackson. "What brings you to our little neighborhood?"

Jackson thought again about his decision to come in here. Why had he thought that it was a good idea? *Oh yeah, because I'm an idiot.* These types of decisions were supposed to decrease as he aged and grew in wisdom. Alas, his wisdom seemed to be a bit stunted. At least that drink was taking some of the edge off.

What the hell. Might as well tell the guy the truth.

"I was following some people from my work," he said.

"You were, huh?" Abner took another small drink, smacked his lips, then downed the rest of the drink, swallowing the onion whole. He slammed the glass down, startling Jackson.

Was he trying to intimidate him? Jackson's anger flared, and he reached for his own jar to slam it down too, but it was gone. Instead he grabbed a napkin and threw it down. "Yes I was," he said. "They claim to hunt Vampires, and I wanted to see what they were up to."

Abner appraised him in silence. Jackson appraised his ass right back. The barman leaned in and did some appraising of his own, though apparently feeling left out, he returned to the two women further down the bar. One of the women appeared to be sniffing the armpit of the other.

"Vampires, around here?" Abner said. "Hmm. I think I would know if there were Vampires around here."

"One would think," Jackson replied, surprised to notice two new filled jars on the bar. He picked his up and took a sip. Erk. It was not much of a sipping drink. He drained it once again, this time accidentally swallowing the onion.

"That's the ticket. Who do you work for?" Abner asked, his expression neutral, though his eyes sparkled like broken shards of glass.

Should he answer that? What if Abner was crazy enough to go after them? Jackson then thought of the barbed wire around the building, the guns, and Buck-Bill's wicked spear. The worst thing Abner could do was get him fired, at least as far as work was concerned. He chose not to think of the worst thing Abner could do, as far as work was not concerned.

"A dude named Talbot," Jackson said.

"Ha! I thought so." Abner downed his drink and stood. "Let's go."

Jackson gripped his pipe. "Where are we going?"

"Me? I'm going to my bed. You? You're going to your car and getting the hell out of here before some creatures of the night creep out and suck you widdle necky-poo." He walked toward the bar exit.

"Wait!" Jackson called, running to catch up. "Do you know anything about what's going on here?"

Abner went outside without turning or waiting. Jackson burst out right behind him and found himself on an empty street. The old man was gone.

"How did he do that?" he asked aloud. *He must have done one of those crazy movie—*

"How did who do what?" Abner called from off to Jackson's left. He was peering at Jackson from behind several boards propped against the building edge. Jackson could hear the splatter of urine against the building.

"Oh, never mind. I thought you, you know, disappeared."

Abner pulled his head back behind the boards and the splattering stopped, though he didn't walk out.

"Abner?" Jackson called, not wanting to peek around the boards and have that image burned into his brain. The darkness and stillness crawled into his brain like a tarantula. The sky could drop on his head at any minute. He even thought he heard something rumble above him.

"See ya Abner! Thanks for the drink!" He didn't stop running until he got to his car. Miraculously, he made it out of the neighborhood without missing a single turn.

CHAPTER 16: THE NUGGET

His dad Victor was watching the news when Jackson came home. Jackson caught the tail end of a news story about another ozone vortex that had briefly opened up west of the city, scorching a thirty-foot swath across a mall parking lot. A female reporter faced the camera in the lot, blackened cars behind her. Next to one of the cars, a pile of ashes topped with black bones smoldered. A charred human skull lay on its side next to the pile, and he wondered if the camera crew had positioned it there for dramatic effect. A mangy dog sniffed it and moved on.

With a cigarette bobbing between her painted red lips, the blond reporter bantered with the anchors in the station, making some comment about roasting marshmallows. She had a good sense of humor, and he felt sorry for her because she always seemed to be sent on the messy assignments, especially those involving GWPs (Grievous Weather Phenomena). On the upside, because of the upsurge in the weather incidents, she'd enjoyed more screen time.

Victor sat on the edge of the couch cushion, shaking his head slightly. Even from behind, Jackson could see that he was agitated, overly attentive. Jackson walked around the edge of couch. His dad's head creaked around toward him, his face pale.

"It's not time yet," Victor said, his eyes far away.

"Time for what? What's wrong, Dad?"

Victor's blank expression vanished. "Huh? What are you talking about?" He looked from Jackson's feet up to his face. "What the hell happened to you? You look like, well, you look as bad as you normally do. You ever wear clothes that you didn't sleep in the night before?"

"What were you...?" Jackson looked at the television which had switched from the newscast to a commercial for "extreme aphrodisiacs." Why had the weather set his dad off? "Are you okay?"

"I'm a hell of a lot better than okay. I haven't looked back at okay since the day you were born."

Jackson was sure that that had been intended as a slam, but his brain was too spent to probe the mysteries of his dad's pronouncements.

"Listen, Dad," he said, wondering how to start. He had to get out of that crazy job, and he didn't know how to explain it.

"You got fired, didn't you? I'm glad your mom's not here to see this."

Jackson needed to sit, but the only close chair was covered in old newspapers. He sat on the pile anyway and slid sideways a few inches, ending up cocked at an angle. "No, I didn't get fired."

Victor ignored him, never one to let a valid counter-argument dampen his tirade. "You know getting fired is the same as quitting, don't you? If you work for a jack-ass, then you find a new job before you kick him in the balls and get canned."

"But—"

"You got to stick with something, anything. And it ain't just work," his dad said, getting so agitated that he tried standing but didn't quite make it out of the low cushions. He dropped back down where he compromised by bouncing as he spoke. "That goes for that crazy broad that you drove off… what was her name?"

"Don't bring Mary into this. She has nothing to do with this."

"You run from everything."

"Dad." Jackson felt the force behind his planned explanation lifting its leg and draining itself on his shoe. "You don't know what I saw today. They went after … people." He almost said "Vampires." He had avoided telling his dad much about his job, preferring for him to think he'd finally found a regular respectable position. Now he was rethinking that position.

"People. What kind of people?" Victor looked like a cop preparing for a whopper from a speeding motorist.

Jackson heard two distinct sucking sounds in his head, one coming from behind the "tell Dad about my Vampire job" door, and another coming from behind the "tell Dad I want to quit" door.

"I just think there's something wrong with these guys," Jackson said.

"No wonder they hired you." Victor sat back and turned his attention to the television.

Jackson walked out of the room.

"Jackson!" his dad called after him. Jackson stuck his head back in.

His dad grimaced at some internal battle, then settled down. "Just… never mind. Try to stick with something for once. You need to grow up, Son."

Jackson slid back out of the room. His dad almost seemed concerned for him. Of course that concern was buried beneath ten feet of disappointment, a few layers of disgust, and steel-reinforced disapproval.

But there was a nugget in there.

CHAPTER 17: THE WATCHER

Seated in his parked car, the strike team leader Avar switched his binocular glasses back to dark tinted sunglasses and made a mental note to check the weather forecast before the assault. Of course, the increasingly unstable weather could flip at a moment's notice, so the plans would need to remain fluid. "Fluid" for Avar meant if conditions were not optimal, the operation would be cancelled. Changing a well-planned assault in midstream was like jumping off of a bridge and trying to tie on a bungee cord on the way down.

Those freaks in the industrial compound 100 meters away were up to something, and if Avar and his fellow Piri clan didn't learn those plans soon, they would have to storm the place. He'd lose most of his team, but he had sustained losses many times before, and it would be worth it if he could disrupt the Goblins' plans. This battle between the Jone-Zen Goblins and the Piri Vampires had raged for hundreds of years, maybe longer. Losing a few pawns and a few of those horsey things that moved like the letter "L" to block a queen was worth it. Maybe even one of those diagonal guys.

Either the Goblins hadn't been in the compound for long, or perhaps they'd just kept a low profile up to this point. For some reason, they'd stepped up their missions, and that had led Avar's people to discover this base. Well, technically they were Tazia's people, but he was only one promotion away from them being *his* people, and that was close enough. Though not well hidden, the compound was definitely well protected, or at least it had some excellent natural attributes that would make a frontal assault difficult. For one, the compound was huge, with the main structure over a hundred meters from the nearest street. Also, the buildings appeared solid, though many had vulnerable windows. Metal pipes and gears abounded, creating a labyrinth of kill zones outside and likely inside the buildings. On top of this, remote soundings indicated that there might be underground passages between the buildings on the compound. It would definitely be a tough nut to crack and grind to dust between his teeth. On top of this topping, the facility squatted in the miserable Tovac Zone, and those humans didn't mess around. His people must keep a low profile if they didn't want battles on two separate fronts.

The increasingly erratic and violent weather patterns spiraled away from the Zone, and it must be the place that the prophecies had predicted would be the final battleground, the place where a great Vampire victory would finally rid the world of the wretched Goblins. The Goblins knew something important was happening here too, and Avar was greatly concerned that they seemed to have discovered this before his own people, as they had already set up the base. Maybe they had just gotten lucky.

He visualized the compound again, weighing the different strike points. One almost entirely windowed building was used during the day as some sort of office. He still didn't know what they did in there, but he could tell that many of the workers were humans, just civilian contractors. A separate team was tasked with capturing and interrogating one of the workers, though he imagined they'd only get a human who wouldn't know the true nature of the facility. The real Goblins would be well protected, and any capture would bring a massive counterattack. Like with his own people, disconnecting the Goblins from their mental hive was almost impossible.

"Exiting vehicle," Avar said, knowing that his team would pick up the audio in a van two blocks away. He didn't bother to broadcast what he saw to the Hive, as the team had video surveillance that was much more detailed and immediate.

After donning a wide-brimmed hat, he reconnoitered the area on foot. There was no need to reconnoiter on foot, but he wanted to be seen with his jazzy new cane with its steel cobra handle. It didn't have a sword hidden in the shaft because a sword was about as useful against his prey as a week-old banana. It did, however, have a nice acid spray mechanism in the tip, enough to slow them down for cases in which a steel club to the head wasn't sufficient.

Even in a hostile free reign zone, he liked the idea of reconnoitering, though not quite as much as he liked saying the word. Any Normal who tried to jump him would end up in the morgue with a cobra-shaped indentation in his skull. Avar pondered this thought – would it really leave a recognizable indention? He made a mental note to try it out the next chance he got.

Run-down two-story commercial buildings that might have been trendy shops twenty years ago dominated the surrounding area. Now they mostly dealt with the necessities: a washeteria (apparently out of business, though it was hard to tell around there), food store, liquor store, drug store, needle shop, assorted filth shop, ammo shop, and one combo drug/ammo/liquor store that claimed to sell "legendary donuts." The gait of the people on the street was primarily of the "slink" variety. In his long black coat, he was overdressed, both for the weather and for the neighborhood, but a fireman didn't rush into a burning building without a little protection. He was too groomed to blend in, but he had no intention of blending in with this crowd. In fact, if he wasn't so close to his target and if the sun was down, he might enjoy a little extra "practice" with a few of the neighborhood inhabitants. They wouldn't be missed.

He scanned the rooftops. As his team members had already reported, the buildings' flat tops were ideal for observation of the compound. He would soon give the final approval for the initiation of the permanent surveillance equipment.

A group of street kids wandered super-chalantly in his direction, the smaller ones actually stretching their fingers to warm them up for pocket diving. A larger one, at about thirteen years old, unfolded a map as he approached Avar. He would likely shove the map in Avar's face and ask a question while the contents of Avar's pockets redistributed themselves amongst ten grubby urchins.

Avar smiled, wondering how many of them he could take out with a single swipe of his cane. The map-wielding leader, apparently realizing that the wounded doe in the tall grass was actually a Kodiak bear with a bazooka and an appetite, suddenly remembered that he had an appointment in the opposite direction.

Avar's smile fell.

Alas. At least the mission was still on target. "Set it up," he said to the air.

CHAPTER 18: IT'S TIME

Did the Alpha Team know that Jackson had followed them the night before?

He wondered if the guards would open fire on him as soon as he pulled up to work Friday, or instead wait until he was trapped inside the office. Probably the latter — they could torture him first then kill him at their leisure. Several images from his most gruesome drawings for the website floated to the top of his mind, many involving barbed hooks at the ends of chains.

The guards waved him in, though they didn't seem thrilled about it. At least that hadn't changed. Come to think of it, he preferred that the men with the guns did *not* smile as they locked him inside the sealed compound.

As soon as he entered the office, Simpson, in full British butler regalia, blocked his way. "Follow me," he said, and then walked toward the management offices.

"What's going on?" Jackson feared he knew the answer. He drifted after Simpson, weighing his chances of escape. A pacing guard peered in at him through the window like a zoo tiger eying some tasty child-sized morsel behind the glass.

He caught up with Simpson just as turned into Talbot's open office. Jackson peeked in. Talbot sat behind his desk as though chipped out of stone, while Simpson did the vertical version to one side of the door. A neon sign flashed in his mind, "Don't enter, fool!" The two would reanimate and fight over his corpse as soon as he crossed the threshold.

His feet would not move.

"Come in, please," Simpson said.

Jackson leaned forward, but his feet still refused.

"You got a problem there, boy?" Talbot asked.

Jackson's head turned of its own accord toward the exit. "No, sir," he lied.

"Well then get yer ass in here."

Simpson raised his eyebrows. "Do you need assistance?"

No. Simpson would likely rescue a child's cat stuck in a tree by throwing a stick of dynamite at it.

Jackson somehow floated into the room and heard the door click behind him – a coffin hinging closed. He stood in front of Talbot's desk, its claw feet perpetually clenched. A blue plastic cup on Talbot's desk filled with brown-soaked napkins was the likely source of the unmistakable odor of wintergreen dipping tobacco.

Talbot leaned forward and spit a brown stream into the cup, then wiped his mouth with the back of his hand. "You know why you're here?"

Because you're going to kill me?

Talbot shook his head slightly.

Did I say that out loud? "No, sir," Jackson said, wondering if Talbot really did shake his head.

Talbot cut his eyes to Jackson's right. Jackson half-turned to find Simpson right next to him. Simpson nodded.

"It's time," Talbot began, "for you to go on a mission with us."

Relief flooded Jackson but quickly drained, leaving behind a frightening new revelation, like a gasping fish stuck on land after a receding wave. They weren't going to kill him here; instead, they would drive him out of town on a "mission" where he would mysteriously disappear.

"Mission?" Jackson said. "I've never really considered myself, you know, a missionary… missionarily inclined, so to speak. More like an artist. Yeah." Were they going to take him out on a Vampire hunt like last night? The options weren't good. They would either attack a group of helpless innocents in an alley, or they would attack a group of crazed fiends who might or might not have a hankering for blood.

Jackson made drawing motions with his hand, in case they didn't quite understand what artists did.

Talbot nodded and the corner of his mouth turned up in possibly a failed attempt at a smile. "Yes," he said. "We go tonight. We'll leave from work."

"I don't know if I want to go. You need to tell me what's going on." Jackson was vaguely distressed at where his anger had taken his mouth.

"Is there a problem?" Simpson asked, leaning close, apparently yearning to solve the problem with the thud of a metal cane on flesh.

"Yeah, there's a problem," Jackson said, turning on Simpson. Something cracked inside. The conservative voice of reason in his head had a sock stuffed in its mouth and now rocked and hugged its knees in a corner up there. "I'm paid to draw pictures," he continued, his voice building. He would have taken a step toward him, but he would have had to step inside of Simpson's body to get any closer to him. "… not to go on missions. I don't have a big-ass Buck-Bill spear. I don't jam stakes into Vampires. I a-makey with-a the pictures." His fingers waggled in Simpson's impassive face.

Simpson flickered, a tiny signal blip in a flatline. Jackson dropped his hands as Simpson's cane blurred through the now-empty space.

"Simpson!" yelled Talbot. "Stand down!"

"You heard the man," Jackson said, not taking his eyes off Simpson. "Stand your ass down. I'm leaving."

Simpson stared with a look of shrewd appraisal. Jackson moved toward the door, half hoping someone would step in his way.

"You'll never learn the truth," Talbot said. He was now standing.

"We're bringing you in. This is a great honor."

"You're *pushing* me in," Jackson said, stopping his walk but still fuming. "I need the job, but there's something not right about you – about all of this place. What the hell is going on around here?"

"Come with us tonight," Talbot said. "And you will know. You can't run from everything."

"I don't run from everything." Jackson's anger flared again — why did people keep saying that? He wished he could have pulled that statement back in. He could hear how hollow his words sounded, could feel how hollow they really were.

"So what will it be?" Talbot asked.

"I'll be at my desk. Come get me when it's time."

CHAPTER 19: THE WRONG FOOT

He knew that kid from somewhere.

Abner was standing on the roof of the 7-story Macmillan Building, a squalid tenement whose opulence had evacuated from the Tovac Free Reign Zone as fast as the high heels and Italian leather shoes of the former tenants. New tenants had moved back in, of course, though they hadn't been quite the "caliber" of the originals. Non-human occupants had also arrived, claiming squatting rights in the hole-riddled walls and stairwells. Abner had the seventh story and roof to himself. At one time, people had challenged him for that space, foolish people who didn't know any better – and who wouldn't have time left in their lives to put their newfound wisdom to good use.

He opened one of the rooftop cages and flicked the wrist of other hand. A dead rat flew off of the end of the kitchen knife he held and tumbled into the cage — it had picked the wrong foot to scurry across during Abner's dinner earlier in the evening. May, a red-tailed hawk that he was nursing back to health, pounced on it. She would have preferred to catch and eat live prey, but carrion, especially if fresh, would do in a pinch. Abner watched her as she peeled the flesh away in strips. She occasionally looked up at him, her viselike talons still clutching her prey, her gaze impenetrable.

Boots, he thought. His old friend Boots would know something about that kid. In fact, there was something about this kid that reminded Abner of his friend. He hadn't seen Boots in over ten years — or maybe twenty — but he knew he had moved back to the area. Like himself, the few members who had left and somehow survived were drawn back to the area. Especially now.

As the efficient killing machine ripped apart the rat, Abner thought about the clueless kid. Did he have something to do with all this, with the magnetic pull of the Tovac Zone, the intensifying weather, and the escalating clashes? He thought so, though he suspected the kid had no clue what was going on or who he was working with. Or who either of them really was.

The hawk ripped away another chunk of flesh.

CHAPTER 20: VAMPIRES AND WHATNOT

By six o'clock that Friday evening, most of the office had cleared out. Gary must have gone home because he finally stopped asking Jackson what he had put into his coffee. Having noticed that his fake "secret project" document had been moved, Jackson had replied to Gary's first query with, "Why would I do something like that?" then conspicuously turned the paper face down. On the seventeenth visit, Jackson just yelled, "No!" even before Gary opened his mouth. The fake document was now a crumbled ball in his trashcan.

His stomach growled for the third time in the last hour. The hunger was distant, a white noise behind the alarm bells of his clattering stress. Why had he agreed to this ridiculous mission? Why was he even here?

He thought back to Mary. He'd done a bang up job screwing that one up.

"Lumber is a growth industry," she had said, missing the pun in her eagerness to throw out some of her newly acquired business knowledge. "You can start in the Arkansas yard across town from my new job, and after only a few years, you can get promoted to assistant manager. My dad will probably get you to run the whole business for him some day."

"Your dad hates me."

"My dad does not. He just wants what's best for me." She smiled and performed a malformed curtsy at that point, inexplicably. Looking back on their picnic now, it seemed so idyllic — the sun glinting off of her smooth blonde hair, her radiant face creased with deep dimples. Back then, though, he just saw a giant mousetrap baited with a small pile of crumpled dollar bills.

"Which explains his hatred of me."

"Hate is a strong word, and it's not good for your aura to speak like that." She looked at the space above his head and gestured with her tofu-melt sandwich.

"My aura is fine. Please stop monitoring my aura. It's private. In fact, I can tell that you're looking at my aura's private parts right now, and it's getting embarrassed."

"So what time are you going to apply for the job?" Her tone gave him the sudden urge to belt sand her. She sipped her bottle of carrot juice through a straw and eyeballed him, waiting.

He had thought about the lumberyard. He envisioned a table saw, an "oops!" and an airborne finger, followed by a festive fountain of blood. Then he pictured himself trying to paint with two missing fingers, and kids laughing at his stubby digits, and failing to pick his nose because the stumps were too fat, with no nails for dislodging the really stubborn ones.

"Err, let's talk about this later," he had said.

"Let's talk about this now. You're going to apply for that job." She actually stomped her foot, a somewhat awkward move when seated on a picnic blanket.

"You know you don't have to literally slap your foot on the ground to 'put your foot down.' It's just a figure of speech."

She threw the half-eaten sandwich at him. Because her dad had spent his time at lumberyards rather than teaching his daughter to throw, the move merely served to ruin a good sandwich on the blanket between them. Well, "good" might be too strong a word. It also became the source of an unpleasant odor for about a month and a half that emanated from the closet where he later stored the blanket.

"It's time," a soft voice said behind him, yanking him from his reverie.

He spun in his seat. Sy was looking at her feet, her black hair hiding her face.

"Time for what?" he asked, though several images produced by unsavory corners of his mind flashed.

"To go." She stepped away from the door of his cubicle, back in, back out again, and then was gone. He pursued her as she headed for the door along the back wall. Off to his left, Buck-Bull talked to a sweat-sheened bald coworker with heavy glasses while watching Jackson. Buck-Bill didn't look too happy, but at least he didn't have his spear with him.

Jackson returned to looking at Sy's backside – rather, to following her. It didn't count as ogling; he was just walking behind her. Though it was impossible (for him, at least) not to sneak a glance down there, if only to admire the shape of God's creation. And perhaps to wonder how it would feel to spank God's creation. God's creation was tight!

Verse one of Jackson's Book of Psalms.

She turned, and his head popped up like a cork fishing float. Had he just been caught? She looked as though she might speak, actually mouthing something, then just turned back and continued through the back door. Her expression had been one of somewhat guarded curiosity. Or, perhaps, she just wanted to ensure that he was following her. Hell if he knew. He couldn't read her at all. She was a blank slate, and no one had chalk. Maybe that look had been one of "loving admiration" or "lustful desires." Either of those would have been okay.

Next to the open doorway along the back wall lay an open cardboard box. She put her cell phone in it on top of a pile of others and gestured for him to do the same, which he did. They then proceeded down a thirty-foot hallway to a solid metal door that opened into the complex behind the office building. He had been curious about the rest of the industrial complex but had never gone past the front office building. His curiosity had been tempered by his aversion to getting shot in the back by armed guards who looked perpetually unsatisfied in the "shooting guys in the back" department. In fact, he imagined that if he had tried to sneak past them and had been shot by one of them, the others would prop his body up so that they could unload a few rounds too. It wouldn't be fair to just let one guy have all the fun.

The darkness outside was broken by two lights – one above the doorway of a metal building slightly to the left, and one on a telephone pole off to his right. Cracked sidewalks lay between corrugated metal shacks that seemed on the verge of collapse. The lit building to the left was larger and more substantial than the others. In fact, it was even a bit larger than the office building in which he worked, though windowless. Sy cut across the dead grass and hard-packed earth that filled in the non-paved areas of the complex. The ground felt almost as solid as the sidewalk.

A light breeze blew across his face, and he could hear the sounds of cars off to his right. This only registered in his mind because of the apparent isolation of his surroundings. He rarely found himself in such a large open space devoid of people. The place felt like a cemetery, and the distant car sounds were reassuring. Of course, they would go on unabated while he was tortured and murdered, their occupants unaware of the carnage within earshot as they talked on the phone to their accountant and tried to dodge the potholes and crack heads that coexisted in this lovely part of town.

In addition to the cars, he heard his own footsteps. Sy was completely silent, though he followed in her exact path. He didn't hear anything behind him, but he had the sudden feeling that someone followed, and he turned. Buck-Bill and a tall thin man walked as silently as Sy behind them. Jackson wondered if the tall guy was the one who'd carried the bleeding man into Talbot's office a while back. Turning back around, Jackson willed his feet to stop making such a racket, and they willed him to mind his own business – they were doing just fine without his help.

Sy opened the metal door of the building and shot Jackson a glance over her shoulder as she entered. He caught the door before it closed and followed her in. A grizzly bear stood in shadow just inside the door, though its silhouette suggested that it might actually be human, albeit one of staggering proportions. Jackson couldn't make out his face at all but decided that it might be best to skip a deeper inspection. Instead, he rushed past, feeling like he was walking under a hulking statue – one that breathed like rumbling thunder. He could feel the man's eyes on him, and he felt an almost overwhelming urge to brush at his own shoulder as though he could repel the intrusive stare that annoyed like a persistent fly.

The old concrete-floored storage warehouse slept in near darkness with the exception of a dim light ahead beyond lanes of eight-foot-high racks of shelves. Sy headed down one lane toward the source of the light. The smell of the place was old, like an aged house, and industrial, with a faint chemical undertone. As they crept deeper into the building, moving past shadowed shelves stacked with unidentifiable equipment, the chemical smell strengthened and took on a metallic odor.

Faint voices and scraping and clicking noises emanated from the source of the light. Around the final corner at the end of the storage row, a group of around ten men and women geared up for the mission. They wore black body suits, and many were sliding thin armored plates into pockets in the suits. Several of the members turned when he approached, all with narrowed suspicious eyes. He'd never seen some of them, though he recognized others from the office. Like Mandy, the Blue-Streaked Jumper. And the aging accountant Archer! What was he doing here?

Well, he appeared to be loading crossbow bolts into a wild weapon of wanton wickedness. What was that thing? Jackson stepped closer. It looked like a Gatling gun, but where each of the barrels should have been, instead there was another miniature Gatling gun, like a spinning gun of spinning guns. Archer popped out one of the miniature Gatling guns and held the circle of barrels up to his eye, looking down their back ends. He grabbed a thin tool and slid it into one of the barrels, cleaning it. Jackson had seen a Marine break down a rifle once, and Archer handled the weapon with the same precision and speed. Archer paused in his work and stared at Jackson, his expression neutral.

Was this really happening?

His pulse ratcheted even higher, and he felt momentarily lost, out of place, like he was floating in a dream. What was he doing there? The pressure of their eyes on him and the weight of his otherworldly situation roared around him like a surging wildfire. His adrenaline exploded, the bubble of pressure bursting, and he felt surprisingly at ease, exhilarated in fact.

A few of the team members, still frozen in place by his arrival, looked at a man off to his left. As they did, he heard incoherent mumbling but could see no speakers. The man was Simpson, fully dressed in a black body suit covered with curved black plates. Unlike the other members' body armor, spikes extended from the shoulders, elbows, hands, and even his back. He looked like a charred porcupine.

Keep him away from my balloon.

As though reading his mind, Simpson looked at him and the spikes retracted. Turning away, he continued strapping on gear. With this, the other team members also lost interest and returned to their own preparations. A man pulled his long straight blond hair into a ponytail, revealing a fresh scar on his forehead, while a dark-skinned squat woman next to him zipped up her body armor. Jackson wondered if they all had the extendable spikes like Simpson, or if they only gave that model to insane butlers with OCD. They would have made good car alarms. He made a mental note not to sit too close to any of them.

Open cases lay amongst the team members next to the benches where they changed. These held an assortment of short weapons, some of which Jackson recognized from his drawings. All were bladed or pointed. There were multiple variations of short swords, some straight and others curved or even hooked. Most had grooves or holes like Buck-Bill's spear. One helmeted man opened a case and pulled out short versions of the spear, these being about three feet long but having the addition of barbs along the shaft and a type of wire attached to the base. The man slid these into sleeves on his back, the wire feeding over his shoulder into a pocket on his hip. In addition to the short weapons in the cases, several members had longer weapons, such as Buck Bill spears, jet black like the rest of their gear.

Sy approached Simpson, and they spoke in soft tones, cutting their eyes in his direction. She shook her head vigorously at one point. After a moment, she returned to him.

"Have a seat there," she said, pointing to a wooden chair outside the ring of team members. She didn't look too happy. "You're going to be an observer on this one."

"How about gear?" he asked, not really sure why.

The corner of her mouth twitched. "Maybe next time." She swung upward the vertical door of a six-foot crate open. Excitement surged at the thought of watching her slide into a black bodysuit and strap on weapons. He was just an observer, after all, and would do his best to fulfill that role. However, to his great disappointment, she grabbed a black bundle out of the crate and ventured around a corner beyond the circle of light. He didn't even dream of following her, much like he didn't dream of getting his groinicles kicked in by biker chicks. Well, he did dream a bit — about following Sy, not about the biker chicks — but he had no intention of doing it. These guys might look upon her as their sister, and there were a lot of poky things around there. The permutations of maiming techniques were limitless with this group.

He kept the corner of his eye on the spot where Sy had disappeared into the darkness. If she returned encased in skin-tight black leather, he didn't want to miss it. At the same time, he watched the team prepare, doing his best not to catch anyone's eye. Several shot glances his way, lingering as they visually probed him. To show them his displeasure and to back them off, he pointedly ignored the stares.

One of those staring at him was Buck-Bill, though that didn't bother Jackson because Buck-Bill seemed to stare at everyone. After suiting up, he climbed onto a wooden crate and squatted there, standing guard — or rather *sitting* guard — the red-headed gargoyle returning to his perch.

These guys were crazy. That thought bobbed to the surface with increasing frequency, no matter how hard he shoved it back down by rationalizing that they were just, you know, creative types. But yet here they were, gearing up for battle against the ghosts of their imagination, a collective psychosis that somehow ensnared him. Not all the way though — he just needed the money. And a way to get his dad off his back. And maybe scoring a date with Sy would be a nice fringe benefit. He watched them. He was definitely in the fringe here. In fact, he was knee deep in fringe. He was rolled and battered and fried in fringe.

While he grasped for more clever "fringe" analogies, she emerged. He felt like he just licked a raw jalapeno with his brain. She was indeed in black leather. The bulky armor couldn't hide her svelte figure as effectively as the loose clothes she wore around the office. He shouldn't stare, but he couldn't stop. Besides the obvious, something else about her exerted a constant pull on him. Maybe it was the danger element.

He wanted gear. He wanted to suit up and grab a spear and gore a Vampire. These guys were insane and scary and now, inexplicably, he wanted in. And not just to impress Sy, who now strapped a knife and sheath to her lower leg. Now that was hot.

Look away.

He again heard a surge of voices but still couldn't see who was talking. The room abruptly quieted, and everyone looked down one of the dark hallways between the rows of shelves. A moment later, Talbot emerged, wearing his regular office clothes.

"Okay, team," he said, "as you know, this one is not a major cell. But it's close — which seems to be a pattern as you probably noticed — and we want a smooth one for our new civilian trainee, Mr. Jackson Krol here." He gestured toward Jackson.

Jackson felt the sharpened jabs of eyes upon him. He stood and nodded, not really agreeing to anything but hoping that that would end the matter. He fought the urge to wave as though he'd just called Bingo.

Why had he called him a "civilian"?

"Though you've no doubt memorized the parameters of this op, as usual, Simpson will brief you on the details again en route. Once again, I want to thank you again for what you're doing for ..." he flicked his eyes over at Jackson, then back to the group – "... for the world by ending this Vampire scourge. This may not be the death blow, but it'll be one of those bunches of cuts that we're inflicting. Remember to be on your guard too. I mean, I'm not sure why they have an active cell so close to one of our bases, so be extra vigilant. It may be a trap, so be ready. Make us proud!" He gestured to Simpson. "Your team." He turned and vanished into the darkness.

Simpson, still dressed in full black body armor and still looking like a butler dressed in full black body armor, rose and addressed the team. "Let's move out. Double-check your gear before we roll."

Jackson felt the urge to pat himself down to verify that his "gear" was double-checked. But he had no gear. Not even his phone. He looked at Sy and was startled to find her staring back. She'd never looked at him so directly before, at least as far as he knew. Unfortunately, the look was less akin to the way a hungry kid looked at an ice cream cone and more like how a mechanic studied a wheezing engine. She jerked her head in a "Follow me" way, and he did so.

The team walked to the back of the building and passed through a door into a garage that held three vehicles and a single metal garage door to the outside. Light spilling from a small office to the right dimly illuminated the space. Most of the team split into two groups and boarded two black utility trucks of the type typically used by plumbers or Swat teams, one with a decal proclaiming "Generic Services" and the other, "Delivery Vehicle."

It was delivering something, all right. What it needed to deliver was all its occupants to a psych ward.

The third vehicle was the extended conversion van, its side repainted with a purple unicorn on its hind legs, rearing up and neighing at a sunset a foot or so above it. Sy approached this vehicle along with Simpson and a gigantic blond man, the probable creator of the grizzly bear silhouette at the building's front door. Sy and Jackson took the back seat captain's chairs while the blond bear drove. Their van lead the convoy out of the small parking lot down a narrow lane past a few more run-down buildings, then a guard shack, and finally to the rear gate. Staffed by four armed guards, the gate was already open. Out on the street, the team accelerated into the night.

Jackson's first "mission." He wondered what he'd see that night. Vampires? Blood? Homeless people? Crazy office workers dressed up like it's Halloween?

Sy turned to him, her leather suit creaking even above the sound of the engine. He liked it.

"What do you think so far?" she asked.

The word, "tight," popped into his head, though he kept it away from his mouth. Conflicting images and emotions battled in his mind. For one, stunning woman in skin-hugging black leather and packing serious heat sat next to him. On the flip side, she was just one more citizen in Crazytown. These opposing thoughts thrust and parried. Another thought pushed its way to the front: if she weren't crazy, then there really were Vampires out there in the night. So, what would be worse, a crazy-but-hot potential-but-not girlfriend, or a sane potential-but-not girlfriend who battled real life blood-sucking Vampires on the loose? Tough call there – hard to say if either one of those could fill even a tiny glass of optimism halfway. Perhaps a glass that had been broken in half, with razor-sharp edges and vicious mouth-ripping shards in the bottom.

She raised her eyebrows at him, and he realized once again that he'd sat silent and expressionless (or at least he hoped he'd been expressionless) while these ideas ricocheted around in his head. "Oh," he said, "I was just considering that. I think this is, uh, the real deal."

"The real deal."

"I mean, you know, before I was just drawing pictures, and I was kind of disconnected with the whole... thing." He waved his hands in an effort to clarify the "thing," but it just looked like he was spreading grated cheese on a pizza. "Now, I mean, this is really happening. Going after ..." it was hard to say for some reason – "Vampires and all. And whatnot. Yeah."

He looked into her eyes and caught her appraising him, a shrewd and penetrating look that he'd first seen on her at the staging area. It made him nervous, like he was talking to the principal. Then her gaze dropped and she was Sy again. "Right," she said. "After this, you're in. Mostly."

"I'm in," he repeated, then silently let that sink in as they drove through the night.

They drove for about an hour before turning onto a country lane to the west of town in a mostly agricultural area. The gravel road led past fields of corn into thickening woods. The darkness grew more intense. Deeper in the woods, the convoy pulled off of the road onto a dirt path that wound still deeper into the black forest. After about ten minutes of twisting and turning along the bumpy path, they pulled to the side and stopped, extinguishing the engines and lights.

Simpson tapped his ear. "Get your gear," he said to no one in particular. "We move in five."

Sy handled Jackson an ear bud with a microphone extension. "I forgot to give you this earlier," she whispered. He put the earpiece in and heard voices from the other team members.

"Alpha team, two minutes."

"Beta team. Two minutes."

Sy whispered, "Hold the middle button down to talk, or you can double click it to leave the mike open, but you probably won't need that."

He nodded.

"Alpha team, ready."

"Beta team, ready."

Simpson looked back at Jackson and Sy. "Remember, you got him," he said to her.

"Yes sir," she replied.

Me? Jackson thought. He felt a little ashamed that he was a newbie who needed someone to watch over him. But then again, he didn't know what the heck was going on here, and she would make a fine babysitter.

The team exited the vehicles. None of the inside lights turned on, and no one slammed their doors. Except Jackson, of course. After he did so and received looks of dragon fire intensity, he realized what he did wrong, and his shame deepened. It had been the loudest door slam he'd ever heard — like he'd fired a shotgun during a moment of silence at church. Except that churchgoers typically didn't have jagged bladed hollow-shafted harpoon guns on them.

He smiled and waved at them. Those loons were going on a Vampire hunt, and he was with them. What did that make him?

This was really happening.

CHAPTER 21: CONTACT

"Okay, team," Simpson said, "to review, intelligence says the Piri are going to hit this community tonight. We're thinking it will be at oh three hundred, but that's not concrete. Teams will spread out according to our preparations, and remember, attacks could come from any position. And some may be decoys, so hold your position until directed to do otherwise. Understood?"

The team nodded and grunted their assent.

Jackson had a sudden premonition that Simpson was going to say, "I can't HEAR YOU!" but alas, that premonition was a fraud. And who the heck were the Peeree?

A kneeling man with one palm flat on the ground and the other holding an electronic tablet said, "All clear. No unusual activity, personnel or weather. We're a go on this end."

Jackson wondered for the 20th time what he was supposed to do. Sketch the action?

"Goji!" Simpson said, "Remember. You take Jackson. Teach him the boards."

Jackson had never heard Sy called that. That must have been her last name. Sy Goji.

She looked from Simpson to Jackson and back again, a look of concern on her face. "But sir," she said, "I've been most effective on –"

"Save it," Simpson said, not looking up. "We already discussed this."

Sy cut her eyes at Jackson, her concern melting into resignation.

He wanted to dig a nice big hole in the ground and shove his head in it.

"Yessir," she finally replied.

The team filed out. They were on a ridge at the edge of the forest overlooking a small village that lay across a sloping field. Sy led him back inside the conversion van. After sliding a curtain behind the front seats, blocking most of the light from the front windows, she sat in one of the rearmost captain's chairs and swiveled to a stiff flat cot that was mounted with a hinge along one wall of the van. In the gloom he could only make out vague silhouettes. When she folded it down, he realized that it wasn't a cot but rather a solid work surface – a fold-down desk. Behind it were mounted four dark flat panel LCD screens that glowed dimly.

The desk looked close to level, but then again, it would depend on what incline the van was on. The pocket holding his level burned, but he just couldn't do it – not here, not now, not with Sy there. He leaned down and looked at the desk from the edge. It bowed up slightly at the right rear corner. He ran his hand along the edge.

She tapped on the desk, and a virtual keyboard appeared on the active surface. The four monitors sprang into life as dim red lights filled the van.

"Nice," Jackson said, pulling his mind away from the desk, though it wouldn't let go entirely.

She didn't respond, still apparently fuming at getting left out.

Maybe he could dig that hole a bit deeper so he could get his entire body in there.

"What do we have here?" he asked, wanting to get out of his swirling head and into the world where it was safer. "What's all this?"

She stared at him as though she didn't know he'd been there. Recognition snapped into her face as she was pulled out of a reverie.

She looked back to the screens. "This is the mobile command center on missions, or at least one of them." She gestured to the panels. "An operator typically mans this station," she paused, probably considering the fact that she was stuck as the operator, "and keeps the team coordinated. Typically, Simpson is here, too, but he's been going out on missions more frequently."

On that night alone, he'd heard her speak more than the entire time he'd been working there. "What about Talbot?" he asked, thinking about Simpson's boss. He seemed more the "mission" type than Simpson, though Simpson did seem handy with that cane of his. Jackson rubbed his knuckles.

"No, he never comes out any more, though Simpson is always in contact with him."

He watched her as discreetly as he could as she tapped away at her virtual keyboard. Screens flickered and danced on the wall, but he only pretended to look at them. They were meaningless swirls of color. He'd never been alone with Sy, truly alone, and he felt strangely outside his own body, like he was only a passenger. He wished he could tell the captain to do something clever, something suave.

Although now was probably not the time for suave. She was dressed in battle gear, angry because of him, and probably hell-bent on killing innocent villagers due to some collective delusion or brainwashing. Definitely not the time. Probably "never" would be the appropriate time to court a potentially murderous psychopath. Probably.

He grabbed the first thought that floated from his subconscious and verbalized it. "So this is real." He still couldn't quite grasp that fact.

She didn't look at him as she tapped a key. "Bumblebee, the tulip is blooming," she said into a mic that hung from her ear in front of her mouth. She tapped a button on the keyboard and said, "What is real?"

It took Jackson a moment to realize that she was now talking to him.

"This," he said, pointing at the electronics, then realizing that that didn't quite cover the breadth of his statement, waved his arms vaguely in the direction of the village and the armed team that now roamed there. "All this. Is it, you know, real?" He knew it wasn't real, but he wanted to get her take. Was she crazy, or did she just need the money?

She paused, cutting her eyes over at him. "You still don't really believe, do you?" she asked.

He had a sudden chill at the thought that she would turn him in, and he'd get fired. Or, somewhat worse, get mounted on a Buck-Bill harpoon in front of the office.

"Well," he started, trying to assemble his words, "Let's just say it all seems... fantastic." That was good. He hadn't planned it, but that word almost made it sound like he thought everything was cool, but he really meant that the entire situation felt more like fantasy than reality.

Her black gaze cut into him, though he didn't look away. There was much hidden behind those depthless eyes.

She turned back to her monitors. "One might think that, but it's true. They exist, and they're not good people. We have to stop them." She froze, like a thought just hit her. She turned back to him abruptly. "You do know that you can't talk about these missions, right? I mean, people know about the Vampires because we want people to know about them. But they can't know about these missions, right?" She looked scared.

"Oh yeah," he replied. "I know." He considered doing the "locking your mouth up with a key, and then throwing it away" motion, but decided that this might not be the right time for that, either. "Locked in a van with a hot psychopath" was not the right time for a lot of things.

She nodded and turned back to the screens. "They're invading our area, and we need to know why."

"So," Jackson said, "do they really do all the Vampire stuff like turn into bats and suck blood and hide from garlic?" He'd wanted to ask these questions since he'd been there but never had the opportunity. Plus he hadn't known who to ask. He wasn't even sure he should be asking her, but he had to know – not just about the Vampires, but about how she felt about all this. Was she really as crazy as the rest of them?

"You just don't get it," she said, a little exasperated.

"No."

"We call them Vampires, but they're not really Vampires like in the books and stuff. You know those drawings you do? Have you seen any that are about wooden stakes or garlic or crosses?"

"No, but—"

"Right. That stuff is all baloney."

"So, who are these guys then?" He was really confused now.

She stood as much as she could, given that this was a conversion van, then walked around her seat and sat back down. "No one told me I could tell you this, but you're here, so I can only assume that you're checked out. If not, I guess they can just kill you later."

"Huh!? Wait! Are you kidding?" She certainly didn't look like she was kidding, though he'd never really caught her in a moment of mirth.

"Yes." No smile.

"Oh, good."

"Perhaps." Slight mouth movement that could have been a smile. Before he could jump in for some clarification on that quite relevant point, she continued. "They're similar to us, though the genetics are a bit skewed."

"Wait… similar to us humans?"

She paused, looking at him briefly but intently. "Uh, yeah, sure. Like us humans. Though they're quite crazy."

Crazy compared to whom? "Then, what are they? What do they want?" He had so many more questions but he didn't want to bombard her and have her skip over the most important ones. Like perhaps the one about whether they would kill him – that one was pretty high on the list.

"Their true name is 'The Piri'."

"The Piri? I think I had some Piri chicken at a restaurant." He thought for a second. "Wait! You don't think that –"

"No," she said without looking up. "Piri Piri is a spicy pepper from Mozambique. So no, you didn't have Vampire chicken."

"Oh."

"And Piri is also a name for Korean double reed instrument made of bamboo."

"Oh. That's unfortunate. I see why they might prefer 'Vampire' over 'Piri'. I'd rather go as 'vicious neck-biter' than 'gay Asian flute thing.'"

"Gay?"

Dang it! He had been trying never to use that word, and now he feared that she'd open a Minority Slander Verbal Assault case against him. Free speech was fine and dandy as long as one didn't toss out a Protected Class Grade 4 Banned Word. People who used harsh language were obviously haters, and hate speech, especially Grade 4 Hate Speech, could get you real jail time. On the other hand, he'd never heard words in Grades 1-3, so any undesirable language that could be perceived to be critical of a Protected Class was straight up Grade 4. "Not that people doing stuff to other, you know, same type people with the same stuff is, you know, bad."

"So you mean 'gay' as in 'happy'."

"Gay can mean happy?"

She looked at him like he was as dumb as he felt. "Yes."

"Well, then, yes. That's what I meant. A happy Asian flute that some might perceive as leaning heavily toward, you know, the feminine side of the spectrum." Man, this conversation had seriously veered into the wrong lane, one filled with oncoming military transport vehicles carrying fuel and explosives and lawyers. He tried to wrench it back. "Wait, I think I remember Simpson saying that name. But what do they want?"

"To kill us," she said, exactly as she might say, "Yes, I *do* want to supersize that."

Jackson wondered who the "us" really were, now suspecting that the people at the office were less than typical, or perhaps more. "You mean, 'us' as in the people in the office, or 'us' as in all people?" he said.

She held up a finger and cupped her other hand over her earpiece, pushing it in. She listened intently for a moment, her eyes unfocused. Then she dropped her hands and looked back to her terminal.

"Us," she said. "Everyone, but mainly us."

"Me too?" he asked, wondering if he was in the Vampires' "leave this loser alone" category, or perhaps the "kill when convenient" or even the "kill toot sweet" category.

She said nothing, though her right hand froze in place for a moment before continuing up to tap a button alongside one of the screens. "We," she finally started. "I mean, I'm not sure. Yet."

Her hand went up to her ear again. "We have movement!" she said, her hands and body animated as she tapped keys. One of the displays switched to infrared. The image was askew slightly, and he guessed that it was one of the temporary cameras that the team had mounted as they had advanced into the town and taken up positions. The unmistakable infrared image of a human staggered toward the camera.

"What's happening?" he whispered, unable to contain himself.

She reached over to his earpiece and made a quick double press motion. The earpiece emitted a single soft tone. He suspected that the team had changed communication frequencies since his earpiece had been silent for several minutes, and she had likely just switched his onto the same channel.

"Contact," a voice said softly in his earpiece.

"40 meters, 3 o'— wait!" she whispered into the microphone, this last word with it off. "I mean," she continued into the microphone, "40 petals, 3 stalks."

"Buzz buzz. Stay on that petal."

He leaned in. On screen, the infrared figure moved, though not with the fluid grace of a vampiric assassin. It looked more like the fluid grace of a person staggering away from a concussion.

Don't kill him, he thought. It's just a guy stumbling out of a bar.

"Possible wasp, uh, flying to ... uh ... he's reaching for something!" a voice said in his ear.

Jackson soon saw what he was reaching for, and after a moment, an infrared glow formed on the wall and ground of the alley as the man relieved himself.

"That doesn't look like a lethal weapon," Jackson said, smiling at Sy. Maybe the guy was Abner.

She cut her eyes at him, expressionless. "That's a negative on stinger," she said into the microphone.

Jackson felt stupid, like an amateur, but that emotion was soon swamped by anger that these crazy people on their idiotic Vampire quest could make him feel that way. What's wrong with a little joke? This whole thing was a joke. But it paid well.

Plus there was Sy.

He looked at her, feeling relatively safe in his inspection while she busied with the terminals. The tight body armor looked like something out of a movie, and in fact probably was inspired by a movie. Despite its bulkiness, he could see real curves there. Her dark hair, pulled back into a ponytail, was a color that was probably shared by over half the planet, but somehow it looked special on her, unique. He imagined himself stroking her cheek, feeling its smoothness beneath his fingers.

Then she looked at him, and not the way he was looking at her. It had a decided "what the hell are you looking at?" vibe to it. But then, apparently reading something in his face, it softened.

Or at least it seemed to from the corner of his eye – he had looked away almost immediately. When Mom walks into the kitchen, you take your hand out of the cookie jar.

"That was..." he started, "not so much.... I mean, yeah. Not a, you know, Vampire. Or Piri or whatever." He suddenly found something that took up all of his attention on one of the screens. It was a motionless black smudge that had been there the entire time. He stared through it intently.

She said nothing, loudly.

Jackson remained in lock-down mode the rest of the evening, channeling his outbursts into inbursts, hoping that extreme laconism might suck his former blathering out of her memory, like the vacuum of space on the air of a punctured spaceship.

After several painful hours, made even more painful by an ever-expanding bladder, the team returned to their vehicles. The mission had been a bust. Faulty intelligence, or perhaps the Vampires had somehow detected them, Simpson mused on the return trip. Or perhaps a spy. One other outlandish possibility that Jackson failed to offer was that there was no such thing as Vampires.

"What do you think about that?" Simpson turned and asked him. "You think a spy tipped them off?"

Jackson felt the implications of that question immediately, though he didn't blurt out what he was thinking.

I'm not a spy, and even if I were, who would I report to? Vampires?! I've got an idea. Maybe you didn't find any Vampires because THERE'S NO SUCH THING AS VAMPIRES!

"I suppose that's possible," Jackson instead said, trying to remain noncommittal.

Simpson stared at him a moment longer, a little too long for Jackson's taste, then turned back.

Back at the office compound, they dropped him off in the parking lot. As he stepped out, Simpson said, "I do not need to remind you that this did not happen. Are we clear?"

"Yeah, of course. Sure," Jackson said.

Jackson swung the van door closed. As it shut, it cut Sy's "Bye" in half before it got all the way out of the car. He said, "Bye" in return as the van pulled away.

CHAPTER 22: THE SNAKE

Avar sat back in the small apartment that served as their remote outpost and staging area. He steepled his fingers and tried to push the sound of the aerobicizing upstairs neighbors out of his mind so that he could concentrate. For the hundredth time that day, he considered sending Bronson up there to silence them, and for the hundredth time he dismissed the idea. He couldn't jeopardize the mission because he was tired of being annoyed.

And this mission grew more critical by the day. The Goblin team had just gone on a mission of their own to a nearby village on the outskirts of the Tovac Zone following a false lead planted by Avar's team. Why had a supposed enemy sighting sent the Goblins out with such haste? Possibly in preparation for their Grand Scheme, the focus of Avar's mission. He had to disrupt whatever they were planning, but he had to discover what it was before he could disrupt it, and his inside man wasn't any help. To top it off, after watching them for days, he'd concluded that their office complex was nearly impenetrable. Storming it would be suicide.

The only shiny coin in this pile of rocks was what he'd learned on the Goblins' last mission — Simpson went with them. If Avar could wipe him out along with that team, he wouldn't exactly cut the head from that snake, but he would at least rip out one of its fangs. And Tazia would be very pleased with him if he could pull this off. A Goblin defeat of this magnitude would surely disrupt their Grand Scheme — or perhaps "grand scheme," though he suspected it probably deserved the capitals.

He didn't have to know what the party was about before he could ruin it.

CHAPTER 23: FAMILY TIME

Seated at her kitchen table, Sy pushed aside her half-eaten Coq au Vin. Cooking was better than eating, she had long ago decided. She scanned the silent apartment, empty, and then took a slow deep breath.

In her heart, she felt a tiny ember, a forgotten feeling, almost foreign, weak. Perhaps with some kindling, it could flare up and share its light and heat, driving away the darkness.

That would never happen; that *could* never happen.

She stood, needing to move. After dumping the remains of her dinner into the trash, she walked into the living room and sat on a low table between the couch and the fake fireplace. She crossed her legs and stacked her hands on her top knee, then gazed at the item on the mantle.

A charred bone rested in an ornate display stand that was designed to hold a Japanese sword. The bone was a big one, approximately the size of a woman's femur.

"I talked to my new friend again today, Grandma," she said, a smile pulling the edges of her mouth.

CHAPTER 24: BAITING

"They bit," Orion said, smoothing down his black slicked hair. He almost wiped off his oily hand on his long black overcoat, then seemed to reconsider, looking around.

He and Avar were standing on the flat roof of their remote command center as a minor electrical physics storm built overhead in the night sky. Clouds glowed in shades of purple and pink as building charges powered the crackling furnaces inside.

Avar nodded. "Yes they did," he said, "and don't wipe that slimy hair juice on me."

Orion looked back at him, a bit startled. "Oh, of course not, sir." He put his damp hand in his pocket.

"The next one, we'll be ready. Did the cleanup team find anything they left behind?"

Orion shook his head. "No sir. As usual, nothing. Not even footprints. One member found a loogie but it might have been from the garbage man. We're analyzing it now."

"I see."

"It was quite sticky."

"That's quite enough. Tell –"

"I think the guy must have a sinus infection, because it was almost –"

"I said," Avar said, forcefully, "that is enough. Now, you and Bronson go prepare the next phase."

Orion clicked his heels, turned, and climbed down the ladder.

Overhead, the storm clouds cracked open, releasing cloud to cloud lightning that split the night with bursts of glowing electricity, the massive arcs holding their position, maintaining the connection. The bolts danced in place as an explosion of sound smashed Avar. He tilted his head toward the flashing, deafening, horrifyingly beautiful show, marveling as the cloud colors morphed from the shifting energy.

He and his brethren would soon unleash such a maelstrom on the wretched Goblins. It didn't matter what the enemy's grand scheme was – one could not execute a scheme when one's head was crushed flat.

No, not messy enough.

One could not act when one's head was cracked open like a coconut.

Too fruity.

One could not act when dead.

Yes, that was it.

The clouds disgorged a sheet of gray rain, but Avar was down the ladder and back in the building before it could even kiss the roof.

CHAPTER 25: REALITY IS FOR SUCKERS

"So explain to me again how you convinced me to start this back up again," Chester panted on Saturday morning, his hands on his knees in the center of a racquetball court. "Oh yeah, you're trying to buff up for the crazy girl, and I just got dragged into it." He straightened up and made a spanking move. "Oh yeah, Jackson likes 'em kinky." Then his face dropped, and he put his hands back on his knees. He appeared close to death.

"You're creating a court hazard there," Jackson said. "Anyone runs through that spot, they'll be on their back in a puddle of nasty Chester sweat."

Chester opened his mouth to speak but just nodded.

"Let's go," Jackson said. The two of them left the court and found some lawn chairs in the health club lobby to sit on. They were in a "squatter club," a health club that was currently embroiled in a legal battle and therefore unable to officially accept customers. In the meantime, it had rented the space out to a group of guys who basically just stood at the door and took money for people to use the facility on a per-usage basis. No jazzy music piped in, no clean towels (or clean anything, really), but it was cheap, and cheap was always high on both of their lists.

"I still can't believe you're going back," Chester said. "I mean, talking about doing all this crazy stuff is one thing, but these guys actually went out to attack some people."

Jackson nodded.

"With big freakin' weapons! Are you sure it wasn't some elaborate hoax?"

"For me? I'm not worth it. Who would spend so much to punk me?"

Chester seemed to consider this, sweat still streaming down his plump face. "Maybe it's a new reality show."

Jackson brightened to this, his mind rapidly connecting pieces. "Yes! That must be it! I'll bet there are several of us who are clueless, and all the others are actors. That explains everything!"

Chester nodded and made a self-congratulatory gesture. "Would I steer you wrong?"

"Yes." Jackson leaned forward. "Think about it. That other attack where I was on the roof was probably staged, right? I mean, I never actually saw anyone hurting anyone else. It was too dark. I just heard a lot of noise, then that crazy Abner guy appeared."

"He must be in on it too."

"Yes, yes! I wonder if the bar guys were too. Man, I wish I knew what the plot was, what they're expecting me to do."

"Whatever you do, don't let them know you're in on it."

Jackson thought about this. "No, you're right—"

"Of course."

"I need to act like this is all normal, like I see this every day." His mind continued to reassemble his memories into this new scaffolding, and he much preferred the new mental image. "I'll act like I'm not scared at all. Which, of course, I wasn't." He gave Chester a look, but Chester was leaning back precariously in the cheap plastic chair and staring at the ceiling, probably still trying to maximize oxygen intake. A sweat puddle had formed under his chair. Jackson continued, "I wonder if Sy is in on it, or if that's even her real name." Her image floated across his mind. "Yeah, it has to be. She *feels* like a Sy."

Chester popped forward. "So what does a Sy feel like?" He had a look, a look that on most faces might be classified as "sly," though on him it just seemed perverted. Jackson knew that look was for show. Well, mostly.

He had no intention of letting Chester sully Jackson's image of Sy with his overdeveloped gift of lewdness, so he didn't say what he was thinking — that she probably felt smooth, and warm. "Like a Spiker car alarm. If you pet her the wrong way, that is," he said.

Chester's eyebrows went up as he nodded, and Jackson knew that he had failed to stem the mental storm of debauchery that now swirled in Chester's head. He moved on. "And that second mission. Nothing happened. Some guys just wandered around in a village with some weapons." He thought about the bony Archer with his massive double spinning Gatling gun; it probably didn't even work. "I'll bet that was an episode that they set up to isolate Sy and me, to see how we would react when we were alone."

Chester stood up, animated. "Dude," he slipped in his sweat puddle but caught himself. "You need to create some conflict! Those guys love conflict. Have you ever watched one of those shows? The jerks are the ones who get all the screen time. You know why? Because nice is boring. Nobody wants to see dudes curtsying to one another. They ..."

"Dudes don't curtsy."

"... want to see people yelling and throwing things. The public wants to watch unhappy crazy people become unhinged and jump across tables. They need action."

"I don't know if that's such a great—"

"You've got to. What's the alternative? If this place is for real, then you'll have to leave soon anyway because they're all crazy and you're too delicate and might get killed."

"What—?"

"And if this place is a reality show set-up, then you need to step it up to get air time. Boring equals no air time equals no cool TV gig after the show is over. You ever thought of that? What are you going to do after the show airs? You'll be out of a fake job."

Jackson hadn't attached that little outhouse to his mental image of his current situation. Once the fake job was over, his very real paycheck would end too.

He needed to step it up.

CHAPTER 26: LIFE IN THE ZONE

On Monday morning Abner went for a walk. It was a good walk. The weather was clear and not too cold, the Tovac SecForce personnel were off somewhere frolicking and extorting, and no one tried to steal his shoes. He didn't even have to hit anyone with a pipe. He walked and walked.

After a time, a pink tear formed in the sky, but it was a small one and quickly disappeared. The Piri and Jone-Zen read prophesy into the weather and thus increased their aggressive assaults on one another. But they had it backwards. As different as they were, both groups were tied to this world, bound more deeply to nature and physical law than humans. Conflict between them threw things out of balance, turned the world in upon itself, like a bogus autoimmune reaction that caused a body's white blood cells to attack the body itself. The laws of the universe were bending, and cracks were forming. God help them all if they broke entirely. The world would puke while he and his fellow citizens bickered at the bottom of the toilet.

Come to mention it, he did have to take a leak.

He walked behind a blackened car that had been blown out of the street – maybe an RPG, but he couldn't be sure unless he looked closer – onto the sidewalk where it now leaned with its roof at a downward diagonal against a gutted movie theater. As he relieved himself against the building, he regretted that he had chosen this neighborhood to do so. The Tovac Zone, like any other region, had its good and bad neighborhoods. This one wasn't the worst, but it was not a good one in which to be caught with your pants down and your pipe (the metal one, that is) in your pocket. Plus, he'd walked so far that most people here didn't know him, making him most definitely "on-limits." He finished up as fast as he could at his age and pulled out his pipe as he continued his walk. He was almost there.

After a few minutes, he saw a group of kids playing "kick the brick" and approached them. Before he got there, one of them saw him and alerted the others. They turned and gave him a scan, determining that he was a low-margin mark. They returned to their game.

"Excuse me," Abner said when he got in range.

"What do you want?" the apparent leader, a kid in his early teens and the biggest of the bunch, said.

Abner continued walking toward them, albeit at a slow mosey. "Just a quick question."

"Get lost!"

"This will only take a second."

"I said get lost!" the kid screamed, picking up the brick and heaving it at Abner.

With a lightning smooth stroke, Abner swung his pipe around and connected with the brick, generating a loud clank and a cloud of brick dust, sending the remaining fragment over a three-story building behind the kids.

Every kid's head followed the arc of the brick, then back to Abner, their eyes satisfyingly round and their mouths half open.

"It seems you lost your ball," Abner said, a bit perturbed by his placement of the brick – back left corner of building instead of back center – but still pleased that he might not need to use the pipe on any of the kids' heads after that demonstration. "I just want to know if you've seen unusual activity here lately."

They stared at him, a few taking steps backwards.

"Like perhaps," Abner continued, "men unloading equipment. Guys wearing black with slicked back hair."

"Oh!" said a red-head in the back, the runt of the group. "What about that guy with the cane?" he said to his compatriots. "He looked like money but smelled like danger."

Wow, a poet. "Well put, young man. So, where did you see this individual?"

"What do you want with him?" the leader asked.

"Are you concerned for his safety?" Abner asked.

"I'd like to kick his ass, if that's what you mean."

Not really, but that answered the question. "Let's just say, we're not friends."

"Up the street on the right," the leader said. "He and some other lugs hauled in some equipment and spent all day walking around and climbing on the roof and watching the old factory."

Bingo. "You boys have been very helpful," Abner said. "Thank you for your time, and please don't let them know I snooped around."

"What's it worth to you?" the lead kid asked.

Abner, having planned for this exact scenario, pulled a ragged baseball out of his pocket and tossed it to the redhead. As Abner turned and walked away, he heard a scuffle from the group. They were probably tackling the kid with the ball to get it from him. It was a tough life, especially in the Tovac Zone.

CHAPTER 27: JUST AN ORDINARY GUY

That same Monday, Jackson had no idea what to do as he sat in his tiny office cubicle amongst the fossils of aging machinery. He had a fresh stack of papers from Talbot detailing new drawings that he needed to make, but he couldn't concentrate on them. Work distractions were like a fly buzzing around a man dropped into a hungry lion's cage. And there were two lions in his cage – one was named Sy and the other had multiple personalities. One of those personalities called itself, "crazy-ass office people are insane and carry big freaking weapons," while the other was named, "funky reality show executives want you to dance." He had flip-flopped over which personality was the true one. It was all surreal somehow. He was in it now, though, and there was no turning back. Severe tire damage lay that way. If this were real, these guys were obviously a bit, er, *altered*, and he'd rather see their weapons from the handle end instead of the little pointy end that he might face should he decide to "quit the team." And if they *weren't* real, well hell, he could just go all out like he had decided earlier.

What he really wanted to do was to talk with Sy. He had seen her leaving the break room as he was about to enter it, but she had only given him a perfunctory wave, like they hadn't shared anything. Maybe they hadn't shared anything, like two people who ride on the same bus but get off on different stops. Being at the same place at the same time doesn't make a connection.

Simpson had blocked him from talking with Talbot, and Simpson himself was about as helpful as a solid iron flotation device. Archer hadn't been at his cubicle all day.

He heard Mandy laughing in the distance. He stood and saw her head bobbing as she jumped in her laughter across a small sea of cubicles. As he headed to see her, a female guard patrolling the opposite wall peeled away and walked toward him, perhaps to "suggest" that he return to his seat. Jackson faked a dramatic stumble, flailing his hands in the air as he dropped down below the cubicle wall, hiding himself from the approaching guard. Crouched, he then made his way over to Mandy's cubicle.

He waited impatiently by the door as she talked and giggled and laughed into her phone, high mirth sending her into jumps, her blue-streaked hair bouncing. She probably had great calves. She was faced away from him, and he wasn't sure how to get her attention, though he needed to do it quickly. He stepped into the cubicle to get out of the hallway, still crouched. He tapped her on her shoulder.

What happened next was, in a word, unexpected. Mandy leapt into the air, sending her phone skyward. She landed on her desk facing him in a fighting stance, her face still frozen in a smile that had somehow morphed into something too frightening to be called a grimace. His breath caught in his throat. Blue-Streaked Jumper was about to eat him.

After seeing him, her face shifted back to a normal state, and she held out her left hand palm up at about shoulder height to the side. Her phone plopped into it. "I'll call you back," she said into it before sliding it into her pants pocket. Then, to Jackson, "Do not do that again."

Jackson nodded vigorously to indicate he understood, but then after considering it, shook his head back and forth with equal vigor, as if to say, "No I definitely won't. You look about as insane as the rest of these people, and I don't ever want to see that face again." Why was he here? What was he about to ask her?

Oh yeah. "Uh, Mandy?" he asked as she climbed down from her desk. "What I wanted to ask was..." He thought about the approaching guard and got to it, though his voice was just a hoarse whisper. "What happened last night? Is this real? I mean, are you in on all this stuff?"

A shadow of crazy face slid in and out, then a big Mandy grin sprouted. "I'm not really sure what you mean," she said.

"I mean —"

"I don't know what you're talking about. We just had a team meeting last night."

"You!" a female voice said behind him. He turned. The spike-haired guard that had approached him earlier stood at the doorway of the cubicle. Tattoos of black tendrils snaked from beneath her shirt onto her neck with one ending in front of each ear, twisting into a loop like a curl of hair. "Talbot wants to talk to you."

"Thanks for your time," Jackson said to Mandy, though he didn't really feel that thankful.

"Anytime sweetie," she said, giving him a wink and a smile that thoroughly freaked him out. It was the smile of a woman who would say, "Welcome home, honey," to her husband, and then plunge an ice pick into his ear while he slept on a recliner in front of a TV playing college football. She was now "The Blue Loon," though the word "loon" in the name didn't really narrow it down in this place.

He followed the tattooed guard. She seemed to have a really sweet voice beneath her gruff tone. She could probably sing a guy a lullaby as she gutted him with a hunting knife. Multi-talented. Plus the tattoo was wicked. He wanted to ask where the tendrils led, but he didn't want her to sing him a lullaby.

She arrived at Talbot's office and gestured with her automatic weapon. "Boom!" she said, then walked back to her post without even a sideways glance.

He stepped in and was met headfirst by a wall of sound.

"Jackson!" Talbot boomed from behind his desk. It wasn't a "Welcome to my office, Jackson" – more like a "Jackson, I'm going to open you up like a baked potato." The door closed behind him, and he was not surprised to see Simpson standing by the door. "Sit!" Talbot continued.

Jackson walked to the seat opposite Talbot and sat. Simpson walked up beside him and removed a glove as he had the first time he came in.

"Don't move," Simpson said. He put a finger to Jackson's temple and inhaled slowly and deeply. After a moment, he exhaled and removed his finger.

As ridiculous as this all was, the possibility that this all was part of a reality show seemed distant and ludicrous somehow.

Jackson heard him mumble something and turned his head to look up at him. "What?" Jackson asked.

Simpson's hand was still closed with the exception of his extended index finger. His confused face changed to one of surprise at Jackson's question, then returned to his neutral angry default. "So, did you just hear something?" he asked Jackson.

Jackson read danger in that question. "No," he lied. "I just wanted to know what you were doing."

Simpson and Talbot exchanged a look.

"Who are you?" Talbot said.

What did that mean? Did they think he was a spy? "I don't understand," he said. "I'm Jackson Krol. Just an ordinary guy. A graphic artist."

"Then why," Talbot said, "are you blank? Simpson thinks you might be masking something."

Simpson walked completely behind Jackson, and Jackson turned his chair sideways so that he could see him in his periphery.

"Nervous?" Simpson asked. He rubbed some antibacterial spray into his hands, then pulled on white gloves.

Jackson had been nervous, but now he just wanted to punch Simpson in the nose. He pictured his nose flattened to the width of his entire face and smiled, then turned back to Talbot. He felt strangely invigorated, much like he had when he was with the team in the staging area.

"What do you mean, I'm blank?" Jackson asked.

"Simpson has a gift," Talbot said, looking from Jackson over Jackson's shoulder to Simpson, then back again. "He's pretty good at sizin' up people, and you got nothing. We read a certain way, regular folks read a different way, and then there's you."

"What do you mean by 'regular folks'? Who are the 'we' in that statement?" Jackson had known something was different about these guys, and his fear and nervousness were now just feeble squeaks beneath the galloping hooves of the questions stampeding through his mind and knocking down vases and crapping on the carpet.

Talbot coughed out a single, "Ha!" that must have passed for a laugh. "Now, I'm telling you this because you're a good artist and because I don't want to break in another. Plus I don't get you, and that means you're an opportunity for me to learn something new. You get me? You're either hiding something from us, or perhaps something in you is hiding from your own self."

Jackson had no idea what this meant, but he kept quiet.

Talbot continued. "And when I figure it out, two things will happen. I'll learn something new, and I'll know what to do with you." That had an ominous undertone that wasn't lost on Jackson. "As for us, you must know that we're not exactly your typical citizens, right? We are the Seven, and we have an important mission to protect the public by eradicating the scourge of the Vampire plague." That felt like a rehearsed sound bite, part of a script. "We have developed some highly specialized equipment and skills that place us in another category of humanity, if you will. Ergo, we read differently to Simpson. You, however, read like a piece of furniture. And that does not happen."

Jackson shrugged. "I don't know what to tell you," was all he could say. He had wanted to ask for clarification about what had happened last night, if this was all real or some media construction. But that would be fruitless. If it really were a reality show, these two would obviously be in on the gag, and he'd just be showing his hand by asking questions. If it wasn't a reality show, then, well, these guys had already told him the company line, and he prayed it wasn't true. Better to have a bunch of crazy Vampire hunters on the loose than a bunch of crazy Vampires, even with sane Vampire hunters on their tail.

However, this whole "reading" bit had some "legs," as they said in show business, and he was now possibly in the biz, right? Maybe. In any case, it seemed like some parlor trick, though if it were one, it was probably the crappiest parlor trick he'd ever seen. There were no ghostly images or knocking sounds or spirit burps or anything. Just Simpson with a finger. It was as exciting as watching an old lady push an elevator button, though this one didn't even have the "Ding."

"As I expected," Talbot said. "So, what did you think of the mission?"

Jackson hadn't expected him to drop the issue so quickly. "Uh, you definitely have an impressive set-up." He felt like he needed to say something else, if only to divert them from the fact that he didn't really answer the question. "So, I know you didn't find what you were looking for, but did you find anything else that might be, you know, important?"

"I'm afraid not, though that in itself might mean something."

"Huh?"

Talbot's gray eyes studied him a moment through his round glasses. "I mean," he said, leaning back in his chair and interlocking his fingers behind his head, "that an absence of something expected can be a clue. Say you go out and whip your dog every day for digging a hole in the garden. Then you go out one day and don't find a hole in the garden. You see something that could be normal – it's just a garden. But the lack of the hole tells you something. It tells you that your dog has learned his lesson."

"Or he's dead," Jackson's mouth added before his brain could stop it.

Talbot's eyes danced in what could have been the beginnings of a smile, though one never came. "Excellent point. I like the way your brain thinks. In any case, the absence of the expected is just as informative. Though we didn't get to kill any of those rat bastards, which is a shame. The bottom line is this: we know that something is up – either they set us up (which I doubt else they would have ambushed us), they have a spy in our organization," long pause here, "or they just got lucky. And I don't believe in luck."

"I see," Jackson said, keeping his head pulled into his shell as much as possible.

"So, we have to be on the lookout. Both outside and in."

"That means you," Simpson whispered in Jackson's ear.

Talbot gave Simpson an exasperated look that seemed to say, "What are you doing?"

"Thanks," Jackson said to Simpson. "I kind of figured that part out." Then to Talbot, he said, "I don't really need to be involved in any of this, you know, stuff. Like I said, I'm no spy. I just want to do my job. In fact, I'm only here because one of my friend's friends mentioned it to him right after I lost my job."

Talbot nodded as though he already knew this. "Hmm. Who was it? What was her name?"

He didn't understand Talbot's reaction. "I don't know. I'll ask my friend about her." How had Talbot known it was a woman rather than a man?

"You do that. We'd like to know that information. We'd also like to know what happened to her."

Now that really confused him. If they didn't know who she was, how could they know that something happened to her. And what did happen to her?

"And Jackson?" Talbot continued.

"Yes?"

"Shut your mouth about the missions out there. Not everyone knows what we do. In fact, our cover story for the people who aren't on the team is that we're having an emergency strategy meeting."

Jackson thought about the shrieking alarm and the lights that preceded the last mission. "That's a pretty big reminder for a strategy meeting."

"Go big or get yer ass home, right?" That line would have been mildly humorous had it not been delivered with a side order of stone face and a pair of large gray "I'm going to murder you" eyes.

"Right." Jackson headed toward the door, exchanging a look of not so great fondness with Simpson.

"Remember," Talbot added when Jackson got to the door, "don't forget what we talked about." His eyes added the "or else" part of that sentence.

CHAPTER 28: SIMPLE FOLK

Abner spotted the guy right away. He must have been a new recruit (which meant less than ten or maybe twenty years on the job) because Abner didn't recognize him. Dressed all in black with black hair – which seemed dyed – slicked back, this guy apparently watched too many Vampire movies and was trying to play the part. He was like a young mob punk imitating the gangsters he saw in movies; the difference was at least that mob guy was a real gangster.

The man was attempting nonchalance as he walked around the building, but a man with clean clothes wandering the Tovac Zone was as inconspicuous as a second nose.

For his part, Abner didn't worry about being spotted. He had no problem playing the part of a crazy old Tovac inhabitant since he'd been practicing that very role for decades. He wandered toward the presumed Piri outpost, situated near the old factory complex that acted as the Jone-Zen base. Grotto must have directed Talbot to set up the new facility at the complex, and that meant something big was happening near here. Apparently the Piri knew this too, else they would have never dared to set up an observation post so close to their enemies.

Abner leaned against a three-story apartment complex and slid down the wall to sit on the sidewalk. It smelled different in this neighborhood, not so much better, though definitely milder. He detected a note of spicy cooking above the stench of rotting trash. Probably a different ethnic group lived here, or at least in that building.

The Jone-Zen base seemed ordinary enough – razor-wired topped solid fence around a non-descript factory complex. He would need to get on the roof to see more, though he doubted he would discover anything interesting. The Jone-Zen weren't that dumb. He'd climb up there later, but first it was time to take a quick nap. He slid off his shoes and tucked them into his grubby jacket, then leaned his head back and dropped out.

Sometime later, he was awoken by something striking the bottom of his foot. He stirred but didn't immediately open his eyes.

"Well, at least he's not dead."

"Someone took his shoes," said a second, deeper voice.

One of them smelled like biscuits, and that made Abner hungry. He opened his eyes. The first talker was the slicked-back, black-haired Piri who he'd seen casing the block earlier, the one who seemed determined to embody the Vampire stereotype. He'd probably scream like a baby if Abner showed him a cross. The other man was much stockier, dark-skinned, and older than the first but still with some serious power in him. That man was crouched, looking at Abner's feet.

Abner stayed in character. "What do you want? Stay away from my shoes! They're my shoes."

The burly man eyed him, his eyes unusually pale. "I already took your shoes, and I ate them!" he said, laughing.

"Now we're going to eat your... socks too!" the slick one added.

"And I'm gonna drink all your booze," said Burly. For a street person, having your booze stolen would be almost as bad as losing your shoes. Maybe worse, depending on your condition.

"And then—" Slick started, but then both men flinched in unison as though someone had just hit them, or perhaps yelled at them. Burly stood, and they looked at one another, a bit concerned.

"So what are you doing out here, man?" asked Burly, now all business.

"Stay away from my booze!" Abner shouted.

"We're not going to take your booze," said Slick. He dropped to a knee and patted Abner's shin in a way that might have been comforting had the situation been different – say, for example, if the comforter hadn't been a murderous Vampire wannabe. Slick had a strange dark triangle of hair on his forehead a few inches in front of his receding apparently dyed-black hair. The man must have seen him looking, as he ran his hand over it and then slicked his hair back. When Abner realized what it was, he almost burst out laughing but disguised it with a hacking cough. The sad sap must have had hair plugs put onto his forehead in the shape of a widow's peak, not knowing that his treacherous hairline would retreat, stranding the triangular peak like a furry island, floating alone on a sea of forehead.

Still trying to look comforting, the man said, "We just want to know what you know about that building over there." He pointed at the Jone-Zen complex.

"Which place?" Abner asked.

"That one," Slick said, waggling his finger.

"That one?" Abner pointed at the wrong building.

"No! That one!" Slick jabbed his finger more emphatically.

"That one?" Abner pointed at a different wrong building.

Burly grabbed Abner's head and turned it to face the complex of buildings. Abner kept his eyes to the side, looking in the wrong direction.

"Straight ahead!" Burly said. "Keep your eyes forward!" He released one side of Abner's head and put his thumb and forefinger under Abner's eyes, then pressed the fingers into his face and moved them side to side.

"I don't have puppet eyes," Abner said. "I'm not a puppet. My eyes don't move like a puppet's." He was enjoying this, but he didn't want them to try to stick needles into his eyes to steer them, so he finally gave in. "Oh, that place. Ah, yeah, I know that place."

"Tell us about it," said Slick.

"Tell us about what?"

Burly's hand tensed into a fist.

"Oh that place," Abner said. "I know that place. What's so special about that old place?"

Slick interlaced his fingers and put them on top of his head, and Burly just turned away. "We don't know," Slick said. "What do you know about that place?"

"Er, it's an old factory complex. Some guys came in an' fixed up one of the buildings to use as an office or something. Just simple folk. Never gave me nothing though."

"Simple folk," Slick said, shaking his head.

"How about this," Abner said, thinking of an idea. "How about I keep an eye on things around here, and I can come tell you when I see something funny." What better way to avoid suspicion from snooping around than to get hired to snoop around?

Slick looked at Burly, and they both shrugged and nodded. "Sure, you do that," Slick said.

"What'll I get?"

"How 'bout I won't tear your throat out?" Slick said.

"That doesn't sound like a very good deal."

"You mean your life is not worth it to watch that place?"

"Huh? Did that make sense?" Abner directed the last question to Burly, who shook his head no.

"What I meant was... Forget it. Bronson! You're up!" Slick said.

"Haven't I been up the whole time?" Burly Bronson asked, a bit confused. "What he's trying to say is," he started, then paused. "Listen, we'll get you some booze –"

"And cigarettes," Abner interrupted.

"And cigarettes," Burly continued. "But you have to –"

"And bullets."

"Okay, and... wait. Why do you want bullets? Do you have a gun?"

Abner examined the end of his long beard. "Well, no," he said, "but if I get bullets, I'm halfway there."

"We're not getting you bullets," Burly said.

Slick punched Burly, speaking in an easily overheard whisper. "We're not giving him the other stuff either, so why not just pretend to throw that in too?"

"We're not?" Burly said.

"Nevermind," Slick said. "I'm out. You're running this asylum."

Burly looked at Slick for a while as though trying to figure out what was approaching him from a distant horizon, then he turned back to Abner. "You snoop around and let us know what you find, and we'll get you booze and maybe cigarettes."

"Tobacco flavored," Abner said.

"Right, absolutely. Tobacco flavored cigarettes. Deal?"

"Deal."

Burly and Abner shook hands, but Slick just walked away, smoothing his oiled hair back with the flat of his palm.

Abner wondered what sound Slick would make if he ran him through with a spear. At his own advanced age, could he still take a guy like that? Back in his prime, there would be no question. But these days, he wasn't so sure.

He'd find out soon enough.

CHAPTER 29: LOSING TOUCH

"You mean she disappeared?" Jackson said into his cell phone as he drove home.

"Well, we just kind of lost touch," Chester replied.

"What does that mean, exactly?"

"It means she stopped returning my calls, and when I went by her apartment one night, no one answered the door. I looked in the window and it looked like she'd moved out."

"Good thing you weren't stalking her. How long did you know her?"

"I don't know. Maybe a month or two? Why are you so interested in all this? Do you think she's part of the reality show? Hey, maybe I'm in the show too!"

Jackson thought for a few seconds. "How did you meet her?"

"Well, that was perhaps a bit out of the ordinary. She approached me at a bar."

"That *is* extraordinary. You went to a bar without me?"

"Hey, I can't babysit you all the time. Sometimes the Chester needs to fly solo."

"I see. So this woman just approaches you and asks if you know a graphics designer?"

"Well, not immediately. She was too dazzled by my presence and overcome with emotion at the bar. She brought that up in a later conversation. Why are you so interested in this?"

"Because they are so interested in it." *And because I want to know how the hell I got into this.* "So, was she too hot for you?"

"What's that supposed to mean?"

"That means, average to below average hotness."

"That's really low. I'm hurt."

"But what's the answer?"

"Ah, man, yeah. I guess so. She was a bit above my usual. But not out of my league! My league is all-inclusive. There've been some all-stars in there."

"And this one would have gone in the first round?"

"Okay! Yes! Are you happy now?"

"No. Not at all."

"At least you still got the reality show angle. She could have been a professional actress."

"Either way, why me?"

Chester had no answer for this one, and neither did Jackson.

CHAPTER 30: SCORING IN GREECE

Fionn whipped his long blond hair out of his face as he strolled down an Athens sidewalk. It hadn't been bothering him, but a gaggle of women across the street had caught his eye, and a little flash of brilliant blond always caught the ladies' attention. Three pair of eyes followed him from across the street. Ha! Works every time.

No time for fraternizing, he thought with a touch of sadness and more than a little pride at his tremendous self-control. He was on a mission for Tazia, and as her right hand man, he needed to deliver. He had everything he needed for the Big Event, having traveled the width and breadth of Europe to find all of the items required. Or maybe that was "length and breadth"... whatever — he'd definitely been through the "breadth" of it, and that was saying something because Europe had tons of breadth. In any case, with what he'd scored, the Big Event would be glorious. Even though she seemed somehow immune to his charm — she was probably gay — there was no way that this wouldn't impress her.

But time was almost up. Something major was going down in the Tovac Zone, and no doubt Tazia needed him to take care of things. After this mission was completed, of course.

CHAPTER 31: SETTING THE TIMER

Jackson almost made it through the next work day without talking to anyone. He kept his headphones on while at his desk, and he tried not to drink too much so he'd not have to go to the restroom and cross paths with anyone who might, say, menace him with their freakish jumping ability. He threw himself into the drawings and created some of his best work. He discovered he had quite a knack for depicting scenes of undead death and destruction. The challenge was to keep the drawings separate from reality in his mind; imagining that these images actually had some basis in truth unnerved him, and he had no idea how to re-nerve himself.

Late in the day, he leaned back and stretched, scanning his surroundings to determine where they might have hidden some cameras for the reality show. His brain grasped at that possibility like a drowning man on a floating tongue depressor. He vowed to do something manly in the office for the cameras the next chance he got, but there really weren't that many manly opportunities in an office building on a day-to-day basis. Perhaps he could manufacture one, but practicing karate in the hallways or pumping iron in the cubicles was probably frowned upon. Besides, he didn't know karate and the only iron he'd ever pumped was, well, he'd never actually pumped anything remotely iron-like at all. He liked to jog, and he'd once done a "squat knee thrust," though that had ended poorly. So he was left to hope for an office fire and a convenient — and preferably light weight — damsel in distress whom he could rescue. In the meantime, he'd get his sketch on. That's good TV there.

If this were a reality show, would there be so much down time? He doubted it.

Finally, the day was over and he headed for the door. Somehow popping into reality between blinks, Simpson blocked his path with his cane and pointed toward the back hallway. A few people determinedly moseyed in that direction, like a bathtub with floating chunks of hair slowly draining. Except the people didn't get stuck in the doorway and gross out a bather. Pausing only to drop his phone into the box, he followed them back to the same staging area. Only a few team members were there.

He looked for Sy but didn't see her. Somewhat lost without her there, he just sat on a bench outside the circle of light, watching the team members mill about, wandering without any sense of urgency, like a cold snake with a full belly. He grew bored, then sleepy, finally leaning against a wood pillar that was as soft as it looked – "hardwood" trees were well named. He drifted off, the images in his mind evolving and slowing.

Battles raged. Vampires with bared pointed teeth leaped onto ash gray warriors, the latter slower but stronger. The Vampires struck with blunt weapons; the Grays fought back with blades. Bloody bodies lay on a green meadow as the bellows of the Grays and the squeals of the Vampires filled the night air. A female Vampire with black hair past her shoulders emerged from the mist, her face slowly materializing.

Jackson awoke with a start as someone spoke in his ear. He looked around in confusion; no one was near him. Ethereal visions swirled in his muddled head. He had been out cold, and one of his legs had fallen asleep. He bounced his foot on that leg to wake it up as his head cleared of the ephemeral images. The team strapped on their gear. Some left the circle to change into their body armor as Sy had. Others, both men and women, just dropped everything except their underwear and changed right there. A few, including Archer, put his body armor on over his work clothes, though he did change out of his work shoes into some black boots. Once again, he serviced the massive Gatlin of Gatling Guns, or G3 as Jackson decided to call it, assuming he'd ever an opportunity to talk about it again. He wondered why one of the scrawniest guys would have the largest weapon.

The giant bear of a man with short blond hair that drove for Simpson walked over to Archer and spoke in a low tone – probably something like, "Hey, why do you get the big freaking gun?" Archer looked up, somewhat aggravated. He grabbed a bundle from the Blond Bear, which seemed to consist of some sort of metallic multipronged hook attached to a coil of metal cable. The hook, which upon further examination looked like a giant fishhook, seemed much larger in Archer's hands than in the giant's. Jackson realized that he'd seen one of these in his inbox of images to draw. Joining the mission might be a great way to get a closer look, but he would have preferred for them to drop off a pile of weapons in the safety of his cubicle. Maybe they brought him along to get a better sense of the battles.

Wait, what was he saying? This wasn't real. This was a reality show. They brought him to see how he would react to a simulated battle sequence. He imagined that this battle would be more active than the last. Possibly season finale-type action.

Archer dropped the cabling to the ground and wound it using a complicated sequence of efficient twists. He then made a twisting movement with the hook that Jackson couldn't see, like he was making some sort of adjustment. He handed the hook with its neat coil of cabling up to Blond Bear, who gave a small bow of gratitude and walked back to his bench. Behind the bear, an older woman with a gray buzz cut stepped up to Archer and, after a few words, handed him two short weapons that looked like miniature versions of Buck-Bill's spears. Archer nodded and bent down into his crate of supplies and pulled out a flat round tin. He popped it open with his teeth and then dipped a black-streaked rag into it, pulling out a dark substance. He rubbed it onto the two spears and held them out to the woman, though when the woman reached to take them,

Archer gestured with them while he spoke. She followed the spears with her hands for a bit, trying to take them from him, then apparently realizing that she wasn't going to get them back until he finished, she dropped her hands and listened. He finally stopped talking, and she reached out again. He held them out to her, but as before, he gestured with them before she could take them.

"Give them to me!" she yelled.

Archer simultaneously threw both of them, one with each hand, at her head. They passed inches from each of her ears and thunked into a solid wooden support beam twenty feet behind her. If she had started off with a normal woman's haircut instead of the bur, she would have ended up with nice bald patches on either side of her head, those chunks of hair repositioned to the support beam, wedged beneath the blades.

The woman's hands went up in supplication and her posture changed to one of subservience. She yelled out her apologies and babbled as she backed away. Archer was leaning forward wearing an expression that screamed obscenities that would make Jackson's dad blush. A few of the members who were near him decided that a different bench would be more comfortable.

Jackson looked closer at the scrawny middle-aged man with his lame combover, wondering if his own eyes were defective. No, that was still Archer the accountant. Jackson put an asterisk by that description in his head and vowed to remember to knock the next time he needed to talk to Archer in his cubicle.

The team seemed ready to go. Like the last mission, Buck-Bill squatted on the edge of a crate, gargoyle-style, watching the others, his spear at his side.

Movement caught his eye from the shadows. Sy emerged, fully geared, her hair pulled back in a ponytail. She didn't look at him, but that was a blessing in a way — he wouldn't have to watch her face drop in disappointment when she discovered that she would have to babysit him again. He wanted to disappear into the shadows.

An image of Talbot popped into his head, and he thought he heard someone say, "Team." He didn't recognize the voice and couldn't locate the source; he must have imagined it.

"Alright, team," Talbot boomed, marching into the circle of light and launching a startled Jackson out of his seat. "This is the one we missed the last time. We think we got our intelligence mixed up, but this one looks solid. Be ready, though, as always. They may know we're coming, and this might be an ambush. But we'll be ready for them. Right, Higgins?"

The older buzz cut woman had been jumping in an attempt to extract her short spears from the support pillar where Archer had thrown them eight feet from the floor. She stopped jumping and turned, blushing. Not a good start to the mission for Higgins.

"Oh," she said. "Of course sir. We'll ambush them like nobody's business."

"Mr. Gorf," Talbot said. The Blond Bear stood and acknowledged him. "Please retrieve Ms. Higgins' weapons and explain to her the mission summary."

Mr. Gorf, a name that Jackson found totally unsuitable and unsatisfying, nodded and lumbered toward her.

"Mr. Simpson, your team," Talbot said, then left.

Once again, Jackson was paired with Sy in the backseat of the conversion van, with Blond Bear Mr. Gorf driving and Simpson in the passenger seat. Sy seemed unusually quiet, even for her. In fact, since she didn't say a single word to anyone and moved with the volume of a stalking cat, she basically pegged the quiet meter. If she were any quieter, she would actually suck in sounds from her surroundings, like an audio black hole. He smiled as he visualized a vortex spiraling into her ... uh..., he wasn't sure where the sounds would enter. The whole vision seemed suddenly unsavory, and he scrubbed it from his thoughts. This of course made it grow larger in his mind.

Simpson spoke over his shoulder as the convoy moved out. "Same drill, people. Jackson, you're here to observe only. We're still watching you," – he turned in his seat to emphasize this point, as though Jackson wasn't exactly clear what "watching you" meant – "so don't do anything foolish."

What, like push a button? There wasn't much for him to do, foolish or otherwise.

Simpson kept staring at him, waiting.

"Oh!" Jackson said. "Right, got it. No tomfoolery."

Simpson held the stare a moment longer, either to express his displeasure at Jackson's flippant attitude (which was built-in and hard to modify), to intimidate him, or because he was curious what products he used to style his hair. Jackson guessed he could strike one of those possibilities.

"Like we discussed, Goji, you're on the boards," Simpson continued, not looking back at her.

"Yes, sir," she said in a tone like a dirge.

His voice softened. "You know we can't have Latents in active combat until their –" He stopped. "Anyway, Jackson here needs to learn the boards so that he can backfill you. Still, don't let him touch anything yet." He turned again and looked at Jackson, though he continued speaking to her. "We still don't know if we can trust him."

"Yes, sir," she said, her voice unchanged.

Jackson scanned the vehicle looking for hidden cameras. He struck a contemplative but brave pose, just in case.

The convoy exited the Tovac Zone via the quick access lane without being stopped, thanks no doubt to the electronic credentials broadcast by each vehicle. They didn't head for the city, however. Instead, they turned at an aging sign that identified the route to an old unincorporated business district that was filled mostly with less agreeable businesses, like battery processing plants and junk yards and unidentifiable factories with smoke stacks that coughed up multicolored clouds that were attractive, caustically speaking. He had driven there in the past to get a newish set of wheels for his car, though he'd turned around before arriving; the unsavory area, combined with the darkness — also combined with either a lack of bravery or an abundance of wisdom — had convinced him that his bare wheels were actually quite stylish. Now he headed back in, this time traveling with a protective coating of armed lunatics.

After passing through several dark blocks of razor-wired, dilapidated (though still operational) business complexes, the group turned off their lights and pulled to the curb. "Goji!" Simpson said. "Take the wheel. Advance to your position. We deploy in ten." He and Blond Bear Gorf exited and joined the rest of the team from the other vehicles. Sy climbed into the driver seat and put the car in gear, pulling away from the rest of the team.

Jackson had two thoughts. Where were they going, and was he supposed to stay back there? He bounded into the passenger seat next to her. "What's up?" he asked.

"You should stay in the back," she said, not turning.

"You're probably right," he said. "I should." He watched her out of the corner of his eye, unable to suppress a slight smile.

She cut her eyes in his direction and then looked back at the road. He thought he might have seen her smile too, but if he did, it was the grin of a phantom in the dark. He was grateful that she returned her attention to the road since she was driving with the headlights off through the dark streets, mostly abandoned at this hour. At what hour? He didn't even know.

Sy pulled the car to the curb, cut the engine, and climbed into the back. He followed. She pointed over her shoulder at the curtain, and he slid it across like he'd seen her do on the previous occasion, sending the back of the van into darkness. Four dim rectangles appeared to his left as Sy folded down the work surface. It lit up at her touch, and soon the back of the van filled with soft red light from a glowing strip along the edge of the ceiling. The four LCD sprang into life. He sat next to her and plopped his level on the desk, leaning down and examining it before he realized what he was doing. He scooped it up and shoved it into his pocket, not looking at her and praying that she was not looking at him.

"So?" she asked.

"So, what?" He feared he knew the question.

"Is it level?"

His face burned. "No. It slopes to the right a bit."

"Ah," she said. "I thought it might. We're pointing uphill." She typed on the keyboard and mercifully said nothing more about it.

He vowed to crush that level the next chance he got. A second later, after visualizing a dismal existence with no level in his life, he modified the vow to keep it in his pocket unless the coast was clear. Idiot.

She tapped keys and pointed at headphones on the wall. He put them on. On one screen was a bland thermal image – probably the facility directly alongside the van. A bright area glimmered near the top right corner of the image. On the next screen, the same image glowed in natural light. She tapped a few keys on the virtual keyboard, and the natural light image brightened, revealing more details, such as a solid fence and a smoke stack off in the distance. After a few more keystrokes, the natural image faded from its screen and merged with the thermal image, the glow brightening the area above the smokestack. The dual image then slid to the right as the camera rotated to point further up the street at a complex surrounded by a solid fence.

"Junkyard," she said, pointing at that image. "Widescreen defensive scan of van." She pointed to the screen that had recently dimmed. It sprang back to life in an image colored similarly to the first, likely another natural light image with a thermal overlay. The image moved in a slow rotation around the vehicle. "Team members," she said, pointing to the bottom two screens. They were still blank.

She tapped on the keyboard and looked at the lower images.

"Cook to cornstarch, plate and kitchen confirmed," she said. "No eyes on toaster or micro. Requesting eyes."

"Cornstarch here. Toaster on," came the static-filled reply. "Micro on. Started the preheat. Meal is still a go. Set timer for five, then update."

Sy cut her eyes over at Jackson for a brief moment. "Ding," she said into the microphone.

"Uh..." Jackson said after a moment of silence.

"Simpson — or maybe it comes from Talbot, I don't know — makes us talk in code." She didn't look at him and seemed embarrassed. "They said that these cameras," she gestured to the two blank screens, "were on and that the mission was still on and that I should contact them again in five minutes."

"So you're the cook? He's cornstarch?"

This time she did smile. "At least that's one good thing. He wanted me to be brown sugar."

If Jackson had been drinking a soda, it would have shot through his nostrils in a fizzy double barrel blast and ruined the electronics. He struggled to stop laughing. Her smile continued, and she even caught his eye once.

This might just be the best mission yet.

CHAPTER 32: UNICORN HUNTING

Avar crouched in the shadows in his black body armor. His team members were in position — taut, ready to pounce. Tazia had given him the honor of this attack, and she would be watching. He had no intention of giving her another set of balls to break. He was neck and neck with pretty boy Fionn, and Fionn had been working on a critical mission, supposedly more so than this one. Avar couldn't imagine what it was – how there could be something more important than crushing the Goblins?

This mission would of course succeed. How could it not? His preparations were impeccable, and his military mind was unrivaled, or at least that's what his autobiography would say if he had written one. That's why he had risen to be her right hand man – or at least one of them – she only had one right hand but two men could be there, right? At least he was the lead Piri/Vampire in the Tovac campaign, and despite what he'd heard, history would prove this the most critical. If they could catch Simpson, that would be a sweet piece of resistance, that's for sure. He'd show that pansy Goblin lump what a real cane felt like. Then he might just drag what was left of him in front of Fionn to see if he could top *that* one.

Surprisingly, the Vampire Smoke Team had done an excellent job of laying a false trail for the Goblins to latch onto like a dripping dog's nose on a scent. He had watched surveillance footage of the Goblins at the village, and their tactics hadn't changed much — roll in quietly in ground vehicles, stop outside of combat zone, deploy forces from that location, then assault their objective with only a small technical team held back for operational support.

The weakest link in their system was their communication system. If the main signal were jammed, then the support vehicle would provide a redundant communication network with enough power to cut through the interference. However, if the support vehicle was knocked out, and the Vampires activated the jammer, the Goblin assault forces would be cut off from one another. They could still fall back on their collective hive communication, but that wasn't at all effective for quick tactical coordination, assuming their hive was similar to the Vampires'. It was great for sharing images, emotions, and memories, but not so good for time-critical specific commands.

A voice in his earpiece said, "Target approaching. Dig?"

"Dig," he replied. He scanned the dark street with his night vision goggles. As expected, vehicles soon approached with their lights off.

"Now?" asked Bronson through the earpiece.

"No, not now, you idiot," Avar whispered hoarsely. Bronson was a good fighter and commanded loyalty of the troops, but he was 100%

Banger, 0% Thinker. Like the Jone-Zen/Goblins, most Piri/Vampires leaned heavily toward one of the great Roles while maintaining lesser abilities in the other areas — some Thinkers could almost Bend, while some Blockers could Pop. Not Bronson. Give him a club and he could swing it hard, but that was about it.

Off in the distance a Tovac security chopper smacked the air as it buzzed low over the area, looking for someone to shoot. 50 mm rounds had an attraction to flesh.

The three convoy vehicles stopped in front of the Vampire position, as planned. The Goblins would exit the vehicle, check their gear, and then head to the assault in two or three separate teams. Meanwhile, the support vehicle would stay behind. A small contingent of Vampires would shadow each Goblin team to ensure that they didn't double back. Two large Vampire groups were stationed at predefined ambush locations. The rest of the Vampires would amass a quick assault force for the support vehicle. Once the Goblin teams were away from the vehicle, he would fire up the jammer with some fake comms to throw them off and then attack the vehicle with vicious precision, obliterating all communication systems and killing or capturing the occupants. After the communication vehicle was out, the vehicle assault team would split and pursue the divided Goblin attack force. The plan was to catch up with them at the predefined ambush locations, trapping them in the crossfire between the vehicle assault force and each prepositioned ambush squad. It would be a bloodbath; the Goblins might be geared up for the battle, but they wouldn't be ready for this.

The support vehicle drove off.

"Support vehicle exiting target zone, you dig?" a voice said in his earpiece.

"Of course I dig it. I'm looking right at it," Avar said. His teams would hold their positions to watch the progress. Hopefully the support vehicle would redeploy in visual range and the plan could move forward as... err... planned.

A new voice spoke through his earpiece. "Is that a unicorn?"

He knew who this was. Bronson. Before he could reply, another voice jumped in.

"Repeat."

"A unicorn," Bronson said again. "On the van. I thought it used to be a sunset. That was cool too, but this is amazing. Maybe we could get —"

Avar cut them off when the support van stopped, its red brake lights disabled and dark. "Teams A and B, send scout contingent to rejoin main fighting force. Vehicle team leaders mobilize to van when clear and stick with original plan."

He kicked himself. Why hadn't he planned for the possibility that the van might deploy in a different location? Could they have known what he was up to? No, surely not.

The Goblin team split into two forces and slinked away. They were good, but nowhere near the caliber of his team. Their formations were looser, their techniques less crisp, and their personal sense of style atrocious. However, he did appreciate the aesthetics of their spiked body armor, if not the efficacy of them.

"Move, you dig?" Avar said.

"Dig," said Bronson.

"Dig," said Orion.

Avar met with the Bronson's team across the street from the van in an alley behind an old dumpster. Orion's team was positioned opposite the van.

"Meedle," Avar whispered. "Ready?"

"Dig it."

That dang Meedle always screwed up the comms. If you don't ask for dig, then you don't give a dig!

"Orion, ready with equipment?"

"Ready."

That's more like it.

"Go in three," Avar said, "starting now."

After two seconds, Meedle said, "Dig!"

Avar moved his team.

Orion's team arrived at the same time as Avar's and Bronson's. Orion leaped atop the van, his cape flapping.

Avar stared in astonishment. A cape? Orion was taking this Vampire thing a bit far. I mean, slick hair and the black clothes, fine, but you don't wear a cape on a mission. Come on!

Orion pumped one arm upward. Success. The van was blind, deaf, and mute, and Avar's attack force had enough heavy siege equipment to tear apart an armored truck like a baked potato with the works in under twenty seconds.

Anyone in the van was in for a world of hurt.

"Go!" Avar yelled. Vampires swarmed the van.

CHAPTER 33: INSTINCT AWAKENS

In the back of the conversion van, the bottom two monitors sprang to life a split second before Jackson's headphones did the same. The dark images on the screens shook violently, and he couldn't make out what was happening.

A voice yelled in his headphones. "We're under – I mean – dinner's not on the table but... argh! Potatoes! Ahh!"

"Mustard greens need vinegar!" yelled another.

"What's happening?" Jackson asked.

Sy tapped on the work surface, looking from screen to screen, her face set.

"Negative visual," she said into the microphone, as calm as Jackson was not. "Cornstarch needs paprika support. Kitchen on fire. I repeat, kitchen fire."

"Send some, ahh, what the... Pickles!" someone shouted. "Send pickles!"

"What are—?" Jackson started, but then decided to stay quiet.

She tapped a key.

"Pickles on the way," she said. To Jackson, she said quickly, "Their commands are all messed up, and I can't tell who's speaking."

Meanwhile, one of the bottom screens changed to a static shot of a two askew unidentifiable solid planes – probably the camera had fallen and now rested against a curb. The other bottom screen's image continued to gyrate as the wearer of the helmet camera either ran or fought or did both at the same time. The junkyard camera was static while the widescreen defensive image scan continued its slow perimeter sweep.

"Cookies, I mean," a panicked voice said over the wire, "Simpson's down! Screw this! Simpson's down!"

"We need to do something," Jackson said, standing as much as he could in a conversion van.

"We *are* doing something," she said.

"*I* need to do something." He reached for the handle at the back of the van.

"You'll get killed! Besides, something's not right about this."

"Then I'll get killed." That exhilarating feeling had returned, and he itched to get out there. Why, he didn't know. Voices shouted and images flashed in his head, and he had no idea what they were saying or where they were coming from. He had to get out of that van.

"The door doesn't open from the inside unless I hit this button." Her black eyes looked alien in this light, but there was something alive in that look that he had never seen from her.

"Then push it," he said.

Something thudded on top of the van, and the vehicle shook for a second. The top screens pointing out from the van changed. The one pointing at the junkyard had two bright pillars cutting vertically through the image, while the other swept past a glowing group of individuals, looking straight into the camera. Their toothy smiles were black in the false color image. Long, pointed teeth.

She pointed at the two bright pillars then looked at the ceiling of the van. "One's on top," she said, her voice finally ratcheting up. The bright pillars must have been someone's legs standing in front of the camera mounted atop the van.

This was no reality show.

The van shuddered with a thunderous impact on its top. The monitors blinked out and the headphones hissed. Jackson threw his off and looked around for a weapon, any weapon. The only weapon he saw, other than two short swords in scabbards crossing Sy's back, was a sleeved dagger attached to the inside edge of the driver's seat. He slid it out and hit the virtual button on the work surface that Sy had said controlled the back door.

The red cabin lights turned blue, but the door remained closed, though he thought he heard a metallic clank from it. He probably just unlocked it.

"Don't go out there!" she said, her eyes and voice frantic. "You're not trained, and the team will be here in a minute."

"There is no team," he said. "Close the door behind me and drive this van out of here. I'll get this loser off the car."

She grabbed his arm, and a jolt of electricity coursed through him. "Don't."

"I have to." He grabbed her head and kissed her. After he released her, she stared at him in shock. "Hell yeah I just did that," he said. "Now go!"

He unlatched the door and kicked it open. It clanged off of something, and a body hit the pavement. A flashing message caught his eye on the desktop, and he turned. A button flashed "emergency lockdown." He tucked the knife into the back of his pants and smashed the button again. The open back doors swung inward. Before they closed, he grabbed the top of the doorframe and threw himself out, his momentum carrying him around in a swinging arc toward the top of the van. Upside down, he pulled his fingers away as the doors slammed shut, his body continuing its rotation to land on his feet on top.

Dark shapes surrounded the van. He heard a distant shocked voice in his head telling him that he'd just done something impossible — for him at least — something that he'd never done in his entire life.

A shadowy figure crouched on the van's roof near the top of the windshield, a misshapen club in one hand and the ruined rooftop electronics in his other. The club looked like something that a cartoon caveman would lug around. The figure rose slightly as Jackson charged, providing a nice target for Jackson's shoulder. He caught the figure in the chest and drove him off the top of the van. The two of them crashed onto the hood and then bounced the ground. Hard.

Someone turned the lights out, and it grew quiet.

CHAPTER 34: VISION

A glossy black beetle scurried across the cooled asphalt of a dark Texas road. It stopped a few inches from a man's face and appraised him in silence.

Jackson stared back, his mind a blur of confusion and agony, his head caught in a vice between the road and the bony knee of his attacker. He wondered what he was doing down there.

"You're screwed," the beetle said, then scurried off.

It was right. Jackson's arm was pinned behind his back, cranked up so high that the excruciating pain had mercifully drifted close to numbness, not unlike his mind.

"I like to pop them first sometimes," his attacker said behind him, his voice like a boot dragging across gravel.

"Uh," a distant voice rumbled, "don't mess up his shoes. Okay?"

"Huh?"

"His shoes. Sometimes these things get, you know, messy."

"So?"

A pause, then the deep voice continued. "I like the shoes. They're classy. Like maybe they're alligator or some other lizard thing. I'd hate if they got, you know, stuff on them. Messy type stuff."

Then a third voice chimed in, moving closer. Jackson could see him kneeling beside him, in front of a van. "Say," the interloper said with obvious appreciation, "those *are* nice. Is that lizard?"

"Ah! No way!" the deep voice — now a notch higher-pitched — called out, his footsteps bringing him closer. "I already called dibs!"

"Enough!" Jackson's attacker yelled.

"I'll take the pants," the interloper said. "Are they boot cut?"

"I said, 'Enough'!" the gravelly-voiced attacker repeated. "We'll deal with this later. We—"

"But—" the deep voice started.

"Can—" the interloper started.

"Okay!" the attacker screamed, loosening his pressure on Jackson's arm. "Bronson, you get the shoes ..."

"Yes!" said the deep voice.

"... and Orion, you get the pants. You'll never fit in them though."

"Hey..." said the interloper, hurt.

"But first," the attacker continued, "We will finish this and rejoin the team. Was this one the only one in the van? Bronson..."

The voices continued, but Jackson's mind had drifted. He saw a van in his mind, a conversion van with a unicorn cutting loose a good old fashioned frolic through a land of rainbows and waterfalls, the rainbows and waterfalls so vivid that the colors shined onto the dark sky above the van, and water poured down in torrents onto the pavement below. The van split open and a shape floated out, featureless. The shape transformed into an image of Sy, her beauty concentrated into black eyes that stared deeply into his own. Her mouth was curled into a wry grin, and her long black hair flowed around her delicate pale face, so mysterious and alluring. Her lips parted to speak, but he could hear nothing. Her face shifted, aging, transforming to another. Her hair, formerly swaying as from an unseen wind, now moved purposefully, alive. It stiffened into segments and writhed and clicked like the legs of the beetle, flailing and stabbing the air. Her eyes widened as black fluid trickled from their corners. She spoke in a gush of black.

The black fluid was not black; it only appeared so in the moonlight. It was red, he knew, and warm. And when it stopped flowing from her mouth, he would see her teeth. Long and pointed, like a tiger's. She would come for him then.

CHAPTER 35: FIRST DANCE

"You just gonna lay there like a pussy?"

The voice was a life raft in a raging sea. His father's.

"What?"

"That's 'sir,' and I think you heard me. I've had dumps with more backbone than you. Now get up!"

He opened his eyes. The world was sideways, with a dark starless void to his left and an infinite wall of black asphalt to his right. Tires and feet extended horizontally from the black wall.

Tires. Van. Sy!

He bucked hard, throwing his head back and pushing with his one free hand. Something light on his back flew off with a yell, and he was on his feet. Shrieking shapes closed in, armed figures with clubs and cannons and fists and bared teeth. He spun into them, and pain streaked and exploded like fireworks. The world blurred.

After a time, sweet darkness returned and hugged him like an old friend, and together they rested once again.

CHAPTER 36: SPY, OR LATENT?

"He's coming to," a voice said. "Get Talbot."

When Jackson opened his eyes, two thoughts hit him. First, he had no idea where he was or what had just happened. Second, he felt like the Vampire stick men on the crest, like he was wearing a shiny new outfit of agony that fit him like a glove.

The stick men — his mind struggled to get solid footing — the crest above Talbot's desk, the crazy leader of the Vampire-hunting Seven, the team that included Sy....

"Sy," he said, his voice coming out much weaker than intended. "Where is she?"

He lay on some sort of cot in Talbot's office. Simpson's bare hands hovered above Jackson's head, like it was a melon soon to be picked. His face wore an expression of deep concentration. Jackson turned his mind inward and felt Simpson there, wandering around like a blind man in a dark room with no doors. Jackson kept the room closed, even dropping it into another closed room to double-insulate it.

What had he just done? How had he known how to do this; or, better yet, what was wrong with him to imagine that this was actually happening? Maybe that's what happened when one suffered head trauma. He tried to remember TV interviews with football quarterbacks or boxers and if they mentioned dropping mental interlopers into isolation chambers. Nope. None of them happened to mention that.

One thing was for sure, if this were a reality show, it was part of the new breed. He had heard about a new law passed that said reality show participants can't sue for getting killed (duh) or getting maimed (mentally or physically or both), even if they were unaware of their participation in the show, as long as the show generated enough profits that the State got at least a million dollars in taxes. Or something like that. Or maybe he was thinking of something else. Or maybe he just made that up because someone had pulled his brain out, jammed thumbtacks into its folds, punched it in its cerebellum face, then dropped it back into his skull backwards and upside down with crumbs on it.

Simpson pulled his hands back like they'd been burned, and he looked as though he wanted to attack Jackson. However, that was the way he always looked, so no big change there. Though Simpson was still in battle gear, his face was shiny and clean. He sported a white bandage across the top right of his head. He'd obviously "freshened up" after their little evening Vampire hunting soiree.

Talbot burst in with Buck-Bill on his tail. The right side of Buck-Bill's face looked like it had been injected with a gallon of red pain, and his eye was swollen closed. Jackson wondered who could manage to do that to such a man. He also wondered what would happen if he stuck a pin into Buck-Bill's bloated face.

Then he remembered the clubs, the teeth – black, then white – the savage attackers. Vampires? Could they have really been Vampires? Maybe they were just lunatics with dental implants. Insanely quick and strong lunatics. He couldn't remember exactly what happened, but images flashed — images of shadowy figures surrounding him, swinging clubs, shrieking like something inhuman, like bats. He would have sworn that some of the voices and messages had been in his head. And he remembered the feel of their bodies as he struck them, the sound of bones snapping. Had that been his own bones?

"Why am I not dead?" Jackson asked Talbot as the man leaned in and drilled him with those eyes of gray steel.

"That's what we'd like to know," Talbot replied. He looked at Simpson, who shook his head. "Still? Well he *has* to be an emerging Latent. How else could he be here?"

Jackson wasn't sure first what a "Latent" was; he thought he remembered Simpson or Talbot saying something to Sy about that. Second, he didn't know what "here" meant – here at the factory complex or here in the land of the living? He suspected the latter. Hoping they would continue talking under the assumption that he would be too groggy to remember, he kept his mouth shut and his ears open.

"But he's still *blank*. If he's a Latent, he should have an aura. Especially if he's emerging."

Talbot crossed his arms and stroked the gray stubble on his chin, thinking. "Are you sure no one—?"

"No one. And yes, I'm sure. I was the first one there. Unless Goji saved him and then evaporated. The van drove away, and they were retreating, some under assistance, and he lay alone on the street. We found the van a few blocks away. It had been trashed."

"Alone?" Jackson asked, unable to remain quiet. "What about Sy?"

They ignored his question. "I don't like it," Talbot said.

"Police officers who make an impressive drug bust will always release their undercover man caught in the sting," Simpson said, his shrewd and suspicious eyes on Jackson. He sprayed his hands with a pump bottle that he pulled from a pocket on his battle armor.

That guy has a problem, Jackson thought, choosing to disregard the level in his own pocket.

Simpson continued, "You do not throw your own man in jail, except perhaps to build some credibility. And you do not kill your inside man when you attack your enemy. You rather superficially damage him."

Talbot stared at Jackson. "I don't think so. I don't like this; I don't understand this. But I don't think so. They could never erase his aura."

Simpson did not look convinced. His motto seemed to be, "When in doubt, just kill the bastard. Then wash up."

"Where's Sy?" Jackson asked again.

"We don't know," Talbot said. "How do you feel?"

"Better than I should, I think."

"Good. Either they didn't rough you up too much, or you're healing quickly," Talbot said, giving Simpson a significant look during the second half of that sentence. "Or both," he continued, his gaze back on Jackson.

"But Sy..." Jackson persisted.

"We don't know," Simpson said. "Where do you think she is?"

"I have no idea. Did you check the van?"

"Gee, we never thought of that," Simpson said.

Jackson felt immediately stupid — of course they looked in the van. His brain was still slow and confused. "Well, that's where I would start," he said.

Simpson took in a deep breath to explosively respond, but Talbot held up a hand to silence him.

"They might've taken her," Talbot said. "They do that sometimes."

Jackson sat up abruptly, spinning his inner ear like a top, and he dropped back flat onto the cot. "Why?" was all he could get out while the world spun around him, and crazed voices mumbled and squealed in his ears. It was not a fun trip.

"You're going to pass back out, son, if you don't take it easy. As for the girl, it's not for ransom. They take other team members for experiments. Try out offensive weapons on them."

Jackson didn't like the sound of that at all. "Like, are they going to kill her?"

"Eventually," Simpson said. "Unless she is their spy. Though that would not explain why they did not terminate you, unless they figured out that your brain was already dead."

"Huh?" Jackson asked. Had he just been insulted? "My brain?" The rotation in his spinning head slowed a bit, but it now drifted sideways too. He tried not to blink because that started it back up.

"Let me ask you an unrelated question, Jackson, " Simpson said. "Do you think you are too good to buy cookies from my daughter? Apparently you are not the only one." He shot a sideways glare at Talbot.

Jackson wondered if he'd blacked out on part of a conversation. Cookies?

"Now's not the time to bring that back up," Talbot said. "In fact, it never is. Drop the damn cookies, Simpson! Your daughter is lovely, but I don't want any cookies, okay? They're gross. They give me gas. Do you really want that? You wanna give me gas, Simpson?"

"No sir." Simpson pointed his glare at Jackson, though it did nothing, like high beams lost in a swirling mist.

Talbot wasn't finished. "No, nobody wants that. That's the last time I let anyone sell those nasty things in the office."

Jackson wondered if he was still passed out and that this was all a dream. Simpson has a daughter? How could someone so fastidious about spraying his hands and sliding on gloves ever impregnate anyone?

One thing he knew was that Sy was no spy. But if she was no spy, then maybe he was. Could he be a spy and not know it? Wait, damn he was confused. He wished the spinning and mumbling and squealing in his head would cut it out so he could concentrate. He had to do something — Sy was in trouble.

"Let's suit up and go get her," he said. He tried to stand, but the world tilted sharply to the right, and he rushed to meet it halfway, fortunately catching up with it on the cot rather than the cold hard floor. He wouldn't have felt it either way.

CHAPTER 37: NOTHING PERMANENT. YET.

"That boy don't listen," Talbot said, shaking his head. What the heck had happened out there? He wished the surveillance hadn't been cut.

"We should take him for more testing," Simpson said. "I am telling you, I do not think he is right."

"You sure the problem's not with you?" Simpson had it out for that kid since he got there. Of course, security chiefs weren't supposed to be the trusting types.

Simpson eyed him, likely aware that Talbot was baiting him to get a reaction. "Yes, there is a problem with my reading. Like I said, I read blank, nothing. He has to have an aura, but I am not picking it up. That is precisely why we should get him to the lab."

"What do you think really happened out there?"

"I think Goji tried to defend that fool as he fled the fight, and she was captured. The Piri then knocked Krol out to make it more convincing. They knew they could not leave him untouched or we would know that he was their spy."

That sounded reasonable, but it still didn't feel right.

"Don't do anything permanent to the kid. Let him rest, then we'll dig a bit deeper."

Simpson did his half nod and half bow and then left the room to get Jackson moved to the Site 4 safe house.

CHAPTER 38: INTO THE DARKNESS

Jackson awoke with a start, feeling somewhat better, though still groggy and a bit "off." He lay in the back of a sedan. Simpson and Buck-Bill talked in the front seat, with Buck-Bill at the wheel.

"Talbot and I do not share a common perspective, shall I say," Simpson said.

"So you think he's a vamp? Does he smell like one?"

"No, he does not *smell* like one," Simpson said, obviously uncomfortable with the word choice. "Then again, he does not read as human either. I posit that perhaps the Piri have developed a technique to obscure their auras. But we need to get him to the Outer Lab to do some tests."

"I thought we were supposed to take him to Site 4 for him to rest."

"Well, he is resting right now, is he not? Talbot just said to let him rest. Please go to the Outer Lab, Ferdinand."

Jackson wondered why Simpson just called Buck-Bill "Ferdinand." Ferdinand didn't sound like a last name, and it sure didn't sound like a nickname. *My name is Buck or maybe Bill, but my friends call me Ferdinand for short.*

"That's a right, right?" Buck-Bill asked.

"No, that would be a left."

"Right, a left. Got it."

Jackson was surprised to discover that they'd been in the parking lot this entire time, not moving, and they were just now pulling away from the complex. He had no idea what the Outer Lab was, and he had no intention of finding out. At a minimum, Simpson would keep him from going after Sy. At a maximum, assuming that "maximum" meant maximum suckiness, they would decide that he was a spy or a Vampire or a general miscreant and then mount him on a grooved Buck-Bill spear and draw a crappy crest to commemorate it.

When the car slowed to make a turn a couple of blocks from the complex, Jackson yanked the door handle and lunged through the door. Or he at least tried to. As planned, the door handle turned as he rushed forward. Not as planned, the door stayed closed. As a result, he thudded into the window, leaving an oily face print.

Buck-Bill slammed the brakes. "What the hell?"

Jackson fumbled the door lock and repeated the maneuver, though this time he didn't lead with his face. The door swung open, and he launched himself onto the dark street.

"Get back in here!" Simpson yelled.

He had no idea where to go, but he knew where he wanted to leave, and he plunged into the darkness at full speed. He thought about throwing a handful of money down so crowds of people would rush into the street behind him, blocking his pursuers. The only problems were that he had no pocketful of money and that there wasn't a single soul on the street. Well, there likely were, but they would be in shadow-hugging night mode, as opposed to his current ass-hauling frantic mode.

A car door opened behind him, and he glanced back to see who was coming. He timed this move perfectly with his arrival at a crater in the sidewalk. As he stumbled and staggered forward, a figure caught him before he could ram his forehead into the side of a rapidly approaching building.

"Wait in there until they pass," the man said in a hoarse whisper, "then run down that alley." He turned Jackson's head toward an area just a hair brighter than the near-total blackness that now engulfed them, and he assumed that the alley must be that way. "I'll meet you back in here in a bit."

The man shoved him, and Jackson again staggered, this time falling onto his hands and knees just inside the doorway of a long-closed business establishment. Dimly sparkling broken glass stuck to his hands but didn't penetrate. The man then ran out of the protective darkness into a better-lit section across the street. Like missiles turning to follow defensive decoys shot from a jet, Jackson's two pursuers peeled away and chased the mystery man.

Gingerly brushing the glass from his hands, Jackson took a few careful steps out of the building and moved toward the alley, breaking into a run when there was enough light. The inky humid alley smelled like a well-aged alley should, with a grimy stench dominated by a pungent sting of rotting trash that made his nostrils spasm in a failed attempt at closing. At irregular intervals, he passed through moist clouds of heat, likely vents in the alley floor. He shuddered to think of what must lurk in the Tovac Zone at night, then his shudders themselves shuddered at the thought of what must be down in the tunnels beneath the alley. Some of the windows overlooking the alley had lights in them, though the only real light reaching the alley floor came from the distant city's reflected glow from the clouds. He exited the alley into an empty street. A few cars were parked at the curb, probably inoperable and possibly now repurposed as people's homes. A street light about a mile to his right seemed garish and out of place. He considered running up the street and then down another alley but figured he had a better chance of getting lost than of getting caught at this point. Whatever choice he made here in the Tovac Zone at night, the chances of getting murdered were well above his comfort limit — that limit always being pegged at zero. He instead ran across the street to another alley, taking cover behind an overflowing trash bin. The odor flowed around him like congealing gravy. He could feel its fingers pushing through his nose and crawling down into his lungs.

Struggling to breathe while sucking in as little of the odiferous air as possible, he counted to 300 and took a single step before spotting a shape emerging from the alley from which he'd come. Jackson froze, still mostly concealed. The man walked with painstaking slowness up the street. Jackson again counted to 300, this time forcing himself to pause between each number. While counting, he concentrated on controlling his breathing, calming himself down. He then thought of Sy, if they had her, if she was okay. To stave off a growing feeling of hollowness and dread, he returned his focus to slow breathing again.

After 300, he moved to the edge of the trash bin alley, ran across the street to the first alley, and then spun around and watched the street for a full minute. Convinced that no one followed, he worked his way back to where he had escaped Simpson's car, but the vehicle was gone.

He had escaped. But now he was alone in the Tovac Zone. At night. Caught between a rock and a frying pan, or something like that.

He remained close to the wall at the edge of the alley for another couple of minutes, watching for movement. Finally, he crept over to the building where the mystery man had hidden him. He stood at the doorway, the opening a pitch-black maw.

"Damn, boy, it's about time you came back," a familiar voice said, the voice of an old man. Abner. He moved closer, though he was still obscured in darkness.

Why am I not surprised?

"They won't send out search parties tonight," Abner said. "Even people in fancy battle gear can't go charging around these parts in the dark of night without attracting a bit of... let's say... *attention*. In fact, you've probably garnered a few new admirers already."

Jackson felt a sudden urge to look back over his shoulder, but he fought it.

Abner continued, "We'd better get off the street. This old man's bladder ain't what it used to be, and I'm not about to cut loose around here at night. Not a good time and place to get caught with your pants down." The man paused for several seconds, then burst into a hearty laugh that was more wheeze that guffaw. "That's a funny paper box."

Jackson was shocked. His dad was the only person he'd ever heard say something was a "funny paper box."

"Where'd you hear that?" Jackson asked.

"Hear what?" Abner said from the darkness.

"Funny paper box."

"Oh, I don't know. Just something I say when something's funny, I guess. Let's go."

Jackson wasn't satisfied, but his aversion to getting murdered trumped his curiosity.

"I invested in some new real estate here very recently," Abner said, leading him away from the building along the street, back in the direction from which the car had come.

"Closer to The Seven's office?" Jackson asked, concerned.

"Right next to it in fact. I haven't fixed it up yet. It's more of a vacation home for me – maybe take the family up here in the summers."

Just two minutes later, they turned a corner to find The Seven's complex, with Abner's building almost directly across the street, as advertised. Jackson didn't like it, but it was better than staying on the street and probably way better than whatever Simpson had planned for him in the Outer Lab or whatever he called it.

Abner led him into a building not unlike the one in which they had first met. They climbed the stairs to an unlocked and partially furnished apartment on the second floor. It smelled of dust, and he was thankful for that, dust being preferable to the alternatives. The only light struggled in through cloth-covered windows along the back of the apartment, and he could just make out the shapes of the furniture, though not what lived on or in them. That was a second item to be thankful for.

"You got the couch," Abner said.

"I'll take it," Jackson said. "Are we safe here?"

"They won't come out here at night. Vamps might get 'em." He smiled, though Jackson couldn't tell if this was a joke or not.

"What about during the day?"

"They'll focus on street level. They won't figure that you'll know what buildings you can safely crash in. And even if they do, we'll be on the roof during the days so we're clear."

"Okay." He wanted to ask why they would be on the roof and how Abner had found him and so many other questions, but he figured he might fall asleep before Abner could answer. He dropped onto the couch, which responded to his encroachment by filling the air with an invisible olfactory litany of its past escapades, apparently involving people with body odor and animals with weak bladders, along with hints of something like incense. "And Abner?"

"Yeah?"

"Thanks."

"Okay. You can pay me back later."

Jackson crashed before he could think through the implications of that.

CHAPTER 39: MANIFEST

"What the hell happened out there?" Tazia screamed. She was in a tear, so agitated that a piece of her long black-streaked gray hair had escaped its ponytail, sliding side to side like a cobra as she raved. Her deep walnut brown eyes shone with menace. She was no Banger, but she could still throw down some serious hurt, and she looked ready to lay it on thick.

Avar looked at his ragtag team strewn about the living room of one of their safe houses outside the Zone. Tabitha, their visual arts and feng shui expert, had decorated the place, and it looked really classy, except of course for the filthy bleeding people scattered about. The walls had decorative textures and designer paint (though he didn't really understand what a paint had to do to be promoted to "designer" status), while the furniture was understated and modern. Some of this fine furniture and a good portion of the hand-scraped Brazilian hardwood floors were now covered with wounded Vampires, oozing blood onto special mats that Tabitha had designed just for that purpose. The mats had been rolled up and stored in the hall closet behind a chest holding a backup supply of the seven types of potpourri sprinkled about the place. Bronson would have really appreciated the place had it not been for his open head wound and general lack of consciousness. He and several others were receiving medical attention, while others lay on their backs in exhaustion or shock staring up at the five bladed "whisper-quiet" fan as it circulated the rotten smell of defeat.

"I... I don't really know," Avar said.

"You don't –" Tazia started.

Avar, realizing that he had misstepped, blurted out, "He was there!"

Tazia's face registered shock. "You mean the boy?"

"Yes, ma'am. In the support vehicle. We didn't know he was in there. When he came out, we got him to the ground. I told him that I was about to kill him... you know... to break his spirits a bit. Or more to see what he was made of – to test his mettle." The look on her face told him that he had shared too much, but he had to keep going, and pronto. "Listen, I knew we weren't supposed to attack him," – but he'd done just that – "or I mean, not supposed to hurt him, but most of the team didn't know about him yet. And when he jumped up, he charged everyone before I could even call them off." He was relieved to get that out; it might give him some cover for this humiliating failure.

"Wait," she said, her face reflecting confusion. "Follow me." They moved away from the groaning men and women into the tranquil kitchen, which smelled vaguely of chocolate cookies. With a lowered voice, she continued, "He attacked you?"

"Yes ma'am." He pulled out a chair and sat as she paced with her arms across her chest.

"Wait wait wait. He did all that?" She gestured toward the team in the other room. "Was he Manifest? Was he alone?"

The memories pained him. Rather, the lack of clarity in the memories pained him. He really wasn't sure what happened; it had been a literal blur.

"Yes and no," he said. "He was definitely Manifest, but... I don't know. I've never seen a Goblin move like that." Who was this guy? Did the Goblins just get the upper hand? "He almost fought like a Vampire — I'm sorry, I mean Piri — but... so fast. I don't even know what he was armed with. And then someone else joined him, and before we could pull in reinforcements from our other teams the main contingent of Goblins returned and we just got the hell out of there." The jagged memory lay in his mind like a sharp burr in his shoe. He had moved to help his team before the other Goblin had appeared and struck him from the side, not knocking him out but severely fazing him. He barely had the wherewithal to pull his team back as the warning came in about the approaching Goblins. He shuddered to think of what would have happened had the main Goblin force found them in that state.

Realizing that Tazia was drilling him with those dark eyes, he revised his last statement. "I mean, we made a tactical retr—... pullback. It was a good thing that the team was so well trained. We didn't leave a single man on the battlefield." *We brought them here to die instead,* he thought.

He was ready to say more, but Tazia's eyes had glazed over, lost in thought. She had warned him not to hurt the boy, but he knew nothing about him or why he should be brought back unharmed should he ever appear on a mission.

"I didn't think they'd bring him in so soon," she said to herself, pacing. "Who was the other one?"

Avar grimaced. "We didn't get much of a look at her, except for long black hair that fell out of her helmet. Maybe a girl?"

"A girl?"

"A woman, I mean. Sorry ma'am."

She stopped pacing and looked at him. "Was she like him?"

"I don't think so. One of the guys said she used double swords, one in each hand. She was good, but not like him. A few thought they got in some shots on her."

"Hmm." The pacing resumed. "We need to slide up the timetable. If he's on missions, he's already in. We need to get him. Avar, your mission has just changed. I want you to bring in the boy. Wait," she said, stopping and leaning toward him, fixing him with a stare like a stake, "Can you handle this one? This one isn't too much for you, is it? I could get Fionn on it. He'll be here from the Balkans tonight. I have him on an important mission, but it will be over soon, and he'd be glad to take over."

"Ah no! Don't do that. I can handle it. I can do this!"

He thought again about the way that guy had moved. He might have just lied to his boss.

CHAPTER 40: VAMPIRES AND GOBLINS

Jackson opened his eyes. Someone had apparently dropped him into a post-apocalyptic cannibal movie, and he had landed on a ruined couch in a creature's wretched den. A fire probably burned in the kitchen beneath a giant pot of Shin Bone Soup, stirred by a lunatic with only one ear and a milky white eye.

He racked his brain, but only random memories surfaced – his dad patting him on the back when Jackson graduated high school, Chester snapping his new suspenders, Sy... oh! The memories slammed into place like the slide of a pistol. He stood, scanned the room, and listened for the old man Abner. A crow cawed off in the distance, and he thought he heard faint voices. As for the old apartment, it had not aged well. The walls were covered with different patterns of peeling wallpaper, showing snapshots in time like geological layers in cleaved mountain faces. Graffiti brightened some. Everything in the room, even the air, was covered with a dull haze, as though someone had smudged every surface with a hunk of gray chalk. Light shone into the room in a dusty beam through two windows covered by a shabby yellow sheet.

"Cozy, isn't it?" Abner said, emerging from a dark hallway. "Wait, who are you?" He frowned.

"I'm Jackson, remember? I worked with those kooks at The Seven." Abner had been his life raft, though it appeared to be taking on water.

"Oh, yeah. I knew that. I was just kidding," he said, smiling.

Jackson tried to believe him.

Abner walked over to the couch and turned out the pocket of his battered coat. A few granola bars fell out, along with a banana peel, a tiny bone, and a couple of wrappers. "Breakfast is served!" he said. "Eat up. We've got work to do."

"Do you know where they took Sy?" He was ready to go.

"Hmm, Sy. Oh yeah. Maybe I do, but you might just have to remind me who she is again." Abner sat on the arm of the couch and grabbed one of the granola bars.

"Oh," Jackson said, thinking back, "I haven't told you about her." He explained who she was and how she disappeared after the last mission.

"Was she a Goblin?" Abner asked.

"Huh? Did you say 'Goblin?'" Bubbles from the submerged life boat floated up and popped at the surface.

Abner's sudden laugh morphed into a coughing fit. Jackson almost slapped him in the back to help. "They never told you?" he asked, once he caught his breath.

Jackson shook his head. Not much would surprise him at this point.

Looking at the old man, he worried that he'd just hitched his wagon to a crazed horse charging toward a cliff.

"Goblins," Abner said, "is what the Piri, or 'Vampires' to you, call the Jone-Zen. People like Talbot and some of the others at the office. Have you never noticed odd things about the folks there?"

"Absolutely, but I didn't think ..." He replayed his time at the office in his head. He had known they were different but not, you know, *different*. "What are the Jone-Zen? And those Piri guys really are Vampires?" Sy had called the Vampires "Piri" too. So had Simpson.

"Have a seat," Abner said, gesturing to the couch. "This might take a while."

"We don't have a while!" Why didn't this guy get it? "We need to get her now!"

"Listen here. You could take off in some random direction, and you might get lucky. Better odds though if you listen to me to learn what's going on here first."

Jackson dropped onto the couch and launched a mini dust storm that rose and merged with the cloud of dust permanently suspended in the room. He barely noticed.

"Okay, there were once a group of people known as the Piri. The new generation calls them 'Vampires,' but I'll get to that. They were almost human, but they had a genetic defect – or maybe the rest of the world had the defect – so they were different, not quite human. Perhaps more than human, let's say. Strong, fast, quick to heal, plus a few other things. Lookers, most of them. I remember this one young thing..." His eyes glazed as he remembered. "She was quite the pistol. One time—"

"Time out," Jackson said. "Can we get back on track?"

"Oh yeah, okay. She really was ... never mind. Where was I? Oh, the Vampires, or Piri. Anyway, they passed their genes onto their children, and some of them were just like their parents. Crazy jumpin' bitin' fools. Some of them were just like regular ole humans. And some were normal until later in life, when they started showing signs of extra abilities like the rest of the Piri. They call those 'Latents,' and when they start getting their abilities, that's 'Emerging.' After you fully emerge, you're 'Manifest.' Got it?"

Jackson had heard some of these terms before, like maybe someone had called him that one time. Oh yeah! Simpson and Talbot had discussed that when he regained consciousness. Did that mean he was a Vampire? Of course not. That was ridiculous. So why did they say it? It must have meant something else. He decided not to ask Abner about that because he didn't want to plant the idea in this old guy's head that he might be a Vampire. Plus he had a feeling that re-railing a derailed Abner would be as easy as doing the same for a train. He'd save that one for later.

"Did I tell you the Vampire part yet? No? Okay, so these guys have been around for hundreds, maybe thousands of years. They look like humans except when they're fighting, and you can't tell from their blood or their cells or anything that they're any different. I think the differences are, you know, smaller than the cells. I used to know a thing or two about cells." Once again, he briefly got a faraway look, though he soon returned. "And there's no test for it, at least that's what they've always told me. I couldn't find a test for it." He seemed startled to discover that a granola bar was in his hand, and he took a bite, crumbs rolling down his gray beard. "Well these fellers change when they get riled up. Their arms get long; their ears get long and pointy; they get all squeaky sounding." Jackson had read about this on the website, and he also had a vague memory of the squeaking cries from his attackers outside the van. "And their teeth," Abner said, pausing for effect, "and... what was I saying?"

"Teeth."

"Teeth? Oh, right, teeth. Their teeth grow long and pointy. Well just a few of them. Not like their back teeth get all long and pointy. That wouldn't work out too well. They're not sharks after all. You know those back teeth are for grinding while the front—"

"I'd like to use my second timeout to get us back on track."

Abner paused with his mouth open, frozen in mid-sentence. Then he closed it and frowned. "You seemed nicer when I first met you. Now, like I said, or was *trying* to say," with a significant look at Jackson, "they've been like this forever, but people occasionally saw them fighting – and boy can those rascals fight — and saw those teeth and called them Vampires. Or maybe someone saw them and made up a story about them that became the story of the Vampire. Who knows? I don't know. Do you know? Probably not. In any case, people called them Vampires and the name stuck. So the Piri are called Vampires, but they're not. That's what they call an executed summary."

"Close enough."

"Huh? Anyway, it probably helped that some of the Piri liked being called Vampires so they sort of fan that flame. Like that guy across the street."

"Who? There's Vampires across the street?" Jackson stood up. "Is that where they have Sy?"

"Who? Oh yeah, your lady friend. No, no. Well probably not. Do you think so? I don't think so. Hmm. Let's go drag some chairs up to the roof and check it out."

Jackson followed him out to the hall. A haggard lady probably twenty years younger than her apparent age of 60 was just exiting her apartment a few feet down the hall on the opposite side.

"Who are you?" she asked, her eyes narrow and the gaps in her teeth wide.

"Your new neighbor," Abner replied.

"Oh!" she said, brightening and losing about five years of her "rough life" age penalty, though no teeth came back. "Welcome to the neighborhood. The washroom is at the corner of the street at the curb during a solid rain, if you're interested. And if you need any companionship, my mother works Tuesdays and Thursdays. Except when they have bingo down at the Z."

Jackson wished he could erase that mental image.

"Thank you, young lady," Abner said. "But we'll just be heading to the roof for now."

"Roof?" she said. "I'm actually, uh, the roof monitor guide person, I mean, the roof monitor, uh, guide person. That will be $17 dollars. Apiece."

She held out her hand.

"Oh, I'm afraid there's been some sort of mix-up," Abner said. "I've already prepaid for six months roof access when I signed my lease." He took her proffered hand, turned it palm down, then kissed the top. "Good day, ma'am." He walked past her as she stood stock still, her hand frozen in place.

Jackson followed. "Nice work," he said.

"Thanks. Now, where are we going?"

"The roof."

"Roof! Right, the roof. Follow me." He yanked open a door to a janitor closet, then closed it. "If you need a mop, or at least a long stick with a moldy frizz at the end, that's your room. Ah, here it is." He opened the door to the stairs, and Jackson followed him in. The sharp smell was familiar. Apparently, this was the official smell of staircases in the Tovac Zone – in addition to being the official smell everywhere else of urine-soaked rotting trash piles in enclosed spaces.

Soon they emerged on the roof to fresh air and a blinding blue sky, though off to the north the color was fading to an ominous orange. That could be bad. It blinked. That could be worse. Several rusted air-conditioning units and a water tower topped the flat roof, in addition to the building extension that housed the roof access from the staircase.

Abner turned and looked at Jackson, appraising him. "Oh!" he said. "I almost forgot. Stand still for a second." Abner ran off behind an air conditioning unit, rummaged around, and then returned with his hands full of dirt and gravel. Before Jackson could ask, Abner threw the glob on Jackson's shirt and rubbed it in with one hand while rubbing Jackson's head with the other grimy hand.

"Hey! What the –"

"Gotta blend in. You're too clean. Gimme your hand."

Jackson held out his hand. Abner rubbed his hands on it.

"Rub your face a little," Abner said. "You look like a shiny penny."

Jackson looked at his hand. It was your standard muck, with bits of unidentifiable solids in a brown gravy, along with some gravel topping. He smelled it.

"Just rub it in!" Abner said. "It's not gonna bite you. And it's not poop." He paused. "Probably not poop. Brown poop is pretty rare on roofs. Definitely not poop."

Jackson tentatively rubbed it into his face.

Abner continued, "At least I don't think it is. The poop, that is, not the biting. Let's find somewhere to set up." He spotted two plastic chairs near the roof's edge and dragged them behind one of the air conditioning units. After sitting, he scooted his chair around until he could see the Vampire building while shielding most of his body. "Come on." He pointed at the other chair. "I think this will work."

Jackson sat in the other chair and tilted precariously to the side. Two of the chair's four legs were split at the bottom. He readjusted in a somewhat futile attempt to straighten it up.

"When do we go after Sy?" he asked. He needed to do something.

"Not just yet. There's nothing we can do for her right now."

"Why not?" he tried to lean toward Abner for emphasis but that only made the chair quiver and almost dump him onto the flat roof.

"I need to finish explaining all this to you first. Once you hear the rest of the story, you'll understand. One of the best things we can do right now is to watch that there building. There's a Piri scouting unit over there and they might just lead us to her. Have I told you about them yet? Oh yeah." He looked over the unit at the building. "No activity yet," he said. He was right. The building opposite looked abandoned. He ducked back behind the unit. "I think that's just a look-out post where they watch the Jone-Zen."

"You haven't told me about the Goblins yet."

"I haven't told you about the Goblins yet? Hmm, I thought I did. Maybe that was someone else. Or maybe I was thinking about telling you but didn't. I'm not as young as I used to be, you know? That's a funny saying because no one is. I mean, even a baby could say, 'I'm not as young—'" He stopped when he saw Jackson making the "time-out" signal with his hands. "Okay, so there was another group of folks, just like the Piri vamps, but different, like a different race or whatever, and they are known as the Jone-Zen. Wait, I did tell you about this, right?"

"Just the name, but not the rest."

"Oh, right. So the Jone-Zen have their own little odd things, like they get really scaly when they fight. More defensive, you know? Stronger but slower too. I like to think of them as the triceratops to the Piri's T-Rex, though both of those guys had sharp weapons, and that's a bit different.

Sharp weapons won't hurt the Goblins in attack mode as long as they stay mostly still because of those scales. Well, like you might guess, these Jone-Zen didn't get along too well with the Piri, and they sometimes fought. One of the Piri Vampire guys started calling the Jone-Zen 'Goblins,' probably because of the scales, and the Jone-Zen hated it. So the Piri called them that even more, and the two groups went to war." Abner shook his head, apparently lost in thought. "If they'd just called them 'Gargoyles' like they wanted, none of this might've happened. Or maybe it would have. It might have been inevitable. Who knows. I mean, both of them are kind of stupid because neither goblins nor gargoyles have scales, do they? Actually I don't know."

Jackson remembered Buck-Bill's gargoyle-style counter squat.

"Then," Abner said, "things begin to cool off and one of the Piri goes and steal's Grotto's girlfriend and —"

"Who's Grotto?"

"Talbot's boss. The big boss."

"Talbot has a boss?"

Abner nodded. "Umm hmm. Or at least he used to. He might have retired."

"Wait," Jackson said, thinking, "is that the same guy that does all the blogging for the site but never comes in?"

"You think I've been doing a lot of surfing out here in the Zone? How the hell would I know?"

"I don't know. Jeez. Sorry."

Abner reacted as though he had totally forgotten that side conversation, a natural reaction that likely resulted from his totally forgetting that side conversation. "So, like I said, one of the Piri goes and steals Grotto's girl — but I don't really think she had a thing for him to start with — Grotto I mean. I mean, she was pretty smokin' and Grotto's this little mean bald dude. But anyway, ... I think she was Italian, or maybe Spanish." He smiled at something floating by in his memories. "Nice. But Grotto goes and starts this campaign against them and later starts this website and it all flares up again."

"What's the deal with auras? They said I didn't have one."

"Well, you don't have a Piri aura, you mean? They had to check you out to be sure you weren't some sort of spy. Both sides have Seers who can read those things."

"No, they said I didn't have an aura at all."

"Everyone has an aura." Abner waved dismissively.

"Simpson said I didn't have one at all. Completely blank."

Abner scrutinized him. "Who are your parents?"

"Huh? What's that got to do with anything?" His parents were none of this guy's business. That was another world, a safe place, and he'd never let this malady of madness infect it.

Abner rose, his face fixed. "What race are they? Are they human?"

"Yeah, of course. I live with my dad but my mom passed years ago."

"But you remember her? You sure she was human? Both sides look human most of the time, you know."

"Of course I remember her," Jackson lied. "She was just a regular mom. She used to make me grits and eggs every morning for breakfast and give me a kiss before I walked to the bus." He was going to continue but... didn't.

"Oh, okay. I guess it wouldn't matter because both sides have auras that the Seers can pick up. That's why they can't really send spies into each other's camps, unless they're civilian contractors. And that's dangerous because they're not in the Hive."

"What? What's the Hive?"

Abner sat down and leaned his chair back on two legs. "I didn't tell you about that either? Each race is part of a 'Hive,' or so they call it. It's just a... I don't know... mental walkie-talkie for the members. They can sorta communicate with the group as a whole that way. Not like words or sentences, but more like just pictures or emotions. And not all the time. You can try to block it out and stay off it, but sometimes it just jumps in and shows you things and other times it seems to just pull stuff out." He stroked his beard, his eyes on the sky. "When I was emerging, I thought I heard voices, but after a bit that all just shifted into the other stuff. It's hard to explain. You sort of 'feel' what the others are feeling, and there's a collective memory that goes back... geez I don't know how far it goes back. Probably all the way. I never looked back that far."

Jackson's breath froze in his chest. "I've got to take a leak," he said, afraid that his shock would be apparent on his face. He got up and walked behind one of the other units.

Abner was one of them. Vampire or Goblin, he didn't know. But he had revealed himself when describing the Hive. But wait, if he were in one of the two races, then he'd still be in the Hive, right? That would mean he'd still have a direct connection with all of the other members, and they'd probably know right where he was. But he had saved Jackson from the Goblins and was now watching the Vampires. One of those was a ruse, but which?

Or maybe he was lying about the Hive. Or, most likely, he was lying about *all* of this nonsense. Jackson tried to process all of what he'd heard, wondering whether to file it under "ridiculous but true" or "ludicrous and false." But true or false, he was in it, and if they believed all this, then it didn't matter. It was real for him either way. And one way or the other, Abner was a liar.

It took a long time for Jackson to finish his business behind the unit.

He didn't really have to go, but he forced himself to do so to avoid suspicion.

As he sat back in his off-balance plastic chair, the orange sky in the distance flashed again, followed several seconds later by a faint hiss.

"And then the storms start again, and it's all centered here, as it's always been," Abner said, as though there had been no pause in the conversation. "That's because the races are from here. This has always been the hallowed ground."

Jackson thought that the races should have searched around for a place a bit nicer than this – the Tovac Zone could be called many things, but probably not "hallowed."

"They had all spread out all over the world, but they know something big is on its way, and it will be here. So they're coming back. But they're the ones causing it all. We're all connected to the earth, and when the groups fight, they tear at the fabric of this place, and the storms are just the symptoms of a world out of balance."

Jackson waited for the sky to flash and hiss again to punctuate that dramatic statement. Nothing. That would have perhaps added a little credibility to the New Age universe fabric crap. His own theory about the weather was that the government scientists had let some of their military experiments get out of hand, and they'd pissed the universe off royally, and it was payback time.

After about five minutes of silence, Jackson decided that Abner was finished telling his story, or perhaps he just forgot that he was talking.

"What now?" Jackson asked.

"We watch. And wait."

"We don't have time to wait! Sy could be in danger!"

"That's the only way we'll ever find her. We don't know where the Piri took her, and the Jone-Zen definitely don't know, or they'd be on their way to retrieve her. We can only watch."

Jackson would rather peel off all his skin than sit and wait. He stared across at the building opposite them and then over to the Goblin headquarters where he had worked.

Nothing. Something better happen soon. He had a feeling that time was running out.

CHAPTER 41: GLORIOUS VISIONS OF GLORY

Fionn directed the forklift operator, a Banger grunt, to set the pallets down at the rear of the loading area in the back of an abandoned store. He originally planned to stage the operation in the heart of the city, but he had learned that the action was going down in the Tovac Zone, so that's where he needed to be.

"Easy!" he yelled to the Banger. "What's wrong with you? Don't you know what's in there? Oh yeah, you don't. You're not in the mission. But you can read, right?" He prepared to zing him about the red "FRAGILE" clearly marked on the wooden crate.

"Der door du deer," the round-bodied imbecile driver replied. "I no read. I just drive ... *and kill people*." He said this last with a piercing stare at Fionn.

Was that supposed to be intimidating? The day he was intimidated by a Banger was the day he'd trade in his staff and make mud angels with the filthy Goblins.

"You jeopardize this mission with your buffoonery, and it will be the last time you regret the day you were born. You got that?"

The driver grinned like an idiot and spun his forklift away.

The building had once been a regular clothing store, then a consignment store, then a used crap thrift store, then a poor loser giveaway stuff store. After a time, it transitioned from a store for vagrants and street people to a home for vagrants and street people. Then when the Piri needed the space, it became a slaughterhouse for vagrants and street people, as well as combat training for the Piri. The training was not that vigorous, as the squatters had the fighting skills of a punching bag, though with added entertainment value. They had made quite a mess, but it was a good time for all.

Everything was coming together, finally. He would announce the onset of the mission to the Hive soon, and his name would be known as the leader of this glorious operation.

"Fionn!" they would shout. "I love you Fionn!" Maybe, "All hail Fionn!" Or even, "That Fionn really has it together. Check out his beautiful blond locks and handsome shoulders!"

He'd ride that wave of fame right over the top of Avar, then pull that idiot's mission out from under him like a bug on a rug.

CHAPTER 42: FINDING THE CENTER

"Ferdinand told me he was driving you and Mr. Krol to the lab," Talbot said, leaning on a stainless steel work counter in the weapons lab in the center of the Jone-Zen headquarters complex. The windowless lab was about the size of a tennis court, with black lockers along one wall and rows of work counters through the middle. Sharpening barbs on a short spear, Simpson sat at one of the benches facing Talbot from across the counter. Archer, the weapon specialist, was welding together a new prototype in a far corner next to a massive ventilation hood. The air cracked and popped from the metal work, permeated with a faint burning metal smell that somehow escaped the droning ventilator like a tiny column of light breaking away from the crushing pull of a black hole. Though Talbot and Simpson were at the opposite end of the room from the unit, they still had to raise their voices to be heard over the distant roar of the system.

"Ferdinand is a fool," Simpson said.

"But is he wrong?" Talbot knew what the answer would be because he knew Simpson. Vicious and paranoid, he made a good security chief, though his excessive independence annoyed the hell out of Talbot. Independence and freethinking could be assets in military operations only when tempered by discipline.

"That's beside the point," Simpson said, unaware of his pun as he sharpened a barb by scraping it across a whetstone. "The point is –"

Talbot pushed himself away from the counter. "*I* decide what the point is, and the point is that you defied my order." He wasn't as furious as he let on. "I told you to let him get some rest before we brought him in for analysis."

Simpson, still focusing on his work, switched to a new barb. "I felt the situation demanded immediate action."

"Sometimes the best action seems like inaction if you don't know the full story. You know that." He had every right to come down hard on Simpson, and he needed to smack him down a bit to keep him in line, though he didn't want to jar him so hard that he'd go rogue and become an obstacle requiring removal.

"I realize that, and I respect your decision. However, I think –"

"You can think all you want, and thinking is a good thing. But you do what I tell you to do, understand? I'm in this position because I'm supposed to be in this position. Don't assume that I make decisions that you don't agree with because I don't know what I'm doing. In many cases I know stuff you don't."

This caused Simpson to pause and look up in alarm. "Like what? What aren't you telling me?"

"There are many things that you don't know, some relevant and some not so much. Like did you know that disposable razors give me a rash? I can stop a barbed arrow fired at 350 feet per second with my bare neck, but a cheap disposable razor blade breaks me out. Not relevant. Jackson Krol is more than just a latent Jone-Zen. Relevant. Do you tell your team everything you know?"

Simpson returned to his barbed spear. "No. My team could not handle everything that I know."

Talbot said nothing for a full minute. "Now, let's address what happened in the car."

"I have Ferdinand's and Mandy's teams sweeping the area. I'm on it."

"I'll get to that. What happened in the car?" He'd heard it from Ferdinand, but he liked to probe from different angles. Scenes didn't gain depth until viewed from more than a single vantage point.

"Krol made a diversion in the back seat so Ferdinand slowed the vehicle, then Krol exited and fled into the darkness of the Tovac Zone."

He mentioned the darkness and Tovac Zone to cover for his failure, Talbot thought. "How did he avoid recapture?"

Simpson focused intently on a barb that was already sharp enough to poke through a brick. "We caught sight of a fleeing figure and pursued him, finally catching him. But he was just an old man."

"What old man?" Talbot asked. Ferdinand had left out that detail. "Who was it?" Jackson might have had an accomplice.

Simpson looked up as though surprised by a new thought. "What? I mean, sir? It was nobody. Just an old man – scared that we were going to take his booze."

"Was he unusually fit for an old Tovac bum?" It could have been a disguise.

Simpson shook his head. "He was definitely old. Ragged too, and he smelled like the Zone. Not someone from outside. I would have known. Though he did seem pretty spry..." Simpson defocused as his mind likely traveled back and re-analyzed the events.

"Probably nothing, but next time bring the guy in."

"We were understaffed at that point, just Ferdinand and I, and I thought Krol might be still in the vicinity, so I let the old man go."

Talbot couldn't argue with a decision made in the field – he wasn't there. There was nothing worse than a soft general second-guessing decisions made by soldiers taking fire while he himself sat in a cozy chair miles from the action with a brandy in his hand. "Okay. So what are your plans to retrieve him?"

"Systematically re-sweep the area. We've already covered the sector where he escaped and we're expanding the search. If he's in the Zone, we'll find him."

"You'd better." The Piri were up to something big, and that kid had something to do with it. He didn't know how yet, but that kid was at the center. "Take Hebert. I need Mandy and her team to set something up." It was time to hit the Piri hard.

CHAPTER 43: MR. SAM

Sy adjusted her pack as she walked upstream alongside a river gurgling on her right. She felt the river knew she was there — that she had returned. It was fated to continue its never-ending march downstream, simultaneously arriving at its destination and starting its journey – a constant flow that had neither beginning nor end. It merely moved forward, driven by an invisible force, sometimes carrying a farmer-tanned drunk guy in an inner tube along with it.

The bus had dropped her off several miles away, and she had camped alongside the river. She caught a few fish but made up the rest of her meals from supplies in her pack. After checking her watch, she took off the pack and sat on a flat rock. It was time to eat, but her mind couldn't bring itself to the task just yet.

She had been around seven or eight years old when her parents had left her with the river people. She and her parents were supposed to go tubing together, with the tour company dropping them off upriver to drift leisurely down the river through magical "tree tunnels" — the canopy of overhanging cypresses that met above the river. Her best friend wasn't allowed to come along because the girl's parents had said that they didn't trust Sy's parents, or so her friend told her. Sy understood the wisdom of that choice only later. Her friend's absence did little to dampen her excitement, though. The cool river would relax her parents, and they wouldn't fight. Maybe they could hold hands through the mini-rapids that interrupted the serenity of the river every fifteen minutes or so. It would be so exciting!

Unfortunately, the tour company only had three inner tubes left, and that was one short. The tour operator said it would be unsafe to put her parents' beer cooler in Sy's lap for the trip downriver, so she couldn't go. Mr. Sam, the bearded leader of the river people, a small camp of nomads who lived along the river, said Sy could stay with them while her parents boozed their way downstream. Her parents could just come pick her up when they were finished, assuming they were sober enough to drive.

"I don't want to stay with these people!" she had yelled. "They're strangers! Why can't I come with you?"

Her dad, or the man she had called Dad, walked off. This was a mom job. "Well, Honey, you saw that there was no room for you," her mom said. "Are you trying to ruin our trip by making us feel guilty?" She put her bony hands on her bony hips and bent at her waist, her black roots peeking from beneath peroxide locks that dangled toward Sy's face, reaching for her. "Well, little lady, you're not going to do that again. You're spoiled enough as it is. These nice people said they'd watch you and you need to be appreciatative of them. Billy just wanted to leave you alongside the river." With that, she turned and followed her husband, or at least the man who lived with her, leaving her tiny daughter alone with a huge grizzled stranger and his merry band of bath-averse vagrants.

"I'm Mr. Sam," the hairy man said, offering his hairy hand.

She recoiled from him, terrified, but with nowhere to run.

"Ah, okay," he continued. "I'm sorry. Here, come meet some of the other kids." He turned and walked toward a grubby group of children who were apparently practicing their slapstick comedy routines, using mud pies instead of cream pies for the requisite "pie in the face" bits. They were as motley as their parents, the latter busying themselves about the tent camp gathering firewood or preparing meals or watching the kids or sleeping so soundly that they appeared dead, assuming they weren't dead.

She followed at a distance.

"Kids!" the man boomed. Several faces turned to him, some older and some younger than her, all with some form of mud on them. "This is Sy. She'll be staying with us for ... well, for a little while." He looked back at her, and she began to cry. "Get back to playing, kids. Sy will be over in a second."

She curled in a ball and buried her face in her hands on the ground and bawled. The tears had been building deep inside her for a long time, even before the trip. Maybe it started back when Billy came to live with her and her mom. She couldn't really remember a time when Billy wasn't around, and even though her mom said to call him, "Dad," Sy knew he wasn't. He never bothered her; he just ignored her. Rather, he treated her like an unwanted cat who occasionally took dumps on his pillow and shredded his favorite shoes. She was tolerated. She was trapped.

By the river, nobody spoke; nobody touched her. After a time, she looked up. Mr. Sam was seated on the ground about ten feet away, carving something. She watched him in silence. What was that? She crept closer. He whistled to himself while he carved. She moved closer, leaning in to see what it was.

"I'm not very good at this," he said without looking up. "I've been doing it for ten years, and I'm the best in the group, but I'm still not very good."

"What is it?" she asked.

"You," he said, holding up a small figurine.

He was apparently an honest man and a good judge of his own skill. The figurine had identifiable limbs and a nub head. The only detail was a deeply carved smile on the head, or perhaps a poorly slit throat.

"Since I'm not very good at whittling, it might be easier to just change you to look more like this."

"You mean I need to look like some sort of sea creature?" she asked.

He guffawed. "No, no! This part." He pointed to the smile and then held the carving out to her.

Though she knew she shouldn't, that she wasn't supposed to take things from strangers, she took it. There was something peaceful about this man.

"Your strength comes from here," he said, pointing at his chest, "not from out there." He waved his hands toward the direction that her parents had taken to the river.

"My strength comes from your chest?" she asked, though she knew exactly what he meant.

He smiled at her. "Exactly. Your strength comes from this rib right here." He pretended to rip it out and hand it to her. "Okay, so now *you* have it. Don't worry about them or me or anyone. There's only God and you, and God gave you all that you need already. He wound you up and set you down. He's watching, but He's not going to step in and change things for you. He wants to give you the freedom to choose, to see how *you* can handle it so He can be proud of you. It's your call, your responsibility. Not those two." Again, he waved toward the river. "They probably couldn't find their way downstream unless the inner tube told them which way to go, right?"

It was her turn to smile.

"Come on. Let's go meet the others." He held out his hand to her, and she shook her head while looking at his outstretched hand. He nodded his approval. "That a girl."

This time, instead of walking behind him, she walked alongside.

CHAPTER 44: DROPPING IN ON THE NEIGHBORS

The sun fought its way through the haze and poked Jackson on the head. He was tired of this. He sat, he watched, he waited, imagining how his skin would feel under his fingernails as he tore it off. Yes, that would definitely be better. Abner sat next to him in the "good" chair, the one with the special equal-length legs, propped back against the air conditioning unit, sound asleep.

Jackson mumbled something about "take a leak," not loud enough to wake him, though perhaps loud enough for him to hear if he were faking it. He headed to the roof door and pulled on it slowly. The volume of the squeak apparently had no relationship to the speed of the door, as it screamed at the top of its tiny metal lungs with every millimeter of movement. Finally, he just yanked it and discovered that he was wrong; it did indeed increase in volume with speed. It made a noise like a pterodactyl passing a stone.

No movement from Abner.

Within minutes, Jackson was down the stairs and out on the street. Despite the daylight, he felt vulnerable. Not just from the Vampires or Goblins, but also from the residents. From the dark windows, he felt eyes tracking him, mouths drooling, with forks and knives emerging from pockets. Without pausing to think, he charged across the street to the Vampire outpost. One of the building doors was off its bottom hinge, hanging diagonally with a single corner propping it up. He squeezed around it. This building looked similar to the one he'd just come from, though this one had a quaint lounging area in the foyer, perfect for visitors who craved a good sit on either a stack of old car batteries or a recliner with its seat cushion replaced with a vertical chunk of flat metal poking up like a shark fin. He walked through this small lobby into the staircase, clearly visible because the door was helpfully propped open with a stained crib mattress. He made the mistake of inhaling as he passed, and his nostrils spasmed in a failed attempt to clamp shut as a flood of old urine stench poured in as through a cracked dam. The staircase had been decorated in the Tovac style, with deep layers of trash at the bottom floor, which thinned as he climbed, the remaining piles mostly concentrated on landings.

At the top floor, he paused and took a deep breath, but not too deep. Abner had pointed out to him the location of the Vampires' apartment unit, or where he thought it was. They would be in there or on the roof.

Wait, what was he doing there? It was ludicrous for him to just stroll in there, but he seemed incapable of stopping himself. He'd done stupid things in the past – too many to count, unless of course you had a long time and were good with numbers – but this one took the cake, ate it, and threw it up all over the birthday girl. He felt like he was two people, with the unpredictable new guy at the wheel. As his legs carried him down the hall toward the Vampires' door, he reached down and picked up a discarded flute that lay on the ground. A pale sadness hit him when he held it, feeling that it must have once belonged to a little girl. Maybe her family had moved out of the Zone into a huge house with a –

Bam!

Incredulous, he watched his foot recoil from a thunderous kick that it had just delivered to an apartment door, causing the doorframe to explode in a cloud of wood shrapnel as the door swung open. Still on auto, he charged into the room, his flute ready to do some serious orbital or nasal damage. The door crashed against the wall and popped a hinge, similar to its downstairs cousin. It creaked softly as it rocked to a stop, and crumbles of trash that had been flung away from the door implosion skittered to a stop across the dark living room floor.

All was silent except for his breathing. Someone had been there, as the old furniture was pushed against the wall and the patterns of dust on the bare wood floor suggested that, until recently, things had stayed quite still there for a while. The layer of dust was marked by drag lines from the furniture, foot traffic, and circular marks likely caused by either desks or perhaps cots. The window had a clear shot to The Seven's factory complex – or rather the "Goblin headquarters," if he was to believe Abner's account.

He searched the rest of the apartment but found nothing. If he were any good, he could probably swipe his finger across the dust, lick it, and say something like, "It's still fresh. They only have a half day ride on us."

Just as he decided to head to the roof, he felt a presence in the apartment — maybe heard a noise, felt the floor vibrate, smelled something. He doubted any of the three, but he knew someone else was in the apartment, though he was in a back bedroom. With the hand not holding a flute, he grabbed a broken child's lamp from a bedside table. The body of the lamp was a ceramic humanoid banana with a grinning "I'm going to eat you in your sleep" face that could inspire a lifetime of nightmares. Though cracked at the top, it had a good heft in his hand. He could heave it at an attacker's head and then follow-up with a vicious flute flogging.

He took two steps toward the bedroom door when something ripped the lamp out of his hand. It shattered on the floor with a sound that would wake the dead, or at least make them flinch. Frozen in place, he spun his head to see what he'd already figured out – the lamp had been plugged in. He stayed stock still listening intently and staring at the door. Nothing moved; nothing made a sound except for the faint whine of the wind against the building. He could feel the other presence in the apartment, unmoving.

Rapid footsteps pounded toward the door. He felt a change inside –
something popped. The room brightened. He tensed.

Bring it!

A male figure charged around the corner into the room with a broken
bottle and froze in his tracks when he saw Jackson. The man squinted at
him and stepped forward menacingly. Abner. The skin on his face and
hands was gray and scaly.

"It's me!" Jackson said, his voice coming out wrong. "Jackson."

Abner lowered his bottle, though with some hesitation. "Are you sure?
Oh, yeah. Your silhouette in front of that window looks a lot like a
Vampire and I couldn't see your face. Plus these old eyes aren't what they
used to be. I could have sworn.... No."

Jackson moved closer to him and looked at the man's skin. Normal.

"What?" Abner asked.

"Oh, nothing. I thought there was something wrong with your skin."
He's a Goblin, you doof, a voice whispered in his head.

"Well, it *is* old. And I haven't made it to the tanning salon in at least a
week." He eyed Jackson. "What the hell are you doing here?"

Jackson felt sheepish. "I couldn't wait any more."

Abner nodded. "You sound like my friend Boots. Maybe I'll introduce
you to him some day. In fact, let's go check out the roof and then go see
him. There won't be a soul up there. Ha! Even if they're there, there still
won't be a soul up there. Get it?" He wheezed and almost slapped his leg
with his broken bottle.

"I got it." Jackson felt deflated somehow, like the other *him* had been
spoiling for a fight. It felt like when he "lost" a sneeze. Worse, they might
have just lost their only lead on Sy.

CHAPTER 45: ENEMY MACHINATIONS

Talbot rammed a pike into a beef carcass hanging from a hook in Archer's weapons lab. Off in another corner, three other Jone-Zen huddled around a Piri club and a section of body armor, trying to work out new defense tactics.

"Now pull it out," Archer said from over Talbot's shoulder.

Talbot pulled it back, leaving behind its hollow tip embedded in the hunk of meat, the tip like a bastard crossbreed between a funnel and a cheese-grater.

Archer stepped around him and gestured at the tip, moving his hand like he was shaking up a pair of dice. "The tip keeps the wound open so air can enter."

"Like the Swiss harpoon?"

Archer waived his hand dismissively. "Psh! That thing's worthless compared to this. You'd have to leave the harpoon in there, but you could reuse this."

"First of all, my great uncle's Swiss harpoon rid the world of a great many Piri. Second," he held the pike up to Archer's face. It was blunt, its tip still stuck in the carcass.

"Oh that?" Archer said. "The tips are replaceable. You can put another one on it."

"Like a coffee filter?"

"Yeah, sure, like a coffee filter."

"So, I say, 'Excuse me fellas, I gotta put a new tip on this bad boy so I can get back to stabbin' ya in the guts.' That about right?"

"Er, no sir." Archer seemed to sense that he'd pissed Talbot off a bit.

Talbot knew himself to be old-fashioned, but these young fellows, even the older young fellows like Archer, should appreciate the sacrifices and contributions of those who came before them.

"I'm working on a quick change device," Archer said. "Maybe we could have a civilian reloading the tips for us."

"Like re-charging up a musket?"

Archer hesitated, apparently not wanting to step straight into another hidden pit bristling with sharpened bamboo spears.

"Sir," Simpson said, rushing into the room in the peculiar run-walk that he favored whenever he was in a hurry. Talbot wondered if the little dandy could actually pick both of his feet up at the same time, or if maybe that would be improper. He always reminded Talbot of the officers fresh out of school, thinking they were soldiers because they had some schoolin'. The difference was that Simpson, besides being one of his best Seers, could unleash a perfectly proper and sanitary smackdown. By the book.

"First," Talbot said. "Hebert find the boy?"

"No sir, not yet. But I have bigger news for you."

"Whatcha got?" Talbot turned his back on him and walked over to the knife board mounted on the wall by the nearest corner.

"I believe we have the Piri. We still have not pinpointed their newest nest in the Tovac Zone, but we know that Fionn is launching a mission from somewhere within the Zone, and –"

"Here?" Talbot asked, wrenching out several throwing knives from the target. "Who's all involved in this one?" He walked to the throwing line about ten feet back.

"All of them. Or at least the major personnel. They are staging a huge operation from an abandoned building in the southeast corner of the Zone, only five miles from here."

"Major personnel? How major?" He threw a knife that hit dead center. Then a second that clinked with the first as its tip slid into the board.

"Tazia."

The third knife missed by half an inch. Talbot slashed the razor-sharp blade of one of his remaining knives across his forearm – he shouldn't have missed just because of the shocking news. Of course, that slash hurt him about as much as slashing himself with a plastic spoon, but it was the principle.

"That's it then," he said, almost relieved that the battle was finally upon them. "This is the big one – this is the mission that they've been planning all this time. It's finally here. But wait, I thought Avar was leading the mission. Was our intelligence off?"

"Not off, I would suggest. I believe the situation has become fluid on their end. Something has shifted their priorities. Our man thought Avar was on point, but he has apparently been pulled off on some other mission, and everyone is talking about Fionn's. He's keeping the details secret from everyone except for his closest inner circle. Even Tazia is somewhat in the dark about the details, though she is the one who sent him off on this mission. I placed the full report on your desk."

Talbot put two knives in his left hand. He slung his left arm across his body and up like a tennis forehand with topspin, releasing one of the knives, then reversed the move in a downward backhand stroke, releasing the second knife. They thudded on either side of the errant knife, as aimed. "What else?"

"Fionn is already back from overseas – the Balkans was his final stop. Remember I briefed you on his travels across Europe. We have followed him of course, but we could not ascertain his intentions."

"But it's related to this mission?"

"We think so. He is likely gathering supplies or intel, but we cannot tell."

"How about our European counterparts? Anything from them?"

"Nothing. One other thing: we do know that Fionn had several crates sent back."

"What's —?"

"We do not know. We know there is metal in one and biological matter in another, but that is it."

"Biological? Like what?"

"We do not know. But there are no air holes, so we do not believe it is living."

"Pull everyone in that we can get. We need to accelerate our timetable. We need to beat them to the stab."

"That would be 'to the punch,' sir."

"I – never mind, Simpson. Just pull in our assets and report when you know something."

Simpson performed his half nod – half bow and walked out of the room, proper and robot-like.

Talbot flicked his remaining knife underhand at the target, the blade wedging itself between the first two knives. Biological matter, Simpson had said. He thought of the ancient histories that he'd read covering both races. One of the Piri legends was that a powerful warrior — what was his name? — could be brought back to life by placing the heart of a freshly sacrificed enemy in his mouth.

Surely it couldn't be that. They couldn't be planning to rip out Sy's heart to revive the legendary Piri warrior.

That would suck to high order, especially for her.

CHAPTER 46: DELICACIES IN THE ZONE

Abner didn't want to tell the kid, but they'd been lucky up to that point. He wasn't really sure how they'd avoided detection so far, despite what he'd told him earlier. Truth was – well, he couldn't really remember what the truth was sometimes. The truth hadn't changed, but his ability to recall it had. His memory wasn't fading like an old picture in the sun; rather, gaps were appearing in it like holes in a paper target. Up until now, the shooters had been using BB guns, but he suspected the caliber was about to ramp up. Maybe he should start doing some crosswords. Or maybe stop eating stuff that really had no business hanging out in a human stomach.

That reminded him of something. They were back in the apartment waiting for nightfall, and he reached above the refrigerator and pulled down two delicacies that he had prepared for dinner.

"Here you go," he said, handing Jackson one of the sticks holding his specialty. Each stick had a cross of two additional sticks attached to the end, and stretched between them was a dried lizard. Actually, it was more of a salted and burned lizard since, while he had access to a fire, he didn't have access to the block of time required for a proper lizard-drying.

"Uh, is that a crucified lizard?" the boy asked, shocked.

Abner smiled, remembering how soft people got outside of the Zone. "No. I'm not a Roman, and he died peacefully before I strung him up."

"Wait, you mean you just found a dead lizard and stretched it out like this?"

"What? No! There's no way a juicy lizard like this would just be laying around dead waiting for me to eat it. I stabbed it with a stick."

"That doesn't sound peaceful."

"Huh?"

"You said he died peacefully. I'd say 'dying peacefully' normally doesn't involve getting disemboweled with a sharp stick."

Abner didn't understand kids these days. "I didn't disembowel him until after I stabbed him with the stick. Anyway, it's better dried but this is the best I could do. Eating them dried is supposed to improve your love life, but it didn't work for me until I rubbed it vigorously on my privates. No, not *that* lizard. And that only worked until one of the sharp claws snagged me in... well, you know." He winced at the memory. "I wouldn't recommend it. Unless of course you scale up first." Oh crap. "I mean, if you were a Jone-Zen you could scale up."

"Those are the Goblins."

"Right. I told you about those, right? Yeah I did. I did, didn't I? Yeah, I think I did." He needed to get to Boots. There was something special about this kid, and Boots would know what to do. He just had to get to him.

CHAPTER 47: CAVALRY CHARGE

Finally, it was time to roll.

Jackson folded up the map that Abner had drawn him. They were heading to Abner's place so he could pick up some supplies and contact his friend Boots. Jackson now wore a hooded sweater that he'd picked up from a pile of discarded junk in one of the bedrooms. The only positive thing that could be said about the moldy odor was that it was "all natural." At least he fit in with others in the Zone now, both visually and olfactorily — at least his old perfume job at the mall had expanded his vocabulary a bit.

They stepped out into the dark crisp air, cool for that time of the year, though above freezing. Dawn would arrive in an hour or two, he figured. Abner lead the way, swinging his lead pipe like he was on deck in a baseball game. Jackson followed a few paces behind, several feet further than the length of the pipe. He held a spear that had started out life as a mop before divorcing its floppy bits as part of an arranged marriage to a steak knife at the apartment. Though he'd tied the knife to the mop handle securely, he imagined it would be a single use weapon. He also carried another knife in his waistband, though this caused him a degree of emotional distress until he figured out that he could put it at his hip instead of in the front or back.

Abner whistled as he walked. Instead of being swallowed by the night, the whistle filled the entire audio spectrum of the dark, mostly abandoned streets – "mostly" instead of "totally" because ghostly figures darted into shadows at their approach like roaches scattering from a midnight muncher flicking on the kitchen lights. Jackson hoped Abner disturbed the silence on purpose, perhaps to indicate to others that they were dominant and not to be messed with. Or maybe he whistled for the same reason that hikers made noise in the woods — to avoid startling dangerous creatures, such as bears. If bears lived here, they'd be drunk and have bear mange and live off of scraps of trash, random animal jerky, and vagrants. Or maybe he just whistled because he was crazy, and in his mind, he strolled down a sunlit beach. Jackson sent up a mental prayer for one of the earlier options. He didn't know why, but he felt that if he talked, he would be exposing himself to the creatures of the night — like a child hanging a juicy leg out of the covers for the monster under the bed to latch onto.

There were no cars on the street. The only sounds above the whistling were Jackson's footsteps – Abner moved in almost total silence – and an occasional thumping from a distant helicopter, similar to the hammering in Jackson's chest. His senses felt inside out, open to the elements and sensitive. Beneath the ordinary, he could hear the faint swish of a night flyer, likely a bat, behind him to his right. The light from the distant city reflected from the low clouds and bathed the streets with an eerie glow, enough for him to see shadows. He'd never seen shadows in the dark, and they didn't look right. In fact, he didn't feel right – not bad, just different. He felt like he was on the edge of a high diving board, itching to take the tiny step that would send him hurtling downward.

Shuffling behind him, faint whispers. He didn't turn. A far-off rumble.

"Abner," he whispered, "I think it's time to go."

Abner turned and smiled. "We *are* going. See?" He pointed at his feet with his pipe as he walked.

The distant rumble warbled and split into separate distinct sounds, growing in volume. "Something is coming," Jackson said, feeling inexplicably more curious than concerned. He knew they needed to take cover, though the urgency came more from detached tactical thinking than from fear. The volume from one of the rumbles stepped upward abruptly as a motorcycle turned a corner onto their street, probably a half a mile behind them.

Abner's smile cracked and splintered into a look of concern. "We have to get off of the street. Now!" They were in the middle of a block, far from an alley. Abner tried a door at the closest building, but it wouldn't budge. He ran to another while the motorcycle revved higher as it sped toward them. Jackson took up a position behind a black metallic block at the edge of the street that might have been the burned-out husk of an inverted van. He could hear Abner cursing under his breath as he tried doors. The motorcycle was almost on them now, with two (or maybe more) not far behind.

Jackson stood stock still, feeling the world morph around him. The light from the city brightened. The roar of the approaching motorcycle split again, dividing into firing cylinders and, beneath this, the whine of tires gripping the road and throwing gravel behind them.

"What ... what are you doing?" Abner yelled from somewhere behind him.

The motorcycle was only a block from them, though Jackson could not see it from behind the van.

"I don't know," he answered, his mind elsewhere, feeling the motorcycle's surging cavalry charge, timing it.

Abner banged his pipe into a metal door. Jackson stepped away from the van. The motorcycle was seconds away, with the driver, like his steed, totally encased in black. He held a blunt mace out to the side, directing it in a trajectory that would send it crashing into one side of Jackson's skull and out the other.

Jackson set the base of his spear on the street and released it to fall forward.

The black mace rushed toward him.

Jackson took two quick steps to his right as the motorcycle roared through the space he had just vacated. As the rush of air hit him, so did a cacophony of sounds – a wet pop, a snapping stick, a shriek of agony, the clanking of a metal mace tumbling down the street, and the grinding and rasping of a motorcycle traveling at well over a hundred miles an hour skidding on its side, shedding pieces of itself as the road tore it apart.

Jackson remained motionless in the road as the screech of the dying motorcycle faded. Up the street, more approached. They should have been too far away for him to see in this darkness. They had less than a minute. He turned.

A short section of the mop handle and the knife that formed the spear tip had gone entirely through the attacker and now lay on the street in a puddle of dark smooth blood. The man himself lay several feet beyond, his limbs unnaturally bent, with the rest of the mop handle sticking out of his chest toward the sky.

Jackson approached him. The man twitched, then raised his helmeted head and turned it toward Jackson.

"Let's move!" Abner yelled. He had righted the half-ruined motorcycle and straddled it, looking back at Jackson.

Jackson ran forward. The injured driver thrashed, and his broken limbs straightened. He leapt to his feet and yanked the wooden stake from his chest, blocking Jackson's path.

So much for a stake through the heart, a distant voice said in his head.

The driver swung the spear handle in an arc at Jackson's head. Jackson slid to the side and, in one fluid movement, took the knife from his waistband and slammed it upward just behind the man's chin, the blade tip popping out a small section at the top of the helmet. The man dropped to the ground, sporting a new metal goatee like something from an Egyptian sarcophagus. Jackson stared at him a moment, then turned toward the approaching motorcycles, his body as alive as the clouds in an electrical physics storm, crackling with energy.

"Let's go!" Abner yelled. "We gotta move now!"

Jackson popped back to reality as though from a waking trance. What the hell was he doing just standing around? He sprinted toward Abner as the motorcycles roared closer behind them. He could feel and hear others approaching on foot too. They only had seconds now. He leapt onto the bike and wrapped his arms around Abner. The tires squealed and the bike lurched dangerously before firing forward, accelerating with such ferocious intensity that he had to squeeze the skinny old man tightly to avoid getting ripped off of the back. The bike clanked and vibrated ominously as it dove into the night.

CHAPTER 48: GETTIN' TUMPED

"Those aren't Jone-Zen!" Abner yelled over the roar of the motorcycle engines.

"Huh?" Jackson asked from behind him. He was lost in thought, watching himself stab the faceless biker under the chin. The memory was detached, impersonal, on the surface, more like the memory of a watched movie than of an actual event.

"Those are Piri! Vampires!" Abner yelled again, his voice almost lost.

Jackson looked over his shoulder. Three motorcycles were gaining on them through the dark streets.

"Hold on!" Abner screamed.

Jackson barely had time to turn his head forward before their bike leaned and attempted to swerve around a metal barrel in the road. They clipped the edge of it, sending it crashing into a car on the curb. The bike wobbled but righted itself.

A screech and grinding crunch sounded behind them. The barrel must have ricocheted off the car and taken out a bike, as both bike and rider were tumbling. The other two bikes accelerated forward, still gaining ground.

"You got one," Jackson yelled. "Two left."

Abner grunted. He swerved the bike side to side now, either trying to avoid getting shot or to kick up more debris. Or maybe because he enjoyed it.

Jackson could feel them approaching. He didn't want to run; he wanted to stand on his bike seat and leap into the air, crashing onto one of the drivers. He could almost feel himself picking one of them up and dropping him on his head. A small voice said that that was ridiculous – he couldn't do that. But he *could* do that. He could feel it. His body tensed.

Something clanked to his left. A grappling hook and chain bounced backwards. The chain led back to the barrel of a gun held by one of the pursuing motorcyclists. The man dropped the gun which tumbled behind him with the chain and hook. He reached down to his bike and pulled out a second identical gun with a barbed hook extending from the front of the barrel.

A heavy object thudded into his back from the other side, closely followed by a quick tug backward, and then a ripping and clanking sound. He knew what it was before he even looked over the other shoulder – the other biker had shot him with one of the hooks, and it didn't bite. Another hook and chain bounced away from them. He was vaguely aware that that should have hurt worse than it did.

"They're shooting hooks at us!" Jackson yelled.

"Tell me which one is about to fire, then tell me when they're about to shoot!" Abner yelled back.

Jackson turned around as far as he could, enough to see both pursuers. "The one on our left is preparing to fire!" Jackson yelled.

Abner veered the bike to the left and decelerated slightly so that the left pursuer was only about twenty feet behind them.

Jackson watched him as the gun wobbled slightly, then stabilized. "Now!" he shouted, gripping the old man even tighter. He felt the intention before the man leaned, banking the bike hard to the right.

Abner wasn't quite fast enough. The hook fired by the left attacker wasn't a direct hit because of the evasive maneuver. But it did hit a glancing blow across Jackson, scraping across his back with a horrific tearing noise, though once again, he felt no real pain. The hook continued off to the left, most of its momentum lost. It hit a signpost and bounced off of the ground, trailing its chain, which whipped like a striking serpent.

And strike it did. The chain hit the tire of the left pursuer and became instantly entangled. The bike swerved as hook whipped around and struck the driver. The front wheel locked and the bike bucked, launching itself and its driver into the air, the crazed hooked chain flailing and slashing the air. They landed in a shower of clattering debris.

Clank!

The final pursuer had shot them with another hook gun, this time missing Jackson but locking into their bike. The driver threw the gun down which exploded on impact, sending up a column of dark debris.

What was – the thought was cut short as the wobbly chain between their bike and the cloud of dust on the street snapped taut. The bike stopped; they did not. As Jackson tumbled through the air, he curled his body, preparing himself. He somehow knew his position; he tracked the ground with his eyes as his body rotated, bracing for the impending impact. In front and to his right, Abner somersaulted above the street, like a man performing a front flip into a swimming pool. Behind him, Jackson heard a metal clank followed by the grinding of metal against the merciless blacktop.

He hit the ground in a roll and bounced forward and up, losing little momentum. He came down again, bouncing and rolling, the world rotating impossibly fast around him. Then again. An image of his tumbling body meeting a cinder block wall flashed across his mind like a burst of lightning. He bounced again. The crunching and groaning of metal and plastic continued behind him, though fading. He bounced one last time, his momentum almost completely spent. Watching the ground, he hit it and rolled again, skidding to a stop on his feet while facing the opposite way from his direction of travel.

Abner's prone body slid to a stop on the ground next to him. His formerly ragged clothes were now mostly cloth strips covering his grayish scaly skin, actually more akin to a shell or a thick hide.

Jackson had been right about him – he was a Goblin!

Behind Abner lay the final pursuer surrounded by the twisted wreckage of his bike. Abner and Jackson's bike must have whipped out from under them and taken him out. Someone hadn't thought through those hook guns that well. Thanks be to God for that one.

Abner! Jackson reached for the motionless man. As he touched him, the old man looked up, peering into Jackson's face, and smiled. "So it seems we are brothers," Abner said. His smile faltered a bit as he scrutinized him. "Well, perhaps cousins."

"Wait, what do you mean, 'cousins'?"

"How do you feel?" Abner asked.

Engines approached. "They're coming! We gotta move!" Jackson dragged Abner to the curb while watching the road for the approaching convoy of vehicles.

The man inexplicably laughed. Well, laughing at such a time wasn't really "inexplicable" for Abner, who tended to shun all things explicable. "You just got dumped off a bike at, what, 120 miles an hour?"

Jackson knew what the man was implying but wouldn't let his mind go near the thought. "I just had a lucky landing. Let's go!" He pulled Abner up as the old man staggered and laughed like a drunk.

"I knew it!" he said. "You're a Goblin!" He looked back at him. "Or at least you have some Goblin blood in you." The old man ambled a few feet over to the final biker's motorcycle and righted it. It was definitely not in riding condition, though still mostly intact.

"Leave it!" Jackson yelled. "It won't run."

"Not now, but someday," Abner said, staring lovingly at the bike, dusting it off.

"Let's go!" he yelled louder, pulling Abner toward the nearest alley. The sound of the approaching convoy of pursuers grew.

"We can't leave it."

"Okay, okay! I got it. Let's get the hell out of here!" He took the bike from Abner and pushed it toward the nearest alley, but Abner grabbed his arm.

"No." He pulled Jackson toward the alley on the opposite side of the street. "This way." He dropped his voice as they jogged down the ever-darkening alley, Jackson still pushing the busted bike. "You might have a bit of something else in you too. But that's impossible. There's no crossbreeding. You must be still emerging so that's why you seem so… I don't know. Not right. But then again…" He looked back at Jackson again in the gloom of the alley.

"What?" was all Jackson could say. That single word covered so many questions. *What now, what are you talking about, what is happening to me, what am I going to do, what am I?!"*

"We need to get to Boots. Let's go. We don't want those Piri wipes to catch us exposed out here. We don't have far now."

They plunged deeper into the darkness as Jackson's world tumped itself right on over.

CHAPTER 49: UNKNOWN

"So what am I?" Jackson finally asked, unable to keep it in anymore. He wasn't a Goblin; his dad wasn't a Goblin; his mom... well she couldn't have been one. Right? But what if his dad left her because he found out what she was?

That was ridiculous. If anyone did any leaving around his dad, it would be whichever person happened to not be his dad. His dad wouldn't leave a sinking boat.

How the heck did I survive the crash? The bike he now pushed was half destroyed. His clothes were in tatters, with his left sleeve constantly sliding down his arm, disconnected at the shoulder. Tired of pushing it back up, he just left it to bunch up at his forearm, like an upper body leg warmer. But then again, people survived crashes all the time. Plus he'd seen a reality police show once where some drug head had jumped out of a fifth story window and landed spread eagle on his face on a cement road – on his face! The police who had been pursuing him into the building called for a medical examiner to pronounce the man dead before they even left the building to inspect his body. When they finally got down the stairs and out into the street, all they found was a small puddle of blood and a bunch of open-mouthed citizens with fingers pointing the way the druggie had run, his only injury a bloody nose.

Then again, Jackson wasn't on drugs. Or was he? Maybe he was in a drug-induced stupor right now, dreaming about a crazy old man taking him on an adventure across the Tovac Zone. But if this were a dream, he'd also have to add the part about the Vampire website, making this the longest dream ever. And that would mean Sy was a dream too.

Her black eyes floated through his mind, not looking at the floor as in real life, but straight back at him. Where was she? What had they done to her? He couldn't fathom something happening to her. Beneath that detached and tough demeanor was a delicate lotus blossom. She wasn't exactly Asian, and he wasn't really sure what a lotus blossom was, but it seemed fitting somehow. If she heard him say that, she would likely "fit" his head into a toilet bowl.

But wait! If she was a Goblin – er, Jone-Zen – then maybe she had been somewhat uninterested in him because he was human, but now.... Was he human? Was he a Goblin? Or something else?

"I don't know," Abner replied, answering at the same moment that Jackson came to the same conclusion.

CHAPTER 50: BOOTS

"You two!" yelled a voice from the shadows ahead.

They froze. His mind afire, Jackson had walked with Abner through the near darkness for about half an hour without incident, other than of course Abner stopping to pee on a wall.

A bright light hit them from the direction of the voice. Releasing the bike, Jackson took two quick steps but stopped as he realized what he was seeing. A man with a curled handlebar mustache, wearing a stovepipe hat, a stained white tuxedo, and cowboy boots waved a cane in front of an old movie theater. The marquis had flickered into life, or at least flickered. "The Flying Water Garden," it announced.

"My bike!" Abner said, catching the motorcycle before it could tip over and crunch to the pavement.

The man pointed his white cane at the sign. "Trapeze artists of the highest order," he announced to them, beckoning them to enter. "Nude so that you may see their true beauty. With the most amazing bladder control, sending spiraling showers to sparkle through the electric air."

"Tell me that's not Boots," Jackson said under his breath to Abner.

Abner hesitated and then whispered, "Well, he *does* have boots on. And that *is* a good show. Pretty amazing actually. You just don't want to sit in the first few rows. Trust me."

Then, to the man, Abner said, "No money."

For a moment, the man's face froze as he cut his eyes from Abner to Jackson. His smile and arms dropped, followed by the lights, throwing them back into blackness deeper than before. Jackson's eyes had previously adjusted to the darkness, but those darn lights had just reset them. Almost immediately, though, his eyes readjusted, and the pitch-black alley was bathed in a dim light.

That's your Goblin eyes, his mind said.

Shut up, he replied.

"I can't see a thing now," Abner said, holding his free arm out in front, feeling for obstacles.

Jackson waved his hand in front of the man's face, and he didn't react.

See, you stupid mind. He's a Goblin, and he can't see in the dark. So I'm no Goblin.

His mind, never one to be outdone by its rebellious self, retorted, *Then you're something else.*

Shut up! he replied again.

"I'll get the bike," Jackson said. "Take my arm. I can just make out the road. We keep going straight?"

Abner looked at him with an odd expression, though that in itself was not odd, as most of his expressions were, in fact, odd. "Yes, straight," he replied.

After about five minutes, Abner released him and again took the lead, weaving through the alleys and thoroughly disorienting Jackson. Soon, dawn broke, and the first rays of sunlight struck the spidery gas tunnels crossing the sky, transferring the light as though by a fiber optic cable, illuminating the sky like green capillaries below the deep purple of the clouds. After a few more minutes, the rising sun lit the clouds, and the green faded into the pink of a beautiful sunrise.

"We're here," Abner said. They stopped at the edge of an alley opening onto a wider street that seemed vaguely familiar to Jackson, though he couldn't quite get his bearings. "I don't think they saw my face so we're probably safe to go in my place – hey that rhymed! What was I saying? Oh, yeah. We go in but not for long. They'll know me soon." Abner leaned out of the alley and peered down the street, squinting. "Ah, good! He got my message. I wasn't sure he would come."

"Boots?"

"No. Father Christmas."

"Isn't he supposed to still be up north making presents?"

"Nah. He works down at the border most of the year making brass fittings for them high end water sprayers."

"You're kind of a smart ass for an old guy."

"Who are you calling old? Leave the bike here. Don't drop it! Gentle." Abner dragged some debris on top of it – urban camo – and then scanned the road. "Let's go."

They ran across the street and into the building, the familiar smell greeting Jackson like an old friend who had gone crazy and now begged at the corner for a single penny so he could buy some Fix-A-Flat for his Bentley. The two shuffled up the dim trash-strewn staircase. Jackson could hear the sounds of people moving around and preparing for a day of... who knew what they did around there – maybe a day of junk-heaving or a day of tending their mold crop.

"Here's where you kicked me," Abner said as they reached a landing near the top floor. "I was just wandering –"

"Okay, okay! I said I was sorry!"

"But did you mean it? I don't think so." At the top floor, Abner stopped and turned, his hand on the handle of the staircase door. "Here we are, the penthouse." Jackson waited for the laugh but then realized that he was serious. "Now, when we get to my apartment, I'm going to go in and talk to Boots. He's a little jumpy, and he really doesn't like coming down here. He was the toughest Bender I ever knew, practically a Banger, so you don't want to get him all riled up. I told you about them, didn't I?"

"Who?"

"You know – Bangers, Benders, Seers, Poppers, err, something else... Oh yeah, Blockers too. Maybe more. I told you about those?"

"Not really." Jackson wanted to know more, but there was still too much to know more about, and not enough time. "This guy's a Goblin?"

"He's a Jone-Zen."

"But isn't that the same –"

"Yes, but we're not Goblins. Goblins are ugly with crooked noses, and they smell funny."

Jackson said nothing.

"Besides, you might be one yourself, so you might want to lay off the derogatories." His face broke into a creaky smile. "Hey, you know if you were half regular civilian human and half Goblin, we could call you a 'Gobman!'"

"I thought 'Goblin' was a bad word."

Abner's face dropped. "Boy you know how to kill a joke, you know that? How funny is Jone-man? Not much."

"I think Jone-Zen is pretty funny already. You know that means something, right?"

"Yes. It means a kick-ass race of genetically superior superhumans. Now let's stop all this crotch-kicking around and get in there." He pulled the staircase door open, and they walked down the hallway to room "7." It had additional digits in the past, but now only the seven remained. "You wait here and then I'll let you know when you can come into the courtin' room and wait." He knocked on the door and pushed it open slowly, calling into the apartment before stepping in. "It's me, Boots. I'm coming in. I've got someone with me, but he's cool." He stepped all the way in the apartment, though his hand remained on the doorknob. "He's gonna hang out in the courtin' room while we talk."

He waved Jackson in. After they were both inside, Abner gestured for him to take a seat in the front room off to the right of the door.

"You do a lot of courtin' in here?" Jackson whispered, eying the couch.

Abner thumped him solidly in the forehead then left him standing there holding his head.

The place was surprisingly clean and almost even cheery. There were paintings of birds on almost every wall, and magazines fanned out on a small end table next to a maroon couch with a green ivy pattern. The top magazine was titled, "Decent Housekeeping," and had a picture of a voluptuous brunette lying on a white leather couch, her bright red lipstick the only punch of color. Apparently, she had servants to do her housekeeping.

He grabbed the magazine and sat on the arm of the couch, only a few feet from the hallway that led into the main area of the apartment. His ears were as open as the mouth of a baby bird when momma landed with a worm.

"Boots!" Abner said, excitement in his voice.

Mumbling. As Jackson strained, the voice became clearer, but still faint. "... your message. Your code stinks. I didn't know if you needed me here or if you needed a chocolate pedicure. Who's your damn friend? I've got enough friends of my own, and I don't need any more. Plus I'm in a hurry. I need to find someone."

Even though it was a whisper, there was something familiar about that voice.

"He's just a kid," Abner said. "Simpson was taking him to the lab for study. He worked at the Jone-Zen's new HQ in the Zone. You know the place I told you about?"

"Oh, is that what you meant? Next time, we need to just meet somewhere, and not in this hellhole. I'm still in the clear. I haven't heard a peep from them in over a decade. I'll bet Grotto doesn't even remember me, and neither does Tazia."

Jackson remembered Abner saying Grotto was Talbot's boss, the one whose girlfriend was stolen by the Vampires, but he'd never heard of Tazia.

"Don't say that. No wait. You don't want her remembering you. She's bad news."

"Yeah. So what's up with this kid? Is he Jone-Zen? How did he end up here?"

Abner briefly told the man about Jackson's escape from the car and their trek across the Tovac Zone. The man said nothing until Abner got to the bike chase.

"You both dumped at over 100?" the man asked.

Abner mumbled something.

"Well then he's *got* to be Jone-Zen. From both sides?"

"His mother left him when he was young, and his dad's nothing."

There was a pause. "Well jam a rainbow up a leper's butt! This can't be..."

Footsteps rapidly approached the front room.

Jackson stood just in time to see his dad turn the corner.

CHAPTER 51: REFLECTIONS ON THE STYX

Sy's grandmother had picked her up from the river people two weeks after she'd been dropped off. No one knew what happened to her mom or Billy, and if it hadn't been for the tour operator complaining to the police about his three lost tubes, Sy might have stayed with the river clan forever. As it was, her grandmother got her a day before the clan packed up and move further upriver.

She had enjoyed her time with the clan. They had treated her well, and she had made friends with Mr. Sam's daughter Cari. Though younger, Cari had been a great mentor for her in the camp, teaching her how to fish and how to kick a boy in the biscuits. They had lived almost as sisters for those two weeks.

Sy hadn't seen Cari since then — over twenty years ago. "What am I doing here?" she thought, scanning the river running past.

She should have taken Jackson with her back at the van, but he might not have wanted a life on the run. She wasn't even sure what had happened. One minute she was in the van with him. The next, he was outside, somehow flipping onto the roof. She frantically called for backup, but the comms were still down. The Vampires must not have known she was in the van, as they didn't even try to get in. When she saw him through the window on the ground, she tried to open the front door, but it was electronically sealed. She ran to the back of the van and hit the door release but it malfunctioned. Terrible shrieks filled the air, and she smashed a fist on the door release and kicked the back door until it crashed open.

By the time she got outside, he was back on his feet, though most of the Vampires were not. Three circling him. She launched herself on the nearest one, jabbing her short spear at a downward angle into his neck. After riding him to the ground, she rose and saw that she was the only one still standing. Jackson was unconscious but still breathing. She dragged him off the road under a low tree canopy. Voices approached, probably Jone-Zen. More Vampires swooped in from a different direction and gathered up their injured, ignoring her and retreating into the darkness.

She had left Jackson then, taking off in the van. The Jone-Zen would take care of him, right? As for her, she hoped the Jone-Zen would assume that the Piri had taken her. The mental pressure of the Hive signaled her impending full emergence. She needed to find a rogue Bender to pull her out, and she would be free at last.

She didn't feel free. Jackson's ghost walked behind her, tapping her with his non-ghostly finger, because of course a ghostly finger would just poke right through and not be that annoying at all. He wore that silly sly grin on his face, like he was up to something. She wondered what he was like outside of "all this" — how he was as a normal person, out in the real world. Now she might never know. Besides, she suspected that he wasn't what most would call "normal" anyway – normal people didn't single-handedly take on a mob of Vampires and pile their bodies up around them.

The Jone-Zen had to have found him by the street and taken care of him. *Please let that be true.*

A lone inner tube floated toward her on the river, cutting through reflections of the overhanging cypresses. She watched it, thinking of the river clan. She hadn't been able to find them. She kicked off her shoes, threw some branches over her pack, and charged into the river after the tube, her sudden splashing causing a crow in the trees to take flight and caw in protest. She caught the tube and climbed aboard.

It connected her to the river, carrying her forward like Charon's boat across the Styx.

Someone was going to lose their tube deposit, she thought as the easy river lulled her to sleep.

CHAPTER 52: COMING AND GOING

Seeing the smile on Victor's face was like finding a glossy penguin sunning himself in the Sahara Desert. He ran across the room and hugged Jackson, thus causing the penguin to fly and recite Shakespeare. Releasing him, he held Jackson's face in both hands and looked into his eyes. Jackson, for his part, was beyond shock at the moment – the needle for his "surprise gauge" had broken.

"You're here! You're safe!" Then, proving the penguin a mirage, he punched Jackson in the stomach, though not too hard. His face dropped into its familiar frown lines. "Scared the hell outta me, you stupid kid."

"What are you doing here?" they both asked simultaneously.

"How 'bout I make us some tea and we can talk about it?" Abner said. "I think we got us some time before they figure out it was me. *If* they ever figure out it was me." He headed deeper into his apartment, and the two followed.

My dad is a Goblin, and I'm half Goblin.

The main room was, in a word, stunning, at least by Tovac standards, with six enormous floor-to-ceiling windows facing the scenic Zone — mostly rooftops and brick walls — and spotless, with more paintings of birds, all nicely framed. In front of a sectional brown leather couch sat a low table with an empty wooden bowl on it.

"I had to get rid of the plastic fruit," Abner said, apparently following Jackson's eye, "because I kept forgetting it was fake! Please, have a seat while I go change. I'll grab you some new clothes too, Jackson. I've got some stuff that will fit you just fine." He left the room.

Jackson sat on the edge of a cushion on the couch. Surprisingly, his dad bypassed the leather recliner and sat right next to him. "You first," his dad said. "Why are the Piri after you? And how did you get mixed up with the Jone-Zen in the first place?"

"Don't know, and didn't mean to." He had trouble talking in one direction while thinking in another. "Remember the new job, how I said they were weird? That was with Talbot's group. I didn't know they were gob— I mean Jone-Zen."

"Wait, you just *happened* to get a job with them? How did that happen?"

"Chester had a friend who told him about the job."

"Who?"

Jackson tried to slide forward on the cushion, but he was already at the edge. "I don't know. But Talbot and Simpson were very interested to find out."

"So they knew about you? About me?"

He considered this. "I don't think so. They said I was 'blank.' That's why Simpson wanted to send me to the lab."

"Simpson? I still can't believe Talbot lets that little prick hang around. He's the one who read you? Laid his hands on you."

"Well, just a finger."

"Oh, yeah. He was a little weird about the germs. He can read people about as good as I can read Chinese squiggles. 'Blank' is just what a Seer says when he can't see nothing. And of course he'd never read anyone like you." Victor appeared suddenly uneasy, and he rose from the couch.

Jackson followed. "What does that mean? Someone 'like me'?"

Victor cut his eyes over at him. "I guess now's as good a time as any to tell you."

"Tell you what?" Abner asked, bursting back into the room. He threw a bundle of clothes over to Jackson. "Did I tell you we have running water here?"

"Wait, tell me what?" Jackson said.

"You go get cleaned up and change first," Victor said. "We need to get ourselves ready first. Go! Just hurry back, and I'll tell you."

Jackson reluctantly left the room, finding a bathroom off a main hall. He ran the water, which started with a brownish tint and stayed that way. He rinsed himself off and dressed himself in the jeans, t-shirt, and jacket Abner had given him. Luckily, the jeans still had a belt in them, as they were a few inches too big in the waist in addition to being a few inches too short. He put his own shoes back on, one of them with a gash on the side that looked like a mouth, with a socked foot for teeth.

Back in the main room, Abner was telling Victor some details about the weapons the Vampires had used. "They were probably meant to be mounted to one of the assault vehicles, but these jokers had rigged explosive anchors to the back ends and were firing them from motorcycles. Those were some nice bikes, though. I'm gonna fix one up as a cruising bike for sunny Sundays. I've got my eye on a sweet little honey down at –"

"Wait!" Victor barked. "Is it here?"

"Oh yeah," Abner said. "I should probably bring that inside before I can get a lock rigged up for it. Wait here and –"

"No, you stupid coot!" Victor yelled. "Where are your supplies? Business supplies."

Abner pointed to a cedar chest topped with a crystal bowl of potpourri next to a floor-to-ceiling bookcase. Victor charged it and flung it open, sending the crystal bowl shattering against a wall and flakes of potpourri raining down like obnoxiously fragrant confetti. He rifled through the chest, throwing out metal boxes, assorted body armor plates, and short weapons similar to the hooked spears that Jackson had seen the Goblins use. Finally, he pulled out a small metal box and opened it up. "Got it!" He pulled something small out, closed and latched the box, then threw the box to Abner. "Hold that! Is this thing charged?" he asked, holding up a small component the size of a penny.

"Is what charged?" Abner asked.

Victor just shook the tiny component.

"Oh that tracker! I think so, it's been plugged into that base unit box thing, and I just got the whole getup two weeks ago. Where is that box part?"

Victor jabbed his finger at Abner, who looked down at the box in his hand. "Oh yeah."

"Pack up quick and leave out the back," Victor said. "They're coming! I'll meet you a mile south at the supply shop." He ran for the door.

"What —?" Jackson started.

"That damn bike!" Victor said, pausing at the door. "They can track it, but so can we!" He ran out.

Abner threw a sheathed knife to Jackson and then took his jacket off. Jackson clipped the knife to his belt while Abner slid a body armor torso piece over his head. He strapped a broadsword onto his back, its hilt hidden by his gray hair, then put his jacket back on. He put several small things into the pockets of his overcoat. "Here," he said, throwing a black tube to Jackson. It was surprisingly heavy. "It's a police baton. It won't faze the Vampires but if those Jone-Zen come after you again, you could stop them in their tracks with a shot to the temple with that bad boy."

Jackson flicked his wrist and the baton extended to its full length. It felt good in his hand, but it was no broadsword. "Where's my body armor?"

"Just tighten up. You won't need it."

"But you –"

"I'm an old man! I like the security."

Jackson could hear engines approaching. "They're almost here!"

Abner ran into the kitchen but returned almost immediately. "Here," he said again. He threw one of the crucified lizards to him. "You gotta eat when you can, and go to the can when you – wait. I forgot how that goes." He took a bite of his own lizard as he headed out the front door, Jackson close behind.

"Ooh!" Abner said as he raced down the hall. "These might be a little, er, off." He spit a greenish glob of slobbery lizard flesh onto the wall where it stuck with a wet splat.

Jackson dropped his lizard. As they plunged down the stairs, the storm of questions in his head swirled around a new target: his dad.

CHAPTER 53: AN OLD MAN AND HIS BIKE

"Sir," Bronson said in his deep bass from the back seat of the SUV, "we have — ah!" There was a rustling and slapping sound.

"I saw it first," Orion said in a whisper, clearly audible to Avar in the front passenger seat. "Where do you get off trying to—ah! Sorry, sir."

Avar had reached back and yanked the tracing display from the two fools in the back seat. He couldn't get rid of them, else Tazia would ask him what happened, and then he'd have to explain to her why he'd misjudged the two men he'd picked for his top lieutenants. They had their strong points; he just couldn't remember any at the moment.

"There!" Avar said to his driver, pointing at an alley ahead to the right. The tracing display said the stolen motorcycle was somewhere in that vicinity within about thirty meters of their car.

A pudgy old vagrant charged from their left across the street toward the alley. The driver slammed the brakes sending the tracing display flying out of Avar's hands, bouncing into the dash. The crazy geezer kept running, oblivious to the fact that he almost got creamed.

"Why didn't you just mow that idiot down?" Orion asked from the back seat.

"Reflex," the driver said.

"Would have messed up the chrome fender," Bronson said.

"Everyone out!" Avar yelled. "Get that man!"

They piled out of the vehicle. Though older and slower, the old guy had a head start on them. Avar had planned to split the team, with some covering the bike and the others detaining the old man, but the guy was making a beeline for the same alley in which the bike was apparently hidden. They charged after him. While running, the old man waved his arms over his head and yelled. They were almost on top of him as he turned the corner into the alley.

"Mine!" he yelled. "Mine! I see it! I saw it! I get it! Mine, mine, mine!" Avar swung his cane at the man's knee, but the man dove out of reach at that exact instant, landing on a pile of old cardboard boxes and filth, setting off a volcano-like eruption of warm rotting trash stench. Something metallic clanked under the boxes as the entire pile shifted and the man tumbled.

The bike lay under the boxes, and the man wrapped himself around it like he was a baby koala on his furry momma. His voice was muffled by the fuel tank against his mouth. "Mine! I see it, I saw it, I get it."

Avar held his hand up to stop his team. "Old man," he said. "Get off my bike."

"My bike! I see it —"

"Shut up!" Orion yelled.

Avar swung his cane so that the cobra handle stopped an inch from Orion's face.

"Sorry sir," Orion said.

"Busted," Bronson said, slapping Orion on the arm.

Avar turned his stare to Bronson, and the big man's smile vanished.

"Sir, please stand," Avar said.

The man kept mumbling.

"Sir," Avar continued. "If you don't stand, I'll have to physically remove you."

After a few seconds, Avar gestured to Bronson who took a knee beside the man and spoke. "Sir? I'm going to pick you up now, okay? Please don't try to poke me or soil your pants while I'm holding you, or I may have to separate the top half of your spine from the bottom half, and that is not pleasant, especially for you." He paused a moment as though waiting for an acknowledgement from the man and, not getting one, leaned over and clamped his arms around him like a Venus flytrap on a tiny, mentally unstable fly. He straightened up and the man came with him, his legs flailing and his eyes wide.

Orion peered at the man's face. "That's not the dude from the motorcycle."

"Thank you, Professor," Avar said.

Bronson struggled to keep the squirming man still. "Little guy's got spunk! I may have to squeeze a little out of him." Bronson's body tightened, and the old man's eyes widened even more. They seemed close to being expelled from his reddening face.

"Don't break him," Avar said. "Yet."

"My bike," the man squeaked out. His eyes started to glaze over.

"Orion, load this up and have it processed like we discussed," Avar said, gesturing to the bike. "Don't touch the handlebars, and leave your gloves on." He walked around Bronson and the man so that if they faced him, Bronson's mass would shield the man from seeing the bike as it was loaded up. "Turn toward me and set him down," Avar directed Bronson. "I don't think he's going anywhere."

The man dropped to the ground, his legs crossed in a position that no longer had a proper name due to concerns for cultural sensitivities. Stray stragglers of hair fell across his haggard confused face. "I won it," the man said to floating ghosts from his memories. "I called, 'Bingo' and I chose curtain number two and the nice redhead with the big jugs showed me my new bike and I got two tacos for five dollars but that gave me diarrhea. Out of paper, no paper, my bike. That's my bike. Where's Johnny?"

"Sir," Avar interrupted, convinced that the ramblings were, in fact, rambling. He sat on his haunches in front of the man. "Who told you about this bike?"

The man looked at Avar like he'd just noticed him there. Behind Bronson, Orion slicked his black hair back and supervised the loading of the bike by one of the junior soldiers. God forbid he should get his black suit dirty. At least the cape was gone. As for Bronson, he stood towering over the old man, probably analyzing the man's fashion sensibilities.

"What bike?"

At least he understood the question. "The bike that you dove on. My bike. It was stolen by an elderly gentleman and a younger man. Did you see them?"

The man frowned, concentrating. This was a good sign. Looking up at Avar, the man nodded. "Definitely."

"Where? Where did they go?"

The man's expression shifted to concern. "Who?"

Bronson slid his blacksmith sledgehammer out of a holster on his hip, its rectangular head almost as large as the man's. Avar had never understood how the guy didn't have back problems, much less keep his pants up. Bronson put the sledge on his shoulder, ready to drive the man into the ground like a railroad spike. Avar gestured to stay his hand.

"Did you see who drove the motorcycle?" Avar asked.

"No?" The man was now paying close attention to Avar's face, obviously trying to read it to know what to say. He probably did that as a sort of survival technique to cover his memory loss or growing dementia, though that technique was failing as bad as a twenty-year-old facelift.

Avar stood and jerked his head at Bronson to say, "Let's go."

"I took a dump yesterday," the man said from the ground, "that was so big that some Injuns floated it in the river and put a casino on it."

Bronson snorted but stifled it.

Though ridiculous, Avar reached into his coat pocket and produced a business card. It read simply "Vlad's Generic Impalation Services" with a phone number on it. He wrote the word "bikers" on it with a black pen from the same pocket, then handed it to the man. "Please call this number if you see the men who were on the bike. See? It says, 'bikers' on it to remind you why you have that card."

Moments later in the car, Avar looked back at the old man, still sitting in the center of the trash-strewn alley. He was cleaning his ear with a tiny tube that looked suspiciously like a rolled-up business card.

He decided to leave a few details out of his report to Tazia. In fact, she didn't have to know about the chase at all. "We have a lead on the boy," was all he had to say, and that was true. Fingerprints of Krol's accomplice from a motorcycle weren't much, but they were something.

CHAPTER 54: FAMILY HISTORY

"That is the supply store?" Jackson asked. He and Abner stood on the sidewalk across the street from a block of interconnected brick buildings that seemed over a century old. A few could have passed for quaint shops selling overpriced antiques around the courthouse square of a small Texas town, but not the supply store — that building was so gutted that it was nearly just an alley, with most of the roof and front glass missing. Inside, a man stood behind a waist-high counter, with eight or ten cardboard boxes behind him. He seemed not to realize that his shop appeared to have been hit by a tornado.

"Well, it's not a typical supply store. It specializes in, uh, somewhat special specialties, so it has to stay mobile. In fact ..." Abner patted his pockets. "Oh, I have no money. Do you have money or stuff to trade?"

"You mean besides my lucky gold brick?"

Abner eyed him. "You are your father's son."

Jackson had never heard anyone say that, and he'd never laid the pattern of his father on himself to see if it fit. He became concerned that parts in fact did.

"Are you sure this is the right place? I wonder what's taking him so long."

"Boots can take care of himself."

"Why do you call him Boots?"

Abner twirled a strip of beard with his forefinger, thinking. "'Cause he used to have these snake boots that he wore. He used to say it was made out of cobras because the Piri like the cobras so much. But I think they were rattlesnake."

Jackson realized that he'd seen snake boots several years ago in the back of his dad's closet. He'd asked him why he never wore them, and his dad had replied something along the lines of, "Because I don't want to wear them." He remembered that conversation because he didn't understand why his dad had seemed so sad. He hadn't worried for long, though, because right after that, he asked if he could wear them himself, and his dad had replied with something sweet and fatherly like, "If you so much as touch them, I'll hit you so hard that your toenails will grow in black for a month." He hadn't understood that one either.

"What happened with my dad? What happened with you? Why aren't you two with Talbot?"

Abner sat on an overturned gray bucket. Jackson dragged over an apple crate and sat beside him. The crate creaked its displeasure at the whole situation.

"Your dad would never tell me why he left, but he just checked out.

Said he didn't want anything to do with the Hive any more. He just disconnected and dropped out. Some of the other guys wanted to go after him to see what happened. You see, the only way you can typically drop out of the Hive permanently is to die, and that's pretty permanent."

"You mean they kill you if you leave?"

Abner waved his hand in a dismissive gesture. "No! Well some guys felt that way. But Grotto was running the show then, and he was a good guy. Crazy, but good. No, the Jone-Zen are all part of the Hive, like a brain channel that connects all of us. Even if you try, you can't disconnect, and you can't block it out all the time."

Should he believe this? "You told me a little about the Hive. Can you like read each other's mind?"

"No, well not really. If they really want you to see something, they can open up to the Hive, and you might get most of it. Just the pictures and feelings, but not like actual words. And everyone will get it. And you can't help but get pieces of everyone else too. It's hard to keep a secret for long. Unless you're a super Bender like your dad."

"Wait, what?"

An attractive and surprisingly clean woman carrying a rifle sauntered in the middle of the street toward them. She was dressed in black jeans and a camouflage jacket, with yellow-tinted shooting sunglasses. Jackson looked from her to Abner to see if he would be concerned. Abner followed his look and saw the woman.

"Now that is nice!" he said. "So beautiful. Looks like a lever-action Winchester. I'm guessing 357 Mag. Walnut stock. Well it looks like walnut. I've never actually seen a walnut tree. Have you?"

"No, I mean, no. What about the woman? Should we be worried?"

"Nah. I mean that's a big ole gun for such a little lady, but she looks like she can handle it."

The woman gave them a sideways glance as she passed and slid the rifle into a scabbard on her back.

The place just got weirder and weirder. "Okay, so what about my dad?" Jackson said. "You said he was a 'Bender.' You talked about that and some other types, but never said what they were."

"Oh," Abner said, still watching the girl, or rather the rifle. "Yeah, the Jone-Zen all have different strengths, but most of the time they fall into major categories. The story is that there were seven brothers, and – well, you probably don't care about the history, and I can't remember it. Anyway, most of the Jone-Zen can fight — I mean, even the weak untrained ones are still better than any human — but the strongest, and usually dumbest, are called 'Bangers.' Thinkers used to be the smart ones, but these days they call anyone who can't do anything else a Thinker because they said it wasn't right that everyone didn't get to be special, so now no one really knows if a Thinker is one of the smart ones or one of the 'not smart but still talented in some deeply hidden way' ones. I think we should come up with a name that means, 'You're special but you can't really do anything special but we still think you're alright' rather than give them a real name that's already taken by real people who are actually good at something.

"Wait, where was I? Oh yeah. Seers can't do much but are good to have around because they're good at spotting imposters and can sometimes tell if people are lying. That part might be a trick, like a fortuneteller. Not like a palm reader though because that's real." He looked at Jackson.

"Okay?"

Abner stomped his foot and slapped his thigh. "Not really, son! You can't believe everything you hear! Palm readers are crooks. Anyway, Poppers can do things with physics, but there aren't many good ones. Most of them don't even pop because they might hurt themselves, like popping the oxygen out of a room or catching themselves on fire or I even saw a guy once generate his own gravity flip. He shot eighty feet into the air before it reversed back the right way. That one hurt!"

"What about the Benders like my dad?" Jackson feared something would interrupt them again, and he'd never hear the story.

"Now, the best Poppers," Abner continued, apparently deaf to Jackson's question, "are also called Blockers. They can deflect projectiles. So each side normally has at least one Blocker that tries to maintain a safe zone from shots. I mean bullets don't normally kill either side but they hurt like hell and can knock you completely out of the action toot sweet. So each side has someone guarding the Blocker, and someone else constantly firing to keep the other guys' Blocker tied up. I told you the Piri have the same types, didn't I?"

Jackson shook his head no, though he wasn't sure if Abner had told him this. A lot of stuff in his head had been jettisoned to make room for this overly heavy cargo that kept growing in size and weight.

"Well, they do. Same deal. What else? Is that it?"

"Benders?" Jackson offered.

"Oh yeah, Benders. You know your dad's a Bender? Best damn Bender anyone's ever seen. In fact, that's how he dropped out. Everyone thought he was dead. He just bent himself right out of the Hive."

"But what is a Bender? What do they do?"

"I don't really get Benders. They're not many of them out there, just like there aren't many true Poppers out there. Did I tell you that's what I was? I haven't done it in a while. Ever since I popped my dog's tail onto his forehead—"

"Benders?"

"Oh, right, Benders. They can... well, first, you know that the Piri and the Jone-Zen aren't all that different, right? Neither are humans. Something about the DNA. I used to understand it a lot better. I think I still have some of my papers back at my apartment. Or maybe it was something in the DNA's DNA, or something like that. But we're all completely the same until you get really small. Well, Benders can somehow shift that." While talking, Abner leaned over and picked up a matchbook-sized ebony fibrous mass from the street, smelled it, frowned, and then flicked it away. "Most of the time, they can't control it, like they might try to bend a Jone-Zen to have more strength but instead they mutate that guy so that he broadcasts to the Hive but can't receive from it. Stuff like that. In a way, they're kind of like the Poppers 'cause most of them can't control it enough to be useful. Luckily most everyone has at least one other strength that they can fall back on even if they're not very good at either of them. So a Bender might have some 'banging' skills too."

"That sounds dirty."

"But not your dad. I mean the 'not control it' part. He bent himself out of the Hive. Oh, I told you that. And he did it for me too. I wanted out. I thought I might start my practice back up, but I'd been treating the Jone-Zen for so long that I didn't have any normal patients. I tried to open a clinic in the Tovac Zone, but I learned you just can't do that here." Abner stroked his beard, gazing at the morning sky. "It's too dangerous. Dope fiends stagger in looking for drugs, no money comes in to support it, and the SecForce fellas try to extort money that doesn't exist. So I just made house calls."

After a few silent seconds looking at the clouds, Abner turned to Jackson and leaned closer. "One problem with leaving was some of the Jone-Zen weren't too happy when a person left, and people who did leave were known to occasionally 'drop off' the Hive without warning. Your dad made sure that I dropped off, but not because I was dead." Abner checked his pulse in his neck. "So when we both went radio silent, everyone thought we were dead. But your dad never believed that they stopped looking for him, and he just kept running. That's why you moved so much as a kid. I finally convinced him to settle down near me, and that's when I found out he had a kid at all. I think *you* had more to do with him settling here than me."

"Why me?"

"He didn't want to keep moving you, forcing you to make new friends at every new school. And if you were anything like him, it would take you a little extra time to make even a single friend."

"Who was my mother?"

"A bitch!" said a voice from behind them in the alley. Jackson's dad Victor emerged from the shadows against one wall. "Boy, you two Coullions sure know how to set up a solid security perimeter. Come on.

I'm parked this way."

"What happened?" Jackson said, running to catch up as his dad walked away down the alley. Abner followed.

"I bugged the bike. Now we can trace their ass right to their headquarters. Stupid Piri."

"Who was my mom, really? Not the fake mom who you said died when I was born; I mean the one who somehow never showed up in any pictures."

They looked at one another. Jackson noticed that his dad had picked up quite a bit of filth since he'd been hangin' in the "Zone." Literally came with the territory. He also seemed ten years younger. Even more shocking, he was almost smiling.

"I always wanted to tell you your story, but I figured it would be easier if you never emerged, because then you could just leave it all behind." He pointed up ahead. "I'll tell you the rest in the car."

Jackson planned to slide into the back seat of his dad's red '72 Monte Carlo, but Abner grabbed his shoulder and pulled him back.

"I need to grab me a quick nap," Abner said as he climbed into the back. "You sit up front with your old man."

"Tell me where to turn," Victor said after everyone was settled in the car, handing Jackson the base unit for the tracking device. It appeared to be integrated with GPS, and he realized that they were represented as a red dot in the center of the device, with the motorcycle represented as a blue dot. The blue dot was near the edge of the screen and flickering.

Victor yanked the steering wheel gear shifter and punched the gas, sending the car lunging forward, throwing gravel in its wake.

"Take a right up here," Jackson said, "and step on it. It looks like they're almost out of range."

"That unit sucks. It's got a range like your throwing arm."

The car accelerated around the corner, the engine's purr growing to a deep growl as Victor pushed it forward.

"Your mom," Victor said. He paused for several seconds. "Your mom was a Piri, a Vampire."

"What!?" Abner spat out from the back seat. "That's impossible!" Then, after receiving a look from Victor, he leaned back in his seat. "Sorry, carry on."

"They're straight ahead," Jackson said, looking at the tracker device, his mind racing like the blades of a blender. "Keep going on this street. They're about... a Vampire?... three blocks up... I mean, really? Did you say Vampire?"

"Abner's right, almost. You weren't supposed to live. Offspring like you never live. Anastazia wanted to get rid of you, but I convinced her that I could bend you in the womb to be a true Vampire, a pure Piri. But I couldn't do it. Not because I was against it; I would have done anything for her, and her for me, at least I thought she would." His words came faster as though he was afraid to lose momentum and stop. Jackson prayed that the blue dot would continue going straight so he wouldn't have to interrupt him.

"We were young and stupid — kind of like you — and the fact that we were supposed to be enemies made it more exciting. Like Romeo and Juliet with knives and clubs. But she worried about what would happen if the others found out about the child she was carrying. It was easier for me to hide our relationship. So I tried to bend you, but it was like twisting an iron pipe, a thick one. It was as though your DNA was set in stone and nothing was going to change it. I couldn't do it. I tried, and maybe I did enough to help you survive – not that I've ever gotten any appreciation for it," he added, with a significant look at his son.

"Offspring always died?"

"Between the races, yeah. And that was only those that took. Most didn't even take.   And between the races and humans, most of the time. But those normally were human. I had no idea what would happen to you. I was shocked that you got conceived in the first place. Then I was even more shocked you didn't die in the womb. But I told her I was able to bend you; I told her you were a Vampire. I lied to her. I think she... she was going to kill you."

They drove in silence for almost a minute. Jackson could see his dad trembling out of the corner of his eye, and Jackson couldn't bring himself to look directly at him. He'd never ask him if he was okay — better to jam a knife into a bleeding man. "Take a left at the next block," he said, his voice barely audible.

"She almost left me, but I told her that I might need to finish bending you after you were born, like I was some dumbass chiropractor giving 'adjustments.' She didn't fully understand how Benders worked, and I wasn't about to tell her."

Jackson couldn't believe what he was hearing. Not just the story, but who was telling it. This was not the person he knew.

"She could tell. I don't know how, but she could. As soon as you were born, she knew that you weren't a Piri. You were an alien to her. She couldn't even look at you. I –" His voice caught.

Jackson looked out of the window, completely at a loss. After a few seconds, he turned and looked at his dad, then put a hand on his right shoulder. Victor reached across his body with his left hand and touched it, giving it a light squeeze. Then he threw it off him.

"Hey!" Victor said. "Stop touching me, you little Nancy." But his face was still caught in a distant sadness. "I never saw her again. That's when I left. I wanted out of all of that stupid mess. I was tired of it. I took my son and we left, together."

Because of Jackson, his dad had lost not only his true love but also his entire tribe. That explained a lot.

"She does sound like a real bitch," Jackson said.

His dad snorted and cut a quick look at him. "That's my boy."

They drove in silence for another minute.

"So tell me about this girl you're making me risk my life for," Victor said.

"She's... she's something, Dad."

"That's really not saying much. I hope she likes you too."

Jackson considered this. "I'm not so sure about that."

His dad grunted, though it was with a smile, or at least what passed for a smile on the crotchety old man's face. "Again, that's my boy. Don't learn from your old man."

Jackson wanted to hug him, but not quite as much as he wanted to avoid getting punched.

The blue dot turned and stopped. "Right there, Dad. At the corner past the fire hydrant on its side, they took a right then stopped."

Just before they passed the same corner, Victor said, "Okay, you two lie down so they can't see you."

"Huh?" Abner said, popping his head up from his nap. "Hey, I think I just saw them! They were right there! By that church!"

Still crouched, Jackson peered around the side of his seat and saw Abner frantically pointing back at the street they just passed.

Victor just shook his head. "Abs, you are the stupidest smart guy I've ever known."

"Thanks, Boots. You're the meanest mean guy I've ever known."

"I think you got that one mixed up."

"I don't think I did."

"Okay, you two lovebirds," Jackson said. "How are we going to get Sy?"

Victor turned a corner. "We're going to watch them. And we're all marked since they've seen us. So we have to be careful."

Jackson tried not to dwell on Sy, wondering what could be happening to her, if she was alone, if she was scared. It hurt to wait, but these old-timers apparently knew this game.

"What can I do?" he asked. "I mean, that crash should have torn me up, but it didn't. So I can make that shell thing, but I don't know how I did it."

Victor looked at him. "I don't know. Your body knows it better than you do, lucky for you. When the time comes, you'll just react. You just need to go with it and follow along. For me, someone tried to stab me, and I knew, just *knew*, that it wouldn't hurt. So instead of dodging it, I just swung my fist at the guy's face. The knife got there first, but it just bounced off like he was poking me with a sponge. As for him, he had nostrils sticking out of each ear. And that was before I knew I had even emerged. I was just ready to come out, I guess. And you're on the edge, with possibly more to come." He eyed him again. "You may have a little of that bitch in you too. They have thin skin, but they heal fast and they move even faster."

Jackson thought of all he'd read about the Vampires on the website. He felt an odd vertigo as his perspective shifted from the human defender to the Vampire attacker. He'd been looking at all that backwards.

"Can you hear them?" Abner asked from the backseat.

"Hear who?" Jackson replied.

"The Hive. You know, I think I told you about that. That was you, right? They have a hive too."

Jackson thought back to the voices he heard mumbling before one of the missions. "I think I can hear the Goblins, er Jone-Zen sometimes. But I haven't seen images. And I've never seen any Piri Vampire visions."

"That's how it starts," Abner said. "The voices. You hear mumbling and then all of a sudden, the images pop into your head. If you concentrate, you might be able to plug in. Boots and I haven't been able to do that for many years, but you might be able to. And you might be able to jack into the Piri hive too. Dang, I never thought of this. Half-breeds have always died. I mean, I always thought that was part of the reason – they were torn apart by their conflicting natures, half of them pulled toward the Jone-Zen and the other half Piri. Yen and yang, but instead of circling, they just kicked each other's asses. If you get closer to a big group, it helps, especially at first. Once you're in, you can plug in from almost anywhere, though it's always stronger when you're close."

"That's it," Victor said. "While we watch, we can try to teach Jackson to plug into the Piri hive. You might be able to see where your girl is. We just need to find a good place to set up camp." He inclined his head to point, and when Jackson looked in that direction, he realized that they'd circled the block and now passed the other side of the parked Vampire convoy.

"I've got an idea," Jackson said. It was a good idea, but he didn't like it in the slightest.

CHAPTER 55: SAGE OF THE RIVER

Sy opened her eyes.

Below the featureless white sky, the overhanging cypress branches surged out and in, like expanding and contracting lungs. The gurgling of the river was the only sound. She raised her head from the inner tube.

"Good to see you again, Sylvia," a voice said at her ear. Only Mr. Sam had ever called her that. Mr. Sam, looking exactly as he had twenty years before, floated in an inner tube alongside her on her right. Like precious stones wedged in a clogged sink drain, his gray-blue eyes twinkled within the brown fur that covered ninety percent of his head and face.

"Whoa, you going to a funeral?" said a second voice. Sy turned to see Cari floating on her left, smiling. She, too, had not aged. "I guess black is in these days."

"Where have you been?" Sy asked, turning her head back and forth. "How did you—?"

"What is your real question?" Mr. Sam interrupted.

"Tell us why you're really here," Cari added.

Jackson sat on the plain white floor of the padded cell of her mind, alone.

"What do I do?" Sy asked. "It's too late to save him."

"It's never too late," Cari said. "Unless of course he's dead. Then I guess that would be –"

"Cari!" Mr. Sam yelled. "You started okay, then what the heck? You don't go talking about the man up and dying. I mean, that's spiritual guidance 101."

"Sorry, Dad. And sorry, Sy. What I meant to say was, 'It's never too late.'"

"Right," Mr. Sam said. "Follow your heart."

Sy looked from him back to Cari, who merely nodded. "That's it?" Sy asked. "'Follow my heart'? I mean, come on. I took a bus down here to find you two, and this is all I get? Do you know how those things stink? And I had to sit across from a guy who wiped his boogers on the seat."

Cari shrugged her shoulders.

"All we have is the truth," Mr. Sam said. "The answer is within."

"Within what?" Sy yelled. "A fortune cookie? A magic nine ball?"

"This is the wisdom of the river," he said. "It does not speak in the King's English. I merely pass its words to you. It's up to you to mold the river's words to your life. It speaks the truth. You just have to accept it, and it will be manifest."

She looked back at Cari, incredulous.

"Yeah, he still talks like that," Cari said. "Have you already forgotten?

Think how I feel. 'Dad, can I have a candy bar?' 'Bars of candy will be as birds in the tree.' 'Is that a yes?' That's all you're going to get. Oh, and you look really cute too. I miss you!"

"Follow your heart," Mr. Sam said. Sy turned, and he was gone. She turned back around and found Cari missing too. She was alone on the river.

Off to her right, she saw a haphazardly placed pile of brush on one bank.

"Impossible." She climbed out of the tube into the waist high water and waded to shore. It was her pack and shoes, exactly as she'd left them. Upriver. Or rather, right here, right where she was.

The tube continued down the river.

Sy packed up and headed back to civilization and the bus stop. And to Jackson.

CHAPTER 56: SOLO MISSION

"Well yeah," Abner said in answer to Jackson's question, "there are tunnels down under the streets for sewage or drainage or something, but that's just creepy. I'm not going down there. That's where the crazies live."

"Really? Have you seen them?" Jackson asked.

"Nah, but I know a guy whose brother's friend dropped a sandwich by the gutter, and a clown reached out and dragged him down there and probably ate him except for his clothes, since those are hard to digest."

Victor thumped Abner in the forehead. "Stop scaring my boy." Then, to Jackson, he said, "There ain't nothing down there but rats, but it *is* pretty dang creepy. I've got some flashlights with my stash in my trunk. We'll check it out."

"No way," Jackson said. "You two have to watch the front. I don't know why, but I think I have to do this myself. I just... I just do."

Abner and Victor looked at each other skeptically.

"What if you get yourself in trouble?" Victor asked. It wouldn't be the first time that had happened to his son.

"I'll cross that bridge and kick some Vampire ass right off it," he said, though he wasn't exactly sure how he would do that. "I've got skills, right?"

"You're untrained and completely without discipline," Victor said. "I say go for it."

CHAPTER 57: DOWN UNDER

An alley ran behind the shops across the street from the church complex where the Vampire convoy had stopped. Victor parked his car in an old parking garage off of the alley behind an abandoned brewpub. The rusting metal back door of the pub yielded to Victor's kick, thudding into an interior wall in a cloud of wood shrapnel from the destroyed doorframe. The decaying interior appeared looted of most everything of value. Even large sections of the eight-foot tall copper brew kettle had been cut away, leaving a skeletal copper shell. Someone had apparently tried to hack the wooden bar apart and cart it off but had failed. Fifteen of its thirty-foot length leaned downward at an angle, its supports chopped away.

"Perfect," Victor said, looking out the filthy front windows.

"You're right about that," Abner said, his back to Victor. He ran his hand along the bar, clearing a small path through the layer of dust. "We just need to figure out how to get this out of here. Do you think this will fit in your car?"

"I don't think he was talking about the bar," Jackson said, pointing toward the front windows. The pub lay directly across the street from the church, providing an ideal vantage point.

"Oh, yeah, that too," Abner said. He continued to caress the smooth wood of the bar.

"How do I get underground?" Jackson asked.

Abner snapped out of his love fest with the bar. "Oh, I saw a grating back there." He licked one of his dusty fingers and made a contemplative expression, apparently considering the freshness of the dirt, and then turned toward the back of the pub.

Victor and Jackson followed him to a square metal grate in the alley about six feet by four feet only a few steps from the back door. Warm moist air surged from it, like the steamy belch of a great beast. Jackson stared at the great maw and hesitated, imaging Sy sinking into its murky depths.

He yanked up the massive grate and threw it aside. The reverberating clang of the sturdy metal grate crashing against the opposite wall of the alley fifteen feet away startled him, and he looked up in time to see a spray of brick fragments and dust flying skyward. Abner and Victor exchanged glances.

"Remember, come back up by nightfall even if you haven't discovered anything yet," Victor said. "We'll maintain watch here." He handed him a flashlight. "Good luck, Son. You might not need it."

"The luck, or the light?"

"Both."

A damp ladder descended into the darkness beneath the streets. Jackson shone his flashlight downward, but the inky blackness swallowed it.

"Time to rock and roll," he said. He put the flashlight in his teeth and climbed down. Drops of water flashed as they fell through the beam of light before descending into the darkness, making tiny "doink!" sounds below.

He splashed down into a horizontal pipe with a diameter of about eight or ten feet, with water running through the bottom few inches. After pulling a piece of chalk from his pocket, he marked the wall behind the ladder. This was not a good place to get lost. Above his head, he heard a metallic clank, and he instinctively jumped to the side to avoid getting cracked in the noggin. Abner had dropped the grate back across the opening, like the sealing of a tomb.

CHAPTER 58: HISTORY REPEATS

Jackson mentally kicked himself for not planning better before descending into the bowels of the Tovac underworld. The situation reminded him of the time he tried to fix a missing roofing shingle on the house. He had climbed a ladder, made that horrifying step onto the evil slanted roof, hovering at the balance point between stability and free-fall-to-agony, and then slid and crawled on the roof as though under razor wire all the way to the bare spot, trembling the entire way. He looked at the hammer in his hand and then back down to the roof. That's all he had brought – a hammer.

Now, he analyzed the ceiling of the horizontal pipe in which he stood. He hadn't figured out how many paces it might take to get across the street, nor how many paces to the left or right to be positioned under the church. On top of that, how was he supposed to "jack in" to the Vampire hive? He didn't even know where his mental ears were.

He flicked the flashlight off and waited, listening and watching. He heard the sounds of water, dripping and flowing. He heard his breath. He heard a distant roar – probably a car passing over one of the grates. Soon, as he had hoped, a dim glow of light appeared from around a corner up ahead. The light was enough that he could see reasonably well, though he kept the flashlight in hand since it had a solid feel to it and would likely make a good first impression on an attacker's skull.

He turned the corner and walked into a circle of light. The light spilled down from a storm drain opening, high over his head. He didn't want to look at it lest his dark-adjusted eyes become blinded, but he had to. There was no ladder. All he saw was sky. He moved from side to side, hoping to catch sight of the top corner of a building or a car or anything recognizable. Nothing.

There was another circle of light further along this pipe, and he repeated the move, arriving at the same result. Another glow came from around a corner, and he followed it. This time, if he leaned all the way against one wall and jumped, he could see the top corner of a building. He didn't know what building it was, but at least it was something. He tried other angles but saw nothing.

Another glow drifted in from a side pipe, and he ran to it. This one actually gave him a clear view of a car tire. So he was next to a street, but where? And which one? He tried to remember which way he had come from. His chalk lay dozing in his pocket, riding the bench as it had for most of his time down here.

His dad would be so proud of him. He was already lost.

CHAPTER 59: BACKDOOR

Sy had been around the Tovac Zone enough to know where the soft spots were. One of them was only a block from the bus station.

Though the checkpoints were well staffed and fenced, the border was more porous away from these. Electronic surveillance along with disproportionate security responses to incursions (and escapes) kept the populace on either side of the border from straying across. However, a few of the buildings straddled the border, and a small percentage of these were unmonitored, at least by Tovac gatekeepers.

She stepped into the front door of the Hotel Golden Spittoon. A scrubbed young man in a bellhop uniform greeted her. He had a mix of African and Asian features and smelled like musk. "Can I help you?"

"I need a room in the very back," she said.

"Ah, like in the back or like *way* in the back?"

"Like way in the back. All the way."

"You mean, like –"

"I need to get into the Tovac Zone."

His eyebrows shot up and tried to hide under the rim of his cap. He glanced at an empty reception counter on top of which stood a sign saying "Be back soon. Pinching a loaf."

"Well," he said, smiling, "that's going to cost."

"I've got money. I know the score."

His smile shifted into something ugly. "It's not money." His gaze rolled to her feet then back to her face, pausing along the way. "I mean, money's not *all* of it. There are certain other –"

He finished that sentence by thudding his head into the floor, following a solid left hook by Sy. She strategically stepped on a rather sensitive part of his prone unconscious body as she passed. He'd feel that last part more than the shot to the head. At the rear of the hotel, she turned left and passed through a door marked, "Employee Only." Along the back right wall was another door beneath a cracked and skewed "exit" sign. She pushed the door open and stepped into the Tovac Zone once again.

CHAPTER 60: GETTIN' ANTSY

"We need to move," Talbot said, stepping into Simpson's small office, furnished with a single chair, a single desk, and air. "How much longer we got until the full team is here?" Time was running out. Striking first was imperative. Though he had a theory, he wasn't totally sure what those Piri bastards were up to, but if he hit them hard and early, he might disrupt their plans — blitz 'em before they could light the fuse.

"We can put together a partial strike team today," Simpson said. "But that is not what you want, is it?"

"We need Brutus. Once he's here, let's roll."

Brutus was the most famous Jone-Zen Banger alive. He fought with twin poleaxes, wielding them with the dexterity of a Chinese villager using chopsticks. One of his forearms was tattooed "kick" and the other was tattooed with "ass," allowing for them to be read in either direction. Or at least that's what Talbot was told they said – he didn't read Italian.

Talbot just hoped the team could be ready soon. He'd been reading, and God help them if the Piri legend was true — if Saldar the Salivator, the great drooling Piri Warlord, could be brought back to life, the Jone-Zen (as well as every non-Piri out there) were screwed.

CHAPTER 61: MEETING NEW FRIENDS

Jackson stopped trying to keep his feet dry and just sloshed through the water running down the center of the pipe. It was probably water. He'd turned back and retraced his steps, but he only succeeded in getting more lost, assuming "more lost" was actually worse than just regular lost.

He arrived at a section of the pipe that opened up into a rectangular vertical shaft like that of a large elevator. The walls were brick here, and a ladder led up to a grate. He climbed up to get his bearings.

He could see more of the sky through the open grate the higher he climbed. Unfortunately, the sky was no help because the clouds blocked the location of the sun. Seeing them made him glad that he was underground; the clouds surged across the sky, like living creatures (as opposed to dead creatures, which of course did minimal surging). And those beasts were hyped up, irritated, pulsing from white to gray to white again. Occasionally one would lose its temper, expelling a spidery mass of copper arcs, which slithered across its face before fading.

A storm was brewing.

He pushed the grate up with his right hand and peered around. A noise roared behind him, and he ducked his head and released the grate to clank down, almost propelling him off the ladder and down twenty feet to the floor of the tunnel. A car narrowly missed him. His flashlight tumbled downward, smashing into the concrete, and then bounced and rolled to a stop, throwing a stripe of light across the brown grime at the bottom of the tunnel.

His heart slid out of the red zone back to yellow, and he poked his head up once again. He recognized nothing. Maybe if he just climbed out and –

"Hey, you!" a man yelled off to his left. "What are you doing down there?"

Jackson didn't even turn to see who it was. He scrambled down the ladder as voices grew louder above his head. Splashing down at the bottom, he reached for the flashlight, but as soon as he picked it up, the front half toppled forward, dangling by a wire. He threw it back down.

"I see him!" a voice shouted above. The grate screeched as it was slid aside.

Jackson kicked the ladder to knock it away from the wall. In return, it clanked loudly, inflicted a nasty bruise on his shin, and stayed right the hell where it was.

"Come here, man!" a different voice yelled. A heavy skull-crushing something shattered on the ground next to Jackson.

He ran into the darkness.

CHAPTER 62: PLAYDATE

Avar smiled as he reviewed the results from the test of the motorcycle fingerprints lifted by the Piri analysis lab in a converted priest's residence at the rear of the church complex. "So he's an old-timer Goblin, eh?"

"Yes, he's a Jone-Zen," the lab tech said.

The tech Thinker was likely one of the old fogeys who still held onto the misguided notion of mutual respect between the traditional enemies.

Avar looked back down at the printout. The old Goblin's name was Abner. "What's his last name?"

"That's all we have on him. Our records show him as deceased for over twenty years."

"He moved pretty good for a dead guy." He took the paper with him out of the small lab into his even smaller office. Why they had to stage the assault on the Goblins from inside the Tovac Zone was beyond him. He'd wanted to stage it outside the Zone and then roll in strong, but Tazia feared Tovac interference. Better to get them accustomed to us inside, and then we strike, or so she thought. But those plans were on hold; he had to catch this Jackson Krol kid first. Tazia had a serious interest in him but wouldn't let on why.

On top of that, Fionn was back flashing his hair and teeth and abnormally toned body, probably getting special treatment from Tazia. And he *still* wouldn't tell Avar what his mission was. The one thing Avar did know — or at least hope — was that Tazia hadn't brought Fionn in for the final Goblin assault. That was supposed to be Avar's mission. Surely she wouldn't do that. Someone didn't get into her position without the ability to recognize a military genius, even if he didn't have flowing locks.

The printout had Abner's last known address, in the Tovac Zone. Not much of a lead, but something.

"Orion!" he yelled. "Grab Bronson and the team." He grinned at the tech. "We're going hunting for some old-timer Goblins."

CHAPTER 63: CHANGE OF VENUE

Something was off. If there was anything that Fionn knew, it was style. And fashion. And fighting of course. But this was a matter of style, and a *thrift store* – the words made his brain pucker – was no place for Tazia.

He had to change the venue.

"Okay, people," he called out to his personal team entrusted to assist him on this mission. "We need to box it back up."

Some disapproving moans and mutterings floated past his ears.

"Who's the leader of this mission?" he yelled. "Me. Whose ass is on the line if it fails? Yours. Not mine of course. But I'm not going to let that happen. I do this for *you*. We're going to get this show on the road to recovery."

A smooth-faced blond of twenty-one raised her hand. "Sir?" she asked.

That's more like it. "Yes, Jenton?"

"Uh, what are we doing?"

"We're taking it underground." He clapped twice. "We're changing the venue to the tunnels under the church at HQ. Let's move. We launch tomorrow."

CHAPTER 64: STAKEOUT

Sy found a good vantage point to watch the Seven's offices at the Jone-Zen factory complex headquarters. While searching for the spot, she had purchased a bicycle from a man who seemed initially inclined to rob her. However, he reconsidered this plan at the tip of her sword, selling her the bike at a fair price. She was a skilled "negotiator."

Now she stood at a window overlooking the facility. Something had drawn her to this observation site in an apartment, but the place somehow disturbed her at the same time. Beneath the odor of decay and trash, it smelled like Vampires, though that was likely her mind playing tricks on her. The dust tracks on the floor indicated that someone had been there recently, but from the smell, they'd been gone for at least a day or more. Just the same, something made her uneasy. But she had little choice – this was the best unoccupied location that gave an unobstructed view of the rear entrance to the facility. She had spent the first day on the street watching the main entrance, looking for Jackson's car. It never came. She planned to return there each morning to watch for it. If unsuccessful, she would return to this apartment to monitor the rear entrance, especially at night. Her bike was just inside the door. She would never be able to keep up with the cars on regular streets, but in Tovac back roads, she might have a chance.

She slid a well-cushioned albeit filthy chair to the window and set her binoculars on the window frame. She was going to be there a while; she might as well be comfortable.

CHAPTER 65: VISIONS OF DARKNESS

Jackson rushed through the inky underground tunnels, senses alert.

Don't charge into dead end. Stick to ledges. I don't have time for this!

Some of the tunnels had raised flat ledges along the side, allowing him to bypass sloshing through the slippery sludge that run underneath. Not as festive but somewhat less precarious and noisy.

Voices of the men who had followed him from the surface echoed behind him.

"Hey, come back here!" one shouted.

"We're not gonna hurt you!"

"Much," another added. Drunken laughter.

These did not sound like Vampires, but that was only a partial relief. Trouble was trouble.

A vision burst into his mind — a woman with dark hair and eyes, almost as dark as Sy's. But this woman was older. And meaner. Her lips moved as she glared at him.

The vision disappeared, popping like a soap bubble. The voices behind him were louder now, closer.

"Come here, you freakin' mutant!"

Jackson realized with a start that he had been running through the tunnels without his flashlight, and had no problem seeing where he was going. A voice in the back corner of his mind tried to offer a theory about this, but he pushed it away – it was just brighter in these parts, even though there were no obvious light sources.

Six feet up to his right a narrow drainage shaft intersected his tunnel, almost hidden in the gloom. Water trickled from it down the wall. He grabbed its slick edge and hoisted himself up, sliding his feet forward and turning so that his head pointed downward toward the main tunnel as he lay prone, like a face down corpse in a long wet coffin. The water soaked his crotch, moved up to his belly, and flowed past his chest, adding a pungent chemical odor to the mold and sewage stench that had been assaulting his nose. He slid forward so that he could peek over the lip of the shaft and watch the men as they passed below.

"I think he went this way," one man said, though still out of sight. A shaft of blinding light danced across the tunnel below. Jackson squinted his eyes.

"I heard all about the Mold Men," another voice said, "but this is the first I've seen 'em. I heard they're blind and their skin is pasty white."

"It's not 'Mold Men'," said the first. "It's 'Mole Men.' Like underground moles."

The light brightened as the men approached. While the two men in front did most of the talking, a massive brute followed in silence, holding a pipe or a bat on his shoulder.

"Wait," said the second man. "What does mold like? Water and darkness. That's what. What do we have down here? Water and darkness. Ego Mold Men."

"Ergo!" the third man snorted, waving his pipe like a baseball batter warming up.

A flashlight beam passed close to Jackson, and he pulled his head back from the edge to stay hidden.

"No, no, no," said the first man. "It's Mole Men because they're underground. Mold can be anywhere. You could have mold in your bathroom. So does that make you a Mold Man?"

They sounded like they were passing Jackson's position.

The second man replied, "Moles live in dirt. They don't live in man-made pipes of water and sewage –"

"Wait!" someone interrupted, likely the pipe-swinger.

Jackson's heart thudded. Had they seen his position?

Clank! Something exploded in Jackson's ears, and he almost cried out. His body remained frozen and tensed, his teeth clenched in anticipation.

"This is sewage?" Pipe Man continued.

Jackson relaxed. The man had just smashed the wall with his pipe.

"It's not supposed to be," said the second man, "but you know, sometimes when there are no facilities and you gotta go... And it all runs downhill."

"Let's get out of here!" said Pipe Man.

"Not until I find my Mole Man," said the first, his voice echoing away as the group continued down the tunnel away from him.

"Mold Man!" said the second.

Jackson held his position, waiting for the men's voices to fade. Would they retrace their steps to leave? He didn't want to get caught down here by three deranged pipe-wielding Tovackers. Well, only one had a pipe, but he was the size of three men smushed together, almost. Jackson felt a powerful yet inexplicable urge to say in position for a bit, despite the flow of water from crotch to chin and the olfactory onslaught. A faint voice in his head screamed at him, but it was far away... so far. His eyes drifted closed.

The woman from his vision returned, older, her hair streaked with gray. She fought, wielding two police tonfa clubs, the length of the clubs flush against her forearms as she held the perpendicular handles and struck out with the short ends. He felt like he knew her, but he couldn't remember.

She disappeared. A desiccated corpse floated through his mind. Hands loaded it into a wooden crate and then picked up hammers to pound the crate shut. Other crates were loaded with small flared tubes like bicycle horns. Somehow, he knew they fired something. But what?

More images lined up behind these, fighting and pushing their way to the front of his mind. Too many, too fast. He struggled to hold back the flood. The mental assault threatened to overwhelm him, and images leaked through – the dark-featured woman, an image of Talbot seen through binoculars, a motorcycle chase from the view of a trailing car. His resistance weakened, faltering. New visions, pressing forward, changing, flashing, pushing into him, tearing at his defenses. A crack — a split.

Darkness dropped.

CHAPTER 66: GNASHING

"We need to get my boy," Victor said, pacing behind the bar at the abandoned brewpub across from the Vampire's apparent base at the church.

Abner lay on his side by the front window, propped up on one elbow as he watched the street. He knew his friend wasn't the outwardly emotional type, but Abner always suspected he had a deep capacity for love, though it was buried even deeper beneath layers of abrasiveness, surliness, and a thick stratum of vulgarity.

Night had fallen, and Jackson hadn't returned. On the plus side, the Piri hadn't done more than drive a few vehicles in and out of the church complex. He would have expected more activity if Jackson had been captured, but that was just a guess. Another guess could be that they were quietly cooking him in a rotisserie oven. Guessing wasn't his strong suit.

"He's probably fine, Boots," Abner said.

"You don't know my boy. He's got no sense, no drive, no ambitions."

"He's got some drive and ambition now. He just dove headfirst into those dark freaky underground Tovac tunnels, and this is the worst free reign zone in the... well, probably the world. Even Tovacs don't like to go down there. Plus he already escaped from the Jone-Zen."

"That still leaves the boy with no sense."

Victor relocated his pacing to in front of the bar, and his voice was a bit loud for a stakeout, but Abner figured now was not the best time to point this out.

"Anastazia had something to do with all this," Victor said. "That bitch wants the boy for some reason. Maybe she found out he was emerging. But why would she care?"

Abner had no idea. He agreed with Victor in his assessment of Anastazia, or "Tazia" as some called her. She wasn't good enough for Boots. Plus she was a Piri, and nothing good ever came out of that bunch, except maybe for Victor's boy Jackson. But those Piri didn't get credit for that.

"What do you think?" Abner asked after several minutes of watching both the Piri headquarters and Victor, his head going back and forth like a tennis spectator during a really slow match.

"We wait. But not for much longer. If we don't hear anything by morning, we move in."

Abner didn't like the sound of that at all. He prayed that Jackson would return, and soon.

CHAPTER 67: MISSION FINALE

"Bronson, you've got point this time," Avar whispered. Avar, Bronson, Orion, and four other Piri agents – three Bangers and one Blocker – crouched outside the old Goblin Abner's last known address. "On three. One, two, three!" Avar kicked the door open, shredding the doorframe on both sides, sending the door sliding into the apartment like a surfboard with a doorknob. Bronson rushed in first, wielding his enormous sledgehammer. Avar and Orion charged in after him, followed by the other members. The Blocker stayed at the rear and generated a deflection field just in front of Bronson, visible as a faint shimmer, like the optical disturbance one sees when opening the door of a car baking in the Texas summer.

An old woman in a bathrobe stood in front of an ancient television set with foil-wrapped coat hanger antennas. She stared at them, motionless, holding a bottle of wine in one hand and a headless doll in the other.

Bronson and the entire team froze.

"Where's the old man?" Avar asked the woman.

"What old man?" she replied.

"Abn—"

"Are you here to violate my feminine wares?"

"Ew!" Bronson said.

"What? No!" Avar said. He felt his solid lead on the old Goblin slipping away. "We're just looking –"

"I won't resist," she interrupted. "I need a good man." She looked at Bronson. "I've never had a big black stallion like yourself before." Her mouth curled in a smile.

"Oh!" Bronson said. "Well the ladies do tell me that I'm quite –"

"Bronson!" Avar yelled. "Stand down. We need to –"

"How about you then?" she asked, pointing at Orion. "You seem like a snappy dresser. Why don't you climb on board the gravy train?"

Orion slicked back his plugged fake widow's peak and receding hair and looked down at his clothes. "That's true. I do appreciate fine –"

"Where is he?" Avar yelled, a bit peeved that the decrepit and disgusting old hag hadn't propositioned him, despite the fact that he was the obvious leader. He was probably just too intimidating.

"Who?"

"Abner!"

"Oh that old coot? He moved upstairs years ago." She rolled her eyes and took a swig out of her wine bottle. "Got the penthouse. Always on about his precious birds." She dropped herself into a recliner. "Doesn't like the coochie. Never wants to see the coochie. I think he's scared of the coochie, if you ask me. The coochie would eat him alive. Alive I tell you!" She gestured with the bottle, and a small burgundy geyser briefly erupted, sending a bolus of wine into the air and onto the carpet, where the stain blended perfectly with the assorted filth down there.

"Sweep the apartment," Avar said. He grabbed the last Banger who passed him. "Jamal, you watch the woman."

Avar searched the apartment with the other Piri. After only a minute, the team reassembled at the door. Jamal appeared relieved at their return.

Bronson said, "It's all clear."

Avar nodded. "Let's move to the top floor. Same formation, except this time Orion's got point."

"Ha!" said Orion.

"Aw, man!" said Bronson.

Avar slashed the air with an open palm. "Zip it."

The team marched over the busted door that lay canted in a bed of wood shrapnel, past the splintered doorframe, and up the stairs at the end of the hall. Moments later, they stood at the door to the top floor apartment.

"Watch and learn," Orion said, looking over his shoulder at Bronson. He kicked the door in and charged forward without waiting for the others.

Barbed spears shot from each side of the entrance hallway, one piercing the right side of Orion's neck and splashing out of the left, while the other embedded itself into his ribs on the left. He dropped to the floor, and the other team members rushed past him. Members called, "Clear!" as they inspected each room, finally returning to the front entry where Orion sat tugging on the spear in his neck. The other spear lay beside him on the floor in a small red pond formed by the blood still pouring from his neck and side.

"So that's how it's done?" Bronson asked.

"Shut it!" Orion croaked. The neck wound had been open for several seconds, and he was looking a little peaked. "I can't ... get it out ... without hurting – Ah!" He interrupted himself by screaming in pain as Bronson grabbed the back of the spear and yanked it out, taking a huge hunk of flesh with it. Orion's eyes rolled up in his head, and he slumped over, splashing down into his blood.

Bronson put the sole of his boot on Orion's open neck wound. After a few seconds, Orion's eyes fluttered and then popped open. Bronson removed his foot, and Orion sat up, feeling his neck and smearing the blood as he probed. The wound was closed, though he had a nasty mark the color of the downstairs wine stain on both sides of his neck. His clothes were slick with blood, and half of his face was drenched in red. His eyes found Bronson.

"I'm going to drill a hole in your ear," Orion said. "While you're sleeping."

"What?" Bronson replied. "I saved your life, mostly. Besides, it's over. It's like pulling off a, er, what are those things humans put on because they heal so slow? Whatever. Never mind. Who cares? It's like that though. Rip! Pain gone. I just wish we could build a fire and roast up some kebabs!" He held up the spear with the chunk of Orion's neck on its tip. "Now that's some good eats!"

Orion tried to get to his feet and slipped, falling onto his face with a splash.

"Enough!" Avar yelled. He'd tolerated those two fools while he'd been rifling through the old man's things, but he'd had enough. "Bronson, take your team and sweep the roof. Orion, stop dicking around and get your team up and then sweep the apartment for anything that might tell us where the old man went. And all of you, watch for more traps."

After over an hour, the only potentially useful discovery was some old photographs. They had found knives and spears and kamas and flails in almost every possible location. The trashcan held tiny bones and empty food cans. One entire cabinet was filled with note cards, each with a bird name on the left and what appeared to be dried bird poop taped on the right. An overturned open book called "How to Pick Up Czech Chicks" lay on a table next to a recliner.

Avar reviewed the photographs for the fifth time. Just a bunch of stupid Goblins posing and smiling or brandishing ridiculous bladed weapons. What the hell was he supposed to –?

The Hive exploded in his mind. It was that blond bastard Fionn. The idiot was summoning him. Avar saw an image of Tazia and one of the church complex. The message was clear. Return to base immediately.

Avar's mission was over. He had failed.

CHAPTER 68: ENTERING THE HIVE

The moist walls of the womb nurtured Jackson, encasing him. He had been protected here, separated from his true reality, allowed to develop far away from the dangers that lay without. But the time had come to emerge. He felt his body sliding forward, being expelled from his place of safety. He vaguely wondered if his head would be squeezed and get all pointy, and some nurse would put a stocking on it so people wouldn't wonder what the heck was wrong with that baby's head, like his dad said had happened the first time he'd been born. Then they'd stick him under a cafeteria heating lamp so he'd stop looking so yellow.

He fell, headfirst. He instinctively twisted and rotated, his feet splashing down onto solid ground along with a surge of falling water. Awake, he opened his eyes, and the memories rushed in, like lake water slamming together to fill the void left by a dropped boulder. Soaking wet, he stood in the center of the underground drainage pipe, now inexplicably brighter. The rush of water that had squirted him out of his hiding spot in the raised pipe slowed to a trickle as the sounds of his dislodgement echoed away.

Thoughts kicked and struggled in his mind, trying to pin one another. But the mental wrestling was less Greek and more "professional," with new thoughts jumping into the ring every few seconds, hitting one another with folding chairs, and trying to throw each other out into the crowd. The Vampires had Sy. His dad was a Goblin, his mom a Vampire. He himself was a "bent" Vampire/Goblin mutt, not fully human at all. And he might have just jacked into the Vampire hive. He held knowledge of situations that felt like memories even though he hadn't been present at them, and they had to be real because he wasn't clever enough to think of all that ridiculousness.

He saw a handsome man, a Vampire, with long blond hair beckoning. Technically his hair wasn't beckoning, but rather the man was, though his hair did seem to be bouncin' and behavin'. Something was about to happen... just out of reach. Another Vampire ran his hands over his close-cropped black hair, his deep-set dark eyes flaring. The man glowed in his rage.

Another thread, somehow different and somehow the same, played through his mind. The two visual threads reminded him of Topher and JL from high school; the twins had looked the same and walked the same, but their voices were different, though not enough for a stranger to distinguish. In this new thread, he saw Talbot and Simpson preparing for battle. With them were the people from his work – Buck-Bill, Archer, Mandy, and the blond bear Mr. Gorf. A man that couldn't be real stood beside them – he made the giant Mr. Gorf look like a schoolgirl next to her dad. With his dark hair, open shirt, and gold chains over his hairy chest, he looked like a New Jersey sumo wrestler – hold half the fat and throw in some extra muscles, please. And maybe a few tattoos. And add a side of chewing gum. His two poleaxes looked like hatchets in his monstrous hands.

Switch. Images blurred. The tonfa-wielding Vampire woman he'd glimpsed in his earlier vision returned, her graying hair now mostly dark again. Younger, her face seemed less hardened, though still with an edge. Power.

Switch. The Goblin images slid backwards, growing rougher but still recognizable. Two young men fought against several attackers. The thinner of the two crouched on one knee, his palms outstretched. A Blocker. A bubble-like field spread around him and his squat partner standing beside him. The stander held a sickle that was attached by a long chain to a spiked ball that he swung around his head, the spikes cutting the air inches from the long bared teeth of a surrounding group of Vampires. A club flew toward the pair, hit the bubble, and ricocheted into another Vampire attacker. It hit that attacker's mace which in turn hit him in his own forehead, knocking him to his backside. His mouth snarled and shouted in silence. Light played across the two Goblins' faces; the stander with the sickle flail was his dad Victor as a young man, with Abner by his side.

Switch. The Vampire woman again, her dark eyes so familiar. So like his own.

Mother.

CHAPTER 69: SHOCKING NEWS

"Why am I here?" Avar demanded.

Blond Fionn stood with his back to him, staring up at the back wall where the crucifix was mounted before the church had been decommissioned. As though burned in, the image of the cross remained, its shadow having protected the burgundy wall behind it from the constant assault of the sun streaming in through the high windows in the vaulted church. The front half of the former church now held racks of equipment and a few tables and chairs. The saints in the stained-glass windows gazed down upon crates of canned food, barrels of balsamic vinegar, computer equipment, and toilet paper, as well as maces, staves, and shoulder-mounted rocket launchers.

"My mission climaxes tomorrow," Fionn pronounced, turning and whipping his hair to theatrical effect. Avar wondered if he'd be cursed if he strangled him in a church, even if it was only an ex-church. "And Anastazia —"

Avar smirked at his use of Tazia's full name, as though Avar wouldn't know who he was talking about.

"—has given me access to the full resources of the Piri nation. Every available Piri is either here now or will be so by morning. That is when we will launch."

Avar had noticed the influx of personnel, though none of them knew why they were summoned from their posts. Most assumed that a massive campaign would be launched against the Goblins.

Fionn meandered across the altar, gazing up at the stained-glass and the arched and cracked ceiling.

The bastard was going to make Avar ask. "What's the damn mission?"

"Ah, that's right, you weren't told yet."

Avar whipped a smooth stone from his pocket at Fionn's head. It struck him in the forehead with a sound like a rap on a wooden door. The stone skittered away across the tile floor. Unfortunately, blunt weapons had little impact on Piri, and Fionn just stared at him.

"Classy," Fionn said. "Perhaps I won't tell you at all."

"Fine. I'll take my team and we'll go. I'll be sure to give Tazia a full report." He strode toward the side door.

"Wait! Okay, I'll tell you so stop whining." And then he told him.

Avar laughed so hard he had to steady himself on the wall.

CHAPTER 70: RIGHT, RIGHT

Sy pulled open the door of a seven-story office building on the opposite side of the Goblin HQ from her apartment vantage point. She'd learned nothing from staring out of the window of that apartment, but she had an idea. Plus, all that still-sitting had been killing her.

"Hello, Sunshine!" said a voice just inside the doorway. A young black man, almost a boy, really, approached her. His teased-out afro added a foot to his six-foot height. He appeared thin enough to slide under a door, with the exception of the hair. Behind him, a slightly older and shorter white man whose fat face didn't match his thin body jogged up, grinning. "What can we do for you?" the black man continued.

"You can let me inspect your roof."

"But ma'am, this is a private establishment. Roof access is prohibited. Right?"

The white guy, named Felks according to his shiny gold name tag, nodded his round face. "Right, Jay, right. That's right, right." He kept nodding.

"So we can't give you access," Jay said.

"No access. No, no," said Felks, shaking his head.

Sy scanned the room. It was definitely not in sparkling condition, but it seemed too nice for the Tovac Zone. They might have some criminal enterprise running from this facility.

"Listen," she said, conspiratorially. She leaned in, and they did the same. Everyone wants in on a secret. "I'm with the Tovacs, I need to see the roof."

Jay whispered back. "You realize that this is already a Tovac building."

"Right, right," added Felks.

Her instinct told her to reach for her weapons, but she restrained herself. She almost lied that she already knew that, but she suspected her face already registered the shock, so she just went with it. "Are you serious?" she said, raising her voice. "Those guys never tell me anything. You know what I mean? A bunch of white men – no offense Felks –"

"For what?"

"—sitting around and sending me out to scout locations for a movie about the Zone, and ... wait, I wasn't supposed to tell you that. No one's supposed to know that I'm scouting this. It's kind of an undercover project, and we're going to surprise the big guy with it."

"You mean Big J?" asked Felks.

"Is he the big one?" she replied, using her one semester of psychology to good use.

"Right, right," Jay said, apparently infected with Felks's speech pattern.

"Listen, please don't tell them. Just let me pop up to the roof, have a quick looksie around, then pop back down. I'll be out in ten minutes. Plus," she dropped her voice again, "we might need some 'talent' on the show, and you two might be perfect for the parts."

Jay rubbed his smooth lip and face. "I want to wear a mustache in my part."

"I want to be a black guy," Felks said. He seemed surprised after catching their looks. "What?" he said.

"The stairs are over there," Jay said. "Don't get out of the stairwell, or they'll be trouble. I hope you're in shape."

"Oh, I can handle myself."

"Right, right," both men said in unison.

CHAPTER 71: T MINUS 3 HOURS

Talbot marveled at Brutus's bulk. He hadn't seen him for years, and somehow the man had grown even larger. The guy must have a thyroid imbalance. No matter. As long as that thyroid kept cranking out muscle hormone or whatever else that big fella had pumping through his veins, Talbot would keep finding him bigger weapons and body armor that fit. The big Italian was like Goliath, though minus the weak spot for pebbles. Even Mr. Gorf shot appreciative glances over at the guy every few seconds as the team geared up. No one, though, was as smitten as Ferdinand. He'd met Brutus at the annual Polearm Enthusiast Conference five years prior, and he hadn't stopped talking about his massive new hero ever since.

"Are we eat before we attack?" Brutus asked Simpson, who was cleaning his weapons in the staging area. "Brutus needs to eat before we attack."

"I'll whip you up some pasta," Ferdinand said, patting Brutus on his shoulder, or at least as close to his shoulder as he could reach. "You like marinara? We got a jar open."

"Brutus likes Bolognese."

Ferdinand's face dropped. "Sure, I'll make you some –"

"Tagliatelle. Tagliatelle al ragù alla bolognese."

"Sure, great, yeah. Maybe I'll just order that one delivered in."

Brutus just looked at him.

Ferdinand raised his eyebrows and nodded for several moments, waiting. Nothing. He walked away.

Talbot stared down at one of his own weapons, a wavy sword known as a kris. Unlike the typical kris technique, Talbot fought using a round shield in his non-dominant right hand. Though quite effective at inflicting deep stabbing wounds, a kris was not a sufficient parrier of a war hammer.

Three hours and counting until the assault, when dawn broke. In recent history, there'd never been a battle of this magnitude, perhaps dating back to that butcher Saldar the Salivater's reign, when blood and drool poured through the streets. This would go down as the Superbowl of Piri Spanking, and Talbot would be the MVP quarterback. He'd been away from solid action for far too long. He'd worry about that boy Jackson later, assuming there would be a "later" for him or any of the other Jone-Zen.

CHAPTER 72: NEARLY-DEAD DOUCHE

Torches lining stone walls cast flickering shadows across rows of Piri dressed in formal battle gear, standing at attention in front of a raised wooden platform near one wall of a large cavern.

Originally the caves under the church had held religious knickknacks, such as blessed relics (like crosses or chalices or garden rakes), bags of gold, and dead guys, the last consisting of members of the religious order whose desiccated bodies now lay in recesses along the older unspoiled areas of the caverns, far away from the main room in which the Piri troops were assembled. That main room had been hollowed out by the grinding pressure of free enterprise after the church sold access to a company that wanted to build a station for a subway that never materialized. A massive concrete pillar supported the roof high overhead, lost in shadows to all but the Piri. Winding tunnels spidered away, the largest ones originally gouged out for the subway tracks. After thirty feet, one of the largest stopped at a stone dead-end. Some of the other tunnels were also man-made – created for water flow and drainage. The oldest, including those housing the holy bones, had been forged by time and the elements.

While Fionn stood on the platform looking down at the troops with his arms crossed, Avar leaned against a side wall, totally at ease while surveying the scene. This was just great. How could Tazia have approved this ridiculous mission? Had she? He prayed that maybe Fionn had misunderstood her, and when she arrived to find well over a hundred Piri waiting, many pulled from their assignments, she would cleave his head from his body. He imagined himself grabbing the head by the ends of its blond hair and spinning with it faster and faster until he released it like an Olympic hammer throw. How far would a head go? Wind might play into it....

"Piri!" Fionn called. "You know why we are assembled here. Most of you did not know – could not know – until the final moment. Security for this mission had to be tight, stricter than any mission in the history of, uh, strict missions.

"We will stand and deliver on my promise to Anastazia, known as Tazia by her inner circle, so most of you don't know that. We will stay the course of history of our great people. We will stick to it, and it will not stick back on us! We do this for Tazia; we do this for the Piri; we do this for all... er, of us Piri. And for Tazia too, like I said.

"She is almost here! Let us rise and greet her!"

Everyone was already standing.

Fionn rhythmically tapped his decorative engraved staff on the platform and gestured for the others to do the same. All of the fighters followed suit, banging their weapons into the ground. Those with short handled weapons took a knee so they could join in, but most of these soon stood back up because others' butts kept hitting them in the head. The tapping grew faster and faster.

"No!" Fionn shouted, though his voice was lost beneath the ever-quickening beat. "Too fast!"

The beat sped until it couldn't be maintained, and everyone just banged as fast as they could. The cacophony echoed off the stone walls, and the warriors yelled and cheered and whistled for a full minute, all eyes on the entrance door, waiting for Tazia. Soon, they grew weary and the sound drifted away. After a few minutes, only Fionn remained tapping, the tiny sound feeble in the massive space, like a lone metronome in an otherwise empty concert hall.

"Too fast, I told you!" he said from the platform. "You can't keep that up. See here, like me."

He tapped alone.

"Where's Tazia?" someone shouted. Several shouts along the lines of "Yeah! Where is she?" followed, and Fionn gestured for them to calm down.

"Well, she's on her way, like I said. But I didn't mean she was, you know, *here* already."

The crowd moaned.

"Wait, wait! Emmett! Where's Emmett? Let's get him and Sharyn up here to play the water glasses. Yeah! Play them like a xylophone! Woohoo! Who's up for that! Avar, bring the glasses!"

Avar made a gesture that could be politely interpreted as, "No, I would prefer not to bring the glasses."

"Dammit! Wait here!" Fionn yelled, running off the stage.

Avar smiled. Fionn was a douche, and when he screwed this one up, Tazia might just make him a dead douche. Let the good times roll.

CHAPTER 73: OPEN INVITATION

Images from the Vampire hive exploded in Jackson's head, overshadowing the Goblin visions that had stabilized into a steady stream. He managed to bind the Vampire hive before it could yank his mind off balance and drag it away. He regarded it like a dog handler struggling with a rabid mongrel he'd lassoed with a pole leash, the feral beast trying to charge rather than flee.

The Hive drew him forward along the murky damp tunnel. Somehow, he knew many, many of them were ahead, all those teeth like so many spines on a cactus. They weren't above him on the surface; they were down here somewhere, with him in these tunnels.

He knew he should return to his dad and Abner, but he didn't know the way. He didn't even know where he was. What he did know was that a massive group of Vampires lay ahead. Something horrible might soon befall Sy, and if he ran back to his dad for help, he might return too late to save her. He couldn't do this alone, but he had to do this alone — though he wouldn't object to a little help, like perhaps a flamethrower.

He crept forward along the dripping tunnel, his mind split between his surroundings and the silent images surging from the Hive. After a time, the images spoke to him, the voices faint at first. They were out of sync, like a horribly dubbed kung fu movie that was so wretched that some people thought it was actually fabulous — these were the same people who thought absurd clothes were ironically stylish, as long as they were expensive and the wearer *knew* they were hideous.

After concentrating, he thought he had shut the Hive out of his mind, but voices remained. A moment later he discovered that they were external, real, echoing through the tunnel. He instinctively crouched but realized that squatting in the middle of a featureless tunnel wouldn't exactly turn him invisible. He stood upright and analyzed the passageway.

The man-made tunnel branched to the left, though light filtered in from a lower natural cavern straight ahead, and this seemed to be the source of the voices. He ducked his head and crept forward through the damp cavern, heading toward the voices, toward the light, toward Sy.

Oh, and toward a buttload of freakin' scary-ass Vampires.

CHAPTER 74: GUTTIN' TIME

"They're rolling!" Simpson called out, one hand pressing in his ear piece and the other held up for silence in the staging area. The entire warehouse was illuminated, with almost every open space filled with Jone-Zen fighters and their gear. The rear parking area was likewise full of assault vehicles. The remote members had drawn straws to see which ones had to roll out in one of the five yellow school buses that had been pressed into service after mysteriously disappearing from an elementary school bus lot in the city. Someone had mounted two ski racks to the roof of each to hold the long weapons. Unlike the buses, the hearse had proven surprisingly popular, and it would be carrying nine members. Brutus, his face and body armor splotched red from the pasta sauce, would ride with Ferdinand in Ferdinand's pickup truck.

"Is Tazia with them?" Talbot asked.

Simpson nodded, listening. He dropped his hands and addressed Talbot. "Dozens, maybe more, maybe a hundred of the Piri are massed under the Piri church complex. Our contact sent over a map to the entrance at the rear of the church. Tazia just rolled into the Zone, presumably heading there. We won't be able to beat her to the complex, but we'll be close behind."

Talbot nodded and then yelled, his voice carrying throughout the entire warehouse. "Remember, Goal 1: save fellow Jone-Zen Sy Goji. Goal 2: open up those Piri bastards like cans of peaches. Gore 'em and gut 'em for the old man. This is what we've worked for." He made a circle over his head as though about to throw a lariat. "Let's move people!"

Simpson looked like Talbot felt – the man grinned from ear to ear.

Time to do this thing.

CHAPTER 75: ROLLIN' AND ROILIN'

As dawn broke, Sy leaned her head against the window frame, struggling to fight off sleep, mostly losing. Her excursion to the roof of the Tovac office complex to look down on the Jone-Zen headquarters parking lot had only confirmed her suspicion – Jackson's car was still there. At least it broke the monotony for a couple of hours, but now she was back in the chair, watching and waiting. Her battle armor was so uncomfortable that it actually helped her stay awake for much of her nighttime vigilance, though its effectiveness was slipping. She tried to let one eye sleep while the other eye remained alert, but because her eyes were unionized, they banded together and refused to cooperate. At the moment, they were technically open, if only a millimeter, though their operator was on break.

Images flickered into existence in her mind like an old fluorescent light warming up, clicking and buzzing before stabilizing and startling her to wakefulness. She was connected to the Jone-Zen hive — at long last, she had apparently fully emerged. She saw many fighters, some recognizable but most not. They called out to her, and to all Jone-Zen, to join them. A great battle loomed – the members were dressed in full battle gear, even Talbot.

Something must be wrong. Talbot didn't fight. Why was he suited up?

Within minutes, she was down the stairs and out on the street with her bicycle. She pedaled furiously as up ahead, a stream of cars exited the Jone Zen complex. She arrived at the rear gate before all the cars had left, so she turned onto a side road and stopped behind a shell of a sedan to wait.

Her breath caught in her chest when she looked up at the wispy clouds stretched across the morning sky. There was something gravely wrong with that sky; it pulsed copper as though alive. A jet-black speck appeared and tore the clear blue, gouging out an ebony wound. Clouds on either side rushed in, disappearing into the void. Then, just as quickly as it had appeared, the rip vanished. But another appeared a moment later, the unzipping black maw devouring the nearby clouds.

She'd seen earth-cloud inversions, cloud drops, and electrical physics storms, but she'd never even heard of something like this. The sky was tearing itself apart. And she was caught under it, with no place to go.

A man approached her as she stared skyward.

"I can do seven pushups," he announced.

She took a cursory glance at him and saw that he appeared harmless – at least compared to the grievous weather phenomenon strengthening over her head. The middle-aged man's scraggly brown hair stood a foot in all directions, defying gravity with the assistance of either a heavy-duty salon product or heavy-duty grime. Not a tough call.

"Good for you. Now please go away."

The man nodded. "You want to see?"

"No. Now please go away before I remove an arm from your body with my sword." She tried to keep watching the exiting convoy while keeping an eye on the stranger.

"You have a sword? Can I see it?"

"If you see it, that will be the last thing you see."

"Ever? Why is that? I don't get it."

She looked closer at him. She couldn't tell if he was messing with her or if he was a bit off. From her experience, approximately 100% of her interactions with men in the Tovac Zone involved at least one of those two. She really didn't want to lop the man's arm off, but she wasn't about to lose that convoy either.

"Let's see those pushups," she said.

"Yes! Now we're talking!" He popped to the ground and grunted out repetitions, his pace slowing with each one.

As he completed repetition six, the final car left the facility, and she stood on her pedals, propelling the bike forward.

"Nice work. Now go inside!" she called back.

"But I've got one more!" he yelled after her.

She pumped the pedals hard to catch up with the convoy, but she had little trouble keeping up. They rolled out slowly, probably to keep the convoy intact. Her breathing and heart rate steady, she pedaled behind them for ten minutes, discovering that the body armor was even less comfortable on a bicycle than in a chair. She made a mental note to tap in some baby powder next time.

The convoy pulled to the curb, and she rolled her bike into an alley a block behind them. She wedged it behind a commercial trash bin, though she expected that it would be gone before she returned. That was the least of her problems.

She squatted at the corner and scanned the convoy through her binoculars, hoping to find Jackson with them. If not, he was either dead or a captive of the Vampires, which would be worse.

The Jone-Zen assembled into squads. When they advanced, she would dive in behind them and seek out Jackson in the confusion of battle.

The sky emitted the sound of a whip crack, followed by deep rolling thunder. Blue clouds poured from one of the ebony sky rips. They rolled in place, with purple regions sliding into view and then back out as they tumbled.

The Vampire attack better start soon, and it better be indoors.

The Hive images strengthened. The excitement and proximity of so many Jone-Zen must have amplified the signal. She tried to experience it fully but felt herself being sucked in, losing reality to the emotional pull of so many years of memories. She snapped it shut. There'd be time for that later.

Right now, it was time to cut some Vampire julienne fries. Grandma would be proud.

CHAPTER 76: SURPRISE!

Fionn held his hand up for silence, though the volume of the room actually increased slightly. One of his lackeys yell-whispered in his ear.

"Positions everyone!" Fionn shouted. The Piri warriors quieted and looked at one another. Idiots, Fionn thought. At least they shut up. "Tazia is here and on her way down. Remember what to do!"

All eyes focused on the main entrance as the flickering torches sent humanoid shadows dancing across the walls and floor. Silence.

Two great Piri twin warriors, their spiked hair bleached shock white, entered the room shoulder to shoulder. Each held a long-handled war hammer, similar to Bronson's though more ornate. The two paused at the entrance and scanned the room. After looking at one another, they each took a sideways step away from the other, leaving room between them.

Even the torches held their breath.

Tazia stepped between the two men, her hands covering her eyes. Her straight black-streaked silver hair was pulled back in a single ponytail. The crowd erupted in cheers.

"No!" Fionn yelled to them, his voice lost in the furor. "You're ruining it!" Then, in a panic, he ran to the edge of the platform just as Tazia arrived at the steps, flanked by the pale twins. "Surprise!" he yelled to her.

Despite the noise, she must have somehow heard him because she dropped her hands and gave him a slight smile. It obviously wasn't anywhere close to a surprise – she could detect it on the Hive as soon as he announced it to the other Piri, not to mention the fact that she herself had assigned him this mission. Just the same, he strove for verisimilitude, even if he didn't know how to spell it or even what it meant.

He reached down to escort her up the three short steps to the main stage. She walked past him without a word as the crowd continued to cheer. He dropped his rejected hand.

She stood at the front of the stage, basking in the adulation like a lonely cold lizard on a rock of hot love. Beaming down on her subjects, she raised her arms, pumping them toward the ceiling, driving the volume higher. She held them in this state, whipped into a frenzy. After a minute of this, she dropped her hands, and the volume followed suit.

"Thank you. I am truly surprised." She looked at Fionn and then back at the crowd. "Not at the surprise party of course, but at the amazing support you've given me. I never realized how much respect and love you all have for me. I worked hard for this position, and we've all fought alongside one another, with me in front, the True Leader. Let us all celebrate the glorious day of my birth!"

After slight pause, the cheers that rang out were a bit lower in volume than before.

Noticing that she shared the stage with a sheet-covered cube about six feet on a side, she raised her hands for silence. "What's this?" she yelled. "A present for me?"

Now was Fionn's chance. He sprang forward. "Indeed it is!" This was only the first of many surprises that he had for her. He reached down and grabbed the edge of the sheet, pausing for effect. He ripped it off to reveal a massive tiered fake birthday cake, the kind typically filled with an uncomfortably crouched stripper. It was painted white with pink "frosting" and decorated with the words, "Happy Birthday Anastazia," the last several letters written progressively smaller as the writer ran out of space. Below that, it said, "Not too old!"

"But that's not the true surprise," Fionn yelled. He beamed at the crowd and Tazia, who stared back at him with a smile made of lips stretched across clenched teeth. "You know how those Goblins always look up to the Piri, how they fear us? How they call us 'Vampires'?" A smattering of laughter. "Well, I bring you, the first true Vampire! He who inspired the legend. The Voivode of Wallachia," and then, under his breath, he added, "Not that Radu guy." Returning to full volume, he continued, "He of the Kickin' 'Stache. Behold Vlad!" Again he dropped his voice, "The third Vlad. Not the Usurper or Dragon one. The cool Impaler one." Raising his arms and voice, he shouted, "Dracula himself!"

On cue, the top section of an open coffin sprang out of the top of the cake, sticking up about four feet. Inside was a desiccated corpse, mostly clothes over bone. Confetti burst from the top of his coffin in a colorful fountain, drifting down and landing on the cadaver's teeth and empty eye sockets. The crowd was completely silent, probably struck dumb in amazement. Those idiots didn't know it, but it wasn't even the real Vlad – Fionn had scoured the whole of Europe for him only to discover that no one knew where he was buried, though theories abounded. The corpse in the box was just some old Romanian peasant that his team had dug up from a family cemetery over there.

The last of the confetti settled to the ground at Tazia's feet. Seconds elapsed as she eased herself around to stare at him, her face warped into something unrecognizable — probably "extreme gratitude", but the expression was inexplicably terrifying.

Ffft! Something ripped the air overhead. Then another and another. A shower of arrows rained down on the stage from multiple angles, plunking into the corpse with dry cracking sounds, launching clouds of wood and bone shrapnel. Tazia dove off the stage. The corpse, his chest a forest of wooden shafts, slumped face down into the cake. More arrows skewered him.

Chaos exploded into the cavern as Goblin warriors rushed in, some yelling, "Death to Saldar! Again!"

"Wait!" Fionn called. "We haven't done the play yet!"

This was the worst birthday party ever.

CHAPTER 77: BREACH

Sy crouched beside her bike, surveilling the church. She had watched as the Jone-Zen executed a perfect entry, disabling the sentries with rapid barbed spear strikes and dragging them back with attached chains. But why was Talbot going in? Generals don't strap on armor and breach the walls! He was probably there for the same reason that the strike force was so massive. Behind him, Simpson ran alongside a behemoth of a man who reminded her of the outermost shell of Russian nesting dolls; Mr. Gorf would be the next layer inside, then Ferdinand, then Simpson. The giant swung an enormous poleaxe in each hand as he ran, once clipping Ferdinand on accident, knocking him into a sedan parked at the curb. Ferdinand's backside shattered the driver window, leaving his arms and legs sticking out like the leaves of a pineapple. He squirmed and only escaped after another team member took his hand and pulled him out. By the time the poleaxe colossus ducked into the church, no one was within twenty feet of him.

She crept closer, debating whether to rush in along with the others and hope they didn't see her, or instead wait until they all entered before following.

She flinched as the sky screeched like jagged metal gears tearing themselves apart, the sound traveling from one horizon to the other over the span of ten seconds. She glanced upward but immediately returned to focus on the Jone-Zen, averting her eyes like she'd just seen some messy roadkill. Several of them looked skyward too, while all of them quickened their pace. She had to get inside, and soon. Something horrific would soon descend, and she'd rather learn about it from the news.

The final team members rushed forward, but no Jackson. Maybe he was still back in the surveillance van, though she saw no movement from the vehicles. She needed to check the van before entering the church grounds.

Rather than continuing into the church like the others, the last two men from the assault team stopped at a small gate leading up to the church and stood guard.

Shoot!

She crept to the surveillance van, now painted with a scene of three wolves howling at a moon. *That would look good on a t-shirt.* She listened. Nothing. She rapped lightly on the door. Still nothing.

The Piri must have him after all.

The sky shrieked again, this time in staccato bursts, like a serrated knife cutting deeper with each jagged peak. Fear dug into her primal core as the sound echoed away, sliding back into an eerie silence.

"Hey, you!" one of the guards yelled.

Sy's chest tried to seize, but it was already pegged at max. Though the van shielded her from view, they must have somehow detected her. She didn't want to fight her own people, but she had no choice. She reached up and slid her swords out with a smooth hiss.

CHAPTER 78: LIKE OLD TIMES

A voice whispered, "Why didn't you wake me for my shift?"

"Huh?" Abner said, startled awake. He'd been keeping watch at the front window. His brain blinked with the first flickers of consciousness. "Is my shift over already?" He dug sleep out of an eye.

"Shitake on a stick! You were asleep!" Boots looked out into the street in a panic. Two men, obviously Jone-Zen, patrolled out front. "Grab your gear, you old coot! It's on! We're missing it!"

Boots threw on the torso section of body armor, the vest not quite fitting as he forced it down. His fat bulged out the top and bottom like the cream from an overstuffed cannoli. He grabbed the kama and spiked ball ends of his modified kusarigama and bolted out of the front door of the shop, knocking it askew as it wedged itself open.

"Hey, wait up!" Abner shouted, stuffing a metal tray from a cafeteria he'd looted into the front of his pants and under his body armor torso piece. It didn't quite fit.

Boots rushed across the street, not waiting for a protective canopy around him, assuming Abner could even remember how to set one up. Abner felt a sick feeling in his gut as he followed his oldest friend across the street. How could he have fallen asleep? He was as bad as Jesus' disciples catching some winks in Gethsemane, except he wasn't quite sure if Vampires were involved in that one. His damn memory!

The sky shrieked as though the clashing blue and purple clouds were made of metal. The fighting down here would cause the world to split – the elements to turn in on themselves. The Piri and the Jone-Zen must make peace.

But first he had to catch up with Boots.

The two Jone-Zen guarding the front of the church complex yelled at Boots to stop, but that fool charged straight at them, roaring like a man burning alive. Abner's body exploded in shivers, the old battle rage rushing back after so many years. The shorter of the guards stole a look at his partner as the man leveled his pike at the charging bull. The short guard also tried to do the same, but Boots snapped the first pike's tip with his forehead and rushed past before the second pike was in position.

Abner caught movement on the roof of a nearby church building and reacted, stopping his run in the middle of the road and throwing out his hands. His protective canopy sprang from his body, its diameter rushing outward even as a volley of projectiles rained down on Boots.

He was too slow. The arrows slammed into Boots, ricocheting off or splintering on contact. They only succeeded in making him stumble a bit.

A sniper opened up with a .50 caliber machine gun from the back of a jeep off to Boots' right. That would have left a mark. Abner felt the powerful bullets pounding into his deflection shield, now just large enough to cover Boots. Abner ran forward because if Boots kept increasing the distance between them, the canopy would have to grow large enough that the gun would be inside the bubble, rendering the shield useless. The shorter guard with the intact pike turned just in time to watch him bolt past.

"You fellas are Jone-Zen?" A roar of .50 caliber gun fire obliterated part of his sentence. "—tell us?"

"No time," Abner yelled back. "Boots' boy's in there!"

The taller guard lamented to no one in particular, "That was my favorite pike."

Boots charged into the front door of the church. The gunfire stopped.

"They're down in the tunnels!" the short guard yelled just before Abner got to the door. "The staircase is behind the altar."

Though the guards were behind him, Abner nodded his thanks and released his canopy. He dove into the dim church, energized for one last battle.

CHAPTER 79: CONVERGENCE

From behind the van, Sy watched the two old men charge across the street, one behind the other. She didn't recognize them, and neither was properly geared for battle. The front squatty one wore some sort of armored vest several sizes too small and held a kama-like weapon chained to a spiked ball, like a combination kusarigama-flail. Only an experienced (or stupid) fighter would attempt to wield such a dangerous weapon in battle. He seemed to be running from the second man, a tall vagrant carrying a single bladed knife with something bulky and metal wedged in the front of his pants. The two old drunk Tovacs must have stumbled onto some gear, and the tall one probably wanted to rob the shorter of his take. She hoped the guards wouldn't hurt them.

Now was her chance. She ran across the sidewalk to the grimy white brick wall that separated her from the church complex grounds, leaped up to latch onto the top edge, and scrambled over it.

Voices shouted at the entrance by the guards. Something crashed, like wood splintering. She sprinted across the grounds, staying near the wall, heading toward the side of the church. A group of Jone-Zen vehicles were parked on the grounds between her and the front door. She ran between them and the wall, momentarily shielded from the entrance to the church grounds where the guards now dealt with the elderly intruders.

A familiar hum filled the air – a Blocker was generating a deflection field back at the entrance to the grounds. Were the old men attacking the Jone-Zen guards with projectiles? She caught movement from that direction and turned her head. The first old man had made it past the guards and was now running in a path parallel to her own – her along the side wall and him directly toward the main entrance. The edge of a deflector bubble rushed to overtake him. She heard the faint whoosh of arrows at the same time she saw men on the roof of a building on the other side of the church grounds. Before the deflection bubble caught up, arrows slammed into the runner, and she wanted to avert her eyes. They ricocheted off of him or shattered on impact, like he was a stone golem. Like he was ... a Jone-Zen!

A deflected arrow cut the air directly in front of her, and she ran on. She didn't know what was happening, but she knew she needed to get into that church before the guards or the sky killed her, before something happened to Jackson.

Gunfire exploded behind her, almost deafening. She froze to maximize her shell, knowing remotely that by the time she heard the shots, the bullets would have already reached her. She could survive small rounds without tightening up, but an unexpected direct hit from large caliber rounds, like the ones speeding away from the roof-mounted Jone-Zen Jeep behind her, would send her sprawling, probably rendering her unconscious.

After another explosive volley, she realized that she wasn't the target. The rounds whined off of the deflector field now enclosing the broad old Jone-Zen, its center somewhere back in the street near the thinner old vagrant. Could he be a Jone-Zen too? Why were the guards attacking them?

She had no idea who these crazy old Goblins were. No time. She ran again. She only had one goal — find Jackson.

CHAPTER 80: THE CHANGE

Crouching in a natural tunnel at the edge of a massive underground chamber, Jackson had gaped at the teeming throngs of Vampires. He remembered going to the zoo with his dad, feeling the raw power of the massive tigers pacing just behind the glass. They were magnificent beasts of muscle and teeth, tuned for killing. The veneration had been one-sided, like a hamburger admiring a hungry laborer in a pick-up truck at a drive-thru. Unlike at the zoo, here there were hundreds of tigers and no glass wall to keep them at bay. Any thoughts of admiration by their potential feast was crushed beneath layers of palpable danger.

At the same time, he felt drawn to them. He could hear them, feel them, see them in his mind. Images and emotions flashed – ancient battles, fear, pain. And love. And at least one of them had to go to the bathroom, but that one was a bit fuzzy.

He couldn't see Sy anywhere. He'd hoped that they would be holding her in a cage in a private corner with the key on a hook a few feet away, with maybe a snoring guard nearby. He needed to get higher so he could see the entire room, but he didn't see how he could do that. She might not even be in there. If all the Vampires stayed bunched up in that chamber, he would be free to search the rest of the tunnels and the compound above ground. He just hoped they didn't all break for lunch and scatter. He'd worry about finding his way out of the base once he found her.

A sheet covered a box on a low stage near him, large enough to hold a cage with a person inside. That might be where she was! But why would she be on-stage? His mind flashed to an image of an Aztec high priest carving the heart out of a shrieking captive. He scanned the huge crowd of Vampires, each one of them powerful enough to rip a man holding a phonebook in half.

Please let that not be her under the sheet.

A long-haired blond Vampire climbed to the stage, his back to Jackson. He spoke to the crowd while making theatrical arm movements before introducing a woman. Even though Jackson only saw her in profile as she approached the stage, he knew her — the woman from his visions. This was Anastazia, or Tazia.

This was his mother.

The man spoke more, but his voice faded. Another channel opened in Jackson's mind, and images poured in again. These were different; they displayed the same battles, but from a different perspective. He saw Talbot and Simpson, Abner and Victor. The Goblin hive engulfed him.

The Goblins are here!

The blond Vampire yanked away the sheet to reveal a huge decorative cake. A wooden box burst from its top, extending out several feet. Though he couldn't see what was in it, he could feel it. It was a corpse. Was it Sy?

Goblin battle rage roared through his mind like a red tsunami. Arrows arched through the air and rained down on the stage, and the other half of his mind exploded in Vampire fury.

The change happened in an instant.

CHAPTER 81: THE CHOSEN ONE

Ass-kicking time.

The underground cavern erupted in light and sound. Projectile deflection bubbles sprang from Blockers in both camps, those from the Vampire camp tinged in red. Along with their archers, Goblin rifleman opened up with automatic fire, their dual Gatling gun designs launching clouds of razor-sharp bolts into the surrounded mass of Vampires. Several Vampires returned fire with rapid-fire mini-cannons mounted under their forearms. Two Vampires accompanied each shooter – a Blocker flanked him, and a smaller assistant fed cannonballs into the back of the shooter's cannon. Many of the initial volleys met their mark, skewering the Vampires or smashing the Goblins. The projectiles careened off deflection bubbles and peppered the walls, sending clouds of dust into the deafening room, filled with the roars of the Goblins and the squeals of the Vampires.

The Vampires' teeth extending to razor tips, their arms lengthened, and their posture hunched, giving them a starving animal appearance. The Goblins' skin turned ash gray. Stray sharp projectiles hitting the Goblins shattered or bounced off without effect, while blunt projectiles had almost no effect on the Vampires. The Vampires were clearly quicker, but the Goblins had them in strength.

Jackson threw himself into the melee, heading for the doorway from which Tazia had come. Sy had to be back there somewhere.

During the Vampire attack outside the van, he had felt as though another force had taken control of his body during the fight. He now recognized that force fighting to again take over, but this time he swallowed it, integrating it into his core while maintaining control. Well, *mostly*.

The room shifted, altered, transformed. Gray clouds of dust became distinct particles, sucked back and forth by the projectiles rushing through the air as they ricocheted from deflection bubbles and walls. He observed fletching lying flat against the shafts of hissing arrows as they corkscrewed through the air past his face, feeling them before he even saw them.

A Vampire rushed at him, swinging a mace in an arc over his head. Jackson leaned his head to the right as a bolt approaching from behind cut through the air an inch from his left ear. It struck the Vampire in the forehead with a wet crack, and he went down, the bolt protruding from both sides of his head.

A tangled mass of two struggling men crashed into him, each holding the other's wrists. Off-balance, they drove him to the left, threatening to take him to the ground. He threw an elbow into the side of the neck of the Vampire whose back was to him. The Vampire's legs went out, and his Goblin attacker released him to fall to the floor. The Goblin's triumphant expression shifted as he stared into Jackson's face, confused. Jackson felt the man's intention, and just as the Goblin flinched to thrust his spear, Jackson slid around it and struck him in the chest. The Goblin's dropped spear, wisely deciding not to follow its owner as he flew backwards into a mosh pit of struggling fighters, stayed aloft long enough for Jackson to catch it. The Vampire at Jackson's feet grabbed him but reconsidered as a spear slammed down into his chest.

Jackson ran on, dodging fighters.

He felt like a professional football running back, hitting the gaps between the other players. Except these players kept trying to stab him or club him or sling a chain around his neck. Both Vampires and Goblins alike attacked him on sight, which simplified tactics – take them all out. He collected and deposited weapons as he passed.

Two fighters squared off near the edge of the room, almost at the passage opening. The Vampire swung two dull gray metal rods while the Goblin fought back with flashing short swords. Sparks flew as their weapons clashed. From the looks of them, each had received a few solid licks. Before he could pass them, they separated, each cutting his eyes toward Jackson. Fear and confusion flashed. They looked at one another and then back at him. Both charged him, the Vampire's teeth bared in a grimace and the Goblin roaring like a berserker. Jackson leaped upward, driving his knee into the center of the spear in his hands, snapping it cleanly in two. As he landed, he saw four distinct arcs in the air, the paths that each of his attacker's weapons would soon travel as they slashed and struck forward. He twisted and crouched like he was stepping through a low gap in a barbed wire fence. As the weapons cut the air around him, he swung the bottom half of the spear into the bridge of the Goblin's nose and the pointed top half up into the Vampire's throat. They both dropped, the clanking of their weapons against the floor lost in the cacophony of battle.

By now, the Blockers proved almost useless because of the close combat. Bolts and cannonballs rained down on everyone alike. Most of the lights had already been extinguished by then, and the Goblins blasted a retreat message over the hive. They wanted to get out before darkness overtook the room.

Out of the corner of his eye, he saw something strike out like a whip. A Goblin Blocker crouched next to a standing Goblin fighter swinging a spiked ball chained to a sickle, fending off four Vampire attackers. The stander surprised one of the Vampires by grabbing the spiked ball and throwing out the sickle end of the weapon, slashing the wrist of the Vampire as the Goblin yanked it back. The Vampire's mace clanked to the ground next to two bleeding Vampires. One of them was on an elbow, crawling away, leaving a bloody trail behind.

Jackson stared at the pair of Goblins.

Abner and Dad.

He was momentarily awestruck. This was the same man who spent the majority of his non-work waking hours attached to a recliner. This was the same man who decided not to read the paper because the paper guy had thrown it more than ten feet from the front door. Now, he attacked a horde of Vampires, whipping them with a vicious chained sickle like a striking scorpion.

Jackson rushed forward. The nearest Vampire jumped back from Victor's approaching strike. Jackson struck him in the back with an open palm, sending him directly into the path of Victor's blade. His neck was sliced nearly in half. The next attacker stuck the barrel of his hand cannon just inside Abner's deflection bubble. Jackson yanked him backwards as the Vampire fired. The burst reflected directly back into the Vampire's face, sending him sprawling across the floor. The final two Vampires noticed Jackson and turned. The first struck out at him with a staff. Jackson blocked the strike with his forearm and then struck the staff as he had his spear, cracking it in two. He grabbed the Vampire's hands holding the two pieces of the split staff, twisted them, then rammed them backward, forcing the Vampire to drive the splintered shafts into his own body. The Vampire crumbled, two shafts of wood protruding from his chest like the masts of a boat.

The final Vampire raised an iron mace and paused, his face frozen in an expression that seemed to say, "Oh, I forgot that old guy was back over there slinging that razor-sharp blade." A trickle of blood ran down his face from the new hole in the top of his head. As he fell, Victor yanked the blade back by the chain and caught it.

"How 'bout that, bitches!" Victor yelled. He patted Abner on the shoulder, though Abner still concentrated on the deflection field around them.

Behind them, the Goblins streamed out of the room, moving backward in a fighting retreat.

"We need to get out here, Son!" Victor yelled to him.

"Not until we find Sy!"

A Goblin slashed at Jackson with a broadsword. Jackson slid to the side and grabbed the man's hair from behind and then kicked the back of his legs. The Goblin's legs flew forward as Jackson drove the man's head downward, slamming his head into the stone floor, the Goblin's body almost completely inverted. The broadsword skittered away from his still body.

"Damn, Son, you're gettin' it from both sides!" Victor yelled as he and Abner ran to his side. Looking into his face, he added, "I can see why. I see a bit of your mom in there."

Jackson ran his tongue over his sharp teeth and was not surprised. His skin was ash gray.

"There!" Jackson yelled, jumping and waving. He could see her. She was trying to enter the room but was being pushed back by the retreating Goblins as they moved up stone steps at the end of the short passageway leading from the cavern. "Let's move!"

Abner and Victor didn't need to be told twice. They ran toward the steps, vigilant for pursuing attackers. Anarchy reigned, the confusion of battle in full force. Flares arced across the room, strobing the room with brief bursts of blinding light. Bolts and arrows and cannonballs and bullets pierced the air and smashed the walls, their sounds mixing with clanking weapons and the screams of battle.

Jackson was separated from them as they struggled toward the exit, and at the doorway, he hit a solid wall blocking his escape. The wall consisted of ash gray skin stretched over a mass of meat topped with curly black hair. The guy could swaddle up Buck-Bill like a newborn. Someone must have smashed and elephant into human form and dropped a gold chain on him. The monster Goblin glared down at him, twirling two poleaxes like a hibachi chef with his knives. And Jackson was about prepped for the grill.

All around them, fighting continued, but nobody stepped between them. A few combatants even stopped to watch.

"He's one of us!" Victor shouted, getting driven up the stairs behind Sy by the mass of retreating Goblins.

The giant sliced his long poleaxes through the air in a figure eight as though he were holding short swords. Jackson watched, timing them. He couldn't wait long. Anyone could decide to attack him from behind while he dealt with this behemoth, and Sy and his dad might need his help. Seeing a gap, he surged forward and struck the giant with a fist to the solar plexus. Big Chops grunted and staggered back, though Jackson caught a glancing blow from one of the axes, sending him skidding into a mass of bloody Vampires and Goblins, knocking them to the ground like bowling pins. Pain spiked up through his ribs.

He scrambled to his feet and grabbed two iron maces from the tangle of bodies and weapons.

Time to stop messing around.

Big Chops bared his teeth in rage and charged, thrusting one spiked axe in front of him like a lance and slashing the air with the other. As before, Jackson could see the paths the weapons would take and he slid through the gaps, striking Big Chops in the right shin with a mace, then the back of his thigh with the other, then a hip, a rib, an elbow. As the giant crumbled on that side, Jackson leaped and finished the mace walk, striking shoulder, neck, and top of the head before his feet hit the ground, less than a second after the giant's head.

The room was quiet. The Vampires stood in a semicircle around him to his rear. The Goblins were frozen in place on the stairs, watching him, shocked. Goliath was down, but David had cheated and used metal sticks instead of a stone. Jackson turned and looked at the Vampires, all of them staring – some warily, others fearfully. The woman whom he knew to be his mother approached him, her eyes intense. She opened her mouth to speak.

"Get him!" a Vampire off to his left yelled.

"Kill him," yelled another.

The crowd of Vampires roared and charged him, weapons raised.

"No!" Tazia yelled.

She said more, but Jackson didn't hear it, as he was at the stairs on the heels of the Goblins before she could finish a sentence. The walls exploded with shrapnel, and he felt painful impacts on his back that knocked him off balance but didn't take him down. The doorway at the top of the stairs was narrower, and he arrived just after the final Goblin squeezed out. He followed the pack across the back of the church outside onto the church grounds, the Vampires close behind. His dad and Sy had to be here somewhere. Now that they were out in the open, he just needed to get them all together so they could escape and let these idiots fight it out.

The sky cracked and buzzed, shrieking in pain.

Before the Goblins arrived at the front gate, he heard something in his head, and the Goblins all spun toward him, weapons at the ready. Talbot emerged from the crowd and held his hands up to stop their attack.

"I thought there was something a bit odd about you." His gray eyes somehow seemed more lethal, even more intense, as though the battle armor had enhanced his entire body. "Now what I want to know is, what the hell—"

He stopped abruptly as a cannonball caught him in the temple, sending him flying backwards into the crowd of Goblins. The Vampires had emerged from the church and were advancing behind Jackson. He was pinned in.

"Take that punk out!" a voice yelled. Simpson.

Jackson needed to find his group, but there was a good chance that they were on the other side of Simpson's soon to be prone body. He charged him, gripping his new maces, remembering Simpson's speed but not caring.

Vampires also charged and engaged the Goblins all around him.

Two Goblins jumped in Jackson's path. The first lunged at him with one of his two short spears. Jackson struck his wrist, knocking that spear to the ground. The Goblin counterattacked with the other spear, ramming it toward Jackson's ribs. Jackson twisted away and felt the glancing blow as the spear tore a gash in his shirt but didn't penetrate his skin.

The Goblin looked up at Jackson, confused. "You're –" the guy started.

"Right. On my dad's side." He hit the Goblin with his mace, though only hard enough to give him a decent headache.

The second attacker was Buck-Bill with his Swiss harpoon. He looked confused, not an unusual expression on his face.

"Hey Buck-Bill. You want to step aside so I can ram this mace up Simpson's nose?"

Buck-Bill's expression didn't change. "My name's Ferdinand." He stared. "Your skin is gray." He stepped aside.

Uncertainty darted across Simpson's face. He charged, slashing the air with his dual broadswords. Swords met maces in a flurry of slashes and crashes. All around them, the battle raged.

"You are an abomination!" Simpson yelled over the din of the battle and the sky. He became more desperate as he attacked, obviously frustrated. Jackson had greater speed and natural ability, but he didn't have Simpson's training, and Simpson surprised him a few times with unexpected spin moves or kicks that Jackson didn't see until almost too late. But Simpson was tiring, and his building frustration made his attacks more reckless.

The sky cracked, and Jackson feigned surprise and looked up, suspecting that Simpson would lunge at him at that exact instant. He could feel it. Jackson slid to the side and swung his mace from the ground upward. Simpson stepped straight into it, helpfully extending his front leg so that his private sensitives hovered in just the right place to cushion the blow from an iron mace to the crotch. Even with a Goblin's resistance and a thick layer of body armor, a shot like that would be felt. The blow raised Simpson off the ground a foot, and Jackson swung his other mace and struck Simpson in the head, sending him tumbling.

Jackson felt a Vampire charge him from behind and slid to the side, narrowly avoiding a metal club to the head.

The Vampire swung with a furious intensity. Something about the guy reminded Jackson of Simpson. The Vampire's strikes were quick and efficient, in perfect control. But Jackson could see them coming. He still didn't quite understand how, but the moves seemed telegraphed. Like Simpson, this Vampire surprised him few times, such as by throwing a kick as he stumbled away. It almost connected.

"Whoa Avar!" a deep voice boomed to Jackson's right, the voice somehow digging through the clashes and roars of battle and the splintering cracks that echoed from the sky. "I thought Tazia said not to hurt him." A huge black Vampire approached, holding what appeared to be an anvil on a stick over his shoulder.

"I won't hurt him," the Vampire Avar said. "Much." He lunged forward. "Help me, you idiots!"

The black Vampire charged forward from Jackson's right, closely followed by a skinny Vampire that seemed to fit the Vampire stereotype, albeit one who might have partied a little too much in school and now worked at an oil change place.

The three had fought as a team before, as they deftly avoided one another's blows and attempted to encircle Jackson, the black hammer wielder in the center. A solid shot from that hammer would flatten his head to his chin and send him into the ground to his shins. But Jackson concentrated on the one called Avar. While the others darted in with little concern for personal safety, Avar sought Jackson's flank, looking for an opening.

Jackson tumbled hard to his right, positioning the scrawny Vampire between the hammer man and himself, with Avar rushing to close the gap to his left. During the roll, Jackson released his useless maces and scooped up a dagger that had fallen during the battle. As he rolled to his feet and lunged forward, the hammer-swinger tried to adjust the arc of his swing, turning it in mid-swing to follow Jackson's roll. Mr. Scrawny didn't even slow the hammer down as it caught him in the head, sending him flying end over end.

"Aw, ma—" the hammer swinger started but was cut short as Jackson plunged the dagger into his neck. The man fell taking the dagger with him. "Nice highwaters," the fallen man gurgled, yanking the knife out of his neck. He'd be down there for a while.

Jackson leaped back just as Avar lunged forward, the Vampire landing on the bulk of the fallen hammer-swinger who grunted his disapproval.

Something clanked directly behind Jackson and he rolled away, turning.

Sy! Her swords flashed as she traded blows with that rat bastard Simpson, who had apparently tried to stab Jackson in the back. Jackson moved forward to help her but saw a movement in his periphery and leaped away just in time. Avar had swung at him with one of his clubs. Jackson was now unarmed. He searched the ground for more fallen weapons, but only saw the giant hammer near Avar's feet. Sy was holding her own but had sustained a few hits. Jackson needed to help. He slid in that direction, pulling Avar with him. The man thrust and slashed. Jackson saw an opening and struck the Vampire with two solid punches, a jab and a hook. The Vampire staggered back from the sheer force of the blows but was uninjured.

"Simpson!" Jackson yelled at the Goblin's back as he fought Sy. "I'm right here!"

Simpson spun quickly to him but continued his motion, bringing his leg up and catching Sy with a heel to her chin just as she rushed in on him. She tumbled to the side, stunned.

"You!" Simpson said, looking toward Jackson. He charged, dropping his swords and reaching over his back to pull out a new weapon. The Vampire Avar also charged, almost directly behind Jackson. Jackson was in a pinch, one of those twisty ones. He rolled out of their paths and spun to his feet.

The Vampire and the Goblin weren't looking at him, though; they watched one another. Simpson now held a cane in front of him, its end tipped with a six-inch blade. Opposite him, Avar assumed a fencing stance with his own cane out in front, his double clubs discarded. The two launched themselves at one another.

Jackson ran to Sy as she made it up to a knee. Battles raged around them. She picked up her swords, and Jackson helped her to her feet.

"We need to take cover!" Sy yelled over the growing roar from the sky. The sounds of battle were almost lost beneath a new sound from the churning copper sky, a deep oscillating moan like Tuvan throat singers. A black dot appeared in the sky with a crisp popping noise. The dot screamed through the air, emitting a sound like ripping cloth, unzipping the cover of the sky and revealing the inky black depths that lay beyond.

Jackson had never agreed with someone more in his entire life. They ran toward the church, dodging slashing sickles and pounding hammers. Above, purple clouds the texture of flowing mercury poured out of the ripped void, leaking across the sky.

They almost made it.

With a shriek, a jet-black tornado stabbed downward from the sky like a twisting dagger. It struck the ground to their right with a cracking explosion. All fighters within ten feet of the swirling inky mass were sucked into it, some clawing at the ground to forestall the inevitable. Weapons flew into the void. The battle ceased as fighters from both sides scrambled away from the lurching column of death.

"Let's move!" Jackson yelled above the din as the rushing wind sucked them toward the void. He reached for her hand, but she was suddenly airborne, launched as though yanked by a rope. She screamed as she tumbled through the air.

Jackson ran with the wind, flying headlong after her, his feet skimming the ground.

The roaring noise of the vortex shifted, like the sound of a frozen lake cracking. Beyond Sy, the top of the black tornado turned ice blue. The blue shot down its length, thrusting out sharp protrusions like jagged icicles from a massive ice column. Still airborne, Sy slammed into the icy spears along with a shower of fighters and weapons. The weapons clanged to the ground, but the fighters were impaled. Jackson skid to the ground just below her feet.

"Sy!"

Her black hair hung across her face and her body sagged, suspended on the spikes. Her skin color shifted, the gray brightening to pink.

The sky roiled above them still, and other black fingers slithered away from the horrid rips, clawing downward. The remaining Vampire and

Goblin fighters stood, preparing to re-engage.

He climbed up the frigid spikes until he was level with Sy. He grabbed her collar and pulled as hard as he could, bracing his feet against the frozen column itself. Her body initially resisted, only shifting slightly before popping out with such force that he was thrown backwards ten feet, crashing to the ground on his back with her on top of him. By the time he hoisted her up, the fighting around him had resumed in full force.

He carried her two steps toward the church before a force like an explosion shockwave struck him. He saw the wave pass his face as it knocked him to the ground, dazing him.

Still stunned, he lifted his head up as he lay alongside Sy, surveying his surroundings from a tilted perspective. The entire field of battle was down except for the ice column and one man, Abner. He held his hands high over his head. Abner shouted something, but Jackson couldn't make out his words over the roar of the sky. Abruptly the din ceased, leaving the complex eerily silent. The rips had closed in the sky, though the copper color remained.

"See?" Abner yelled. "Like I said. Have I said it?" He looked down at a man on a knee beside him. Victor. "You see that?" he said to Victor. "Bam. I still got my pop." Victor said something. "No, I know. I just thought it was pretty cool. Like dominoes they went down. Bam!" He looked at the stunned fighters from both races. "Listen to me! You are tearing the world apart! We are one with the earth, one with the sky, one with... something else but that's not important. What's important is that we stop fighting. You see how the storm stopped when we stopped fighting? As long as our people are at peace, the ..."

A low guttural growl started at one point in the sky.

"... world will be at peace."

Jackson got to a knee. Talbot stood next to him. He had a giant welt on the side of his head from the cannon ball.

"You're the one," Talbot said. "You can stop all this."

Multiple points in the clouds now growled.

Abner continued speaking. "So if we can just all get along..."

"I can stop this?" Jackson asked Talbot.

Talbot nodded. "That Abner is a kook. He was crazy back before he got senile. Now he's got it double. Only you can put the world in order. You are the Chosen One."

Jackson nodded. *I am the Chosen One.* He concentrated and held his open hands out toward the sky. He could feel the energy of this place, the spirits of the Vampires and Goblins, the electricity and raw power of the clouds, the solidity and eternality of the earth beneath his feet. Intertwined, alive. He sought their secret, seeking a way to harness this great power, a way to heal the world.

Abner looked to the sky as he spoke. "... then the natural order ..."

Black dots filled the churning sky.

Jackson had the universe in his hands.

"... will be restored ..." Abner's voice drifted away. The rips started, not just in one place, but across the entire sky. The guttural growl intensified, echoing and harmonizing. "Okay, so maybe not. Let's get the hell outta here!"

The universe gave Jackson the finger.

"I guess I'm not your man!" Jackson yelled to Talbot as he hoisted Sy onto his shoulder and ran.

Black writhing tendrils burst from the gaping rips in the sky, heaving the ground as they crashed around him. He wasn't going to make it.

CHAPTER 82: FADING

Almost there.

As Jackson reached the doorway to the church, a single thunderous detonation flattened all other sound on the deafening battlefield. He tried to throw Sy to the ground so he could cover her, but he didn't make it. Searing bolts of pain tore through his back, and a shockwave hurled him and Sy into the church to slide across the stone floor.

His ears rang as he lay near her. She would heal quickly – not quite as fast as the Vampires, but she would likely be mostly recovered by the morning. He didn't know why he knew that. His own body howled in agony. He almost couldn't bring himself to look at his wounds, afraid of what he might find.

On his side, he twisted his head around as far as he could, searching for the source of the pain. He regretted it. He was a pincushion, a porcupine with inverted quills of ice, the dull thick ends out and the pointy bits in — way in. Consciousness drifted, held with fingertips. Those spikes had to come out. His head sank to the floor.

Sy's eyes fluttered open, and she gazed at him as they both lay with their cheeks on the cool stone floor. For a moment, the rest of the world faded; he was alone in her eyes.

Then fear snapped into her face, and she propped herself up, staring at him in alarm. He wondered vaguely why she looked so worried.

Abner ran to her as Victor kneeled by Jackson.

Hey, Dad. I'm just gonna rest my eyes a sec...

"This is gonna hurt, Son," Victor said, reaching behind Jackson.

Wait. Are you about to yank...?

A wet splashing sound drowned out by a shriek that filled his head. Incredible pain, unfathomable. The world wavered, fading. Darkness surged in.

Hold on. Hold....

With torturous slowness, the darkness slinked away, though the pain remained pegged at near max. He opened his mouth to speak, but the words were pinned in his chest beneath the spikes.

As Victor reached for another spike, something struck him with a clank and knocked him to the floor. Abner too was down. A flurry of movement. Someone grabbed Jackson. Pain exploded. Darkness returned.

CHAPTER 83: AS ONE

Agony engulfed him.

Jackson opened his eyes and tried to make sense of his surroundings. He sat bound and propped against an inside wall of the Vampire church. Ice spears lay at his feet, meltwater mixing with the blood. He was thankful that he'd been out for that part. Through the open door across from him, he heard more fighting outside and wondered how long he'd been out. Several Vampires were stationed at the entryway, weapons at the ready. Victor, Sy, and Abner sat gagged and bound against a rack of equipment off to his right, watching him.

Tazia kneeled next to him. "You'll heal now, but that was quite a shot, huh?"

He looked into his mother's eyes, and he saw flint, both harder and older than the woman of his visions. *Mom.* The word tasted like metal in his mouth, like blood.

With great effort, he asked, "Why?"

"Such a short question with such a long answer." She stood and paced before him and then flicked her eyes to the open doorway where the battle raged despite the storm. "I'll make it quick. You are half Piri and half Jone-Zen. I'm sure you know that already. But you were in my body; I carried you. You are more Piri than barbarian. You belong with us."

Jackson's dad yelled out something beneath his gag.

"I'm sure that you must be very disappointed about how your own father lied to you for all these years, and I imagine that you have quite a bit of shame at your impure status, but you can make all that right." She dropped to a knee, blocking his view of the others. "I saw you emerging. We found you and your dad years ago, and I watched and waited. I knew that if you worked with the Jone-Zen, your emergence would quicken. You've probably noticed that the Hive presence strengthens when you're close to the others, right? Well I knew those bastards were up to something, and I didn't have time to wait for you to emerge on your own, so I sent you in. If we sent a regular spy in there, they'd spot him right away." She stopped pacing and stared at him. "You, though, you're perfect. You are a Piri who can jack into the Jone-Zen hive." She resumed her pacing and gestured with her arms. "You can see both hives. I know, because I've felt you in the Piri hive. You can tell me everything that the Jone-Zen are up to or have ever done. You have their entire history at your fingertips. You can open up their whole race to me, and we can finally rid ourselves of this scourge. You do this, and you'll never have to worry about anything. You'll never have to work again." Again she turned to him. "Just think, no jobs, no responsibility. You're finished. And you'll be a hero to your people. You are a Piri. What do you think?"

Her black eyes bored into his, and he saw both strength and familiarity there. He could see why men would follow her, why his dad would fall for her. His mind flashed an image of how his life could be.

"You know," he said, his voice a hoarse whisper, "Dad was right. You really are a bitch."

Her face hardened as she slapped him. Her words passed through long, pointed teeth. "Kill the girl!"

"Wait!" Jackson yelled. "I'll do it. I'll plug you in. I'll open up the Jone-Zen hive."

All three of the bound Goblins yelled behind their gags. Sy tried to get to her feet and was kicked back to the ground by a thin Vampire with greasy black hair.

Jackson closed his eyes. He felt the two hive streams in his mind, shut away as though in drawers. They opened. He pushed this moment onto them, what was happening in this very church. He felt minds on both hives awaken, connecting. The channels were open.

Vampires at the doorway yelled out. Goblins were attacking, forcing their way in. They would probably rather see him dead than allow him to do as Tazia asked.

He kept his eyes closed. He felt Tazia's presence close to him, so powerful. He could plug her into the Goblin hive with barely an effort.

"Do it!" she yelled. The battle noise advanced into the church. There wasn't much time.

He knew what he had to do. He didn't know if it was right, but it was the only option he could think of. He would have preferred to flip into the air and kick everyone's asses with his feet while his hands were tied behind his back, but he doubted he could even stand at this point.

He crossed the streams. Visa and versa. Images and emotions flowed between the hives, like the rush of water out of Chester's waterbed that time when Jackson had tried knife juggling. He held the connection open as the sensations poured across, mixing and churning, accelerating. He knew he could no longer stop them even if he tried.

The hives merged; two races had become one. He felt a surge of confusion from both sides as the mental reverberations spread.

He opened his eyes. Silence. Goblins and Vampires stared at one another, shocked.

"Kill them all!" screeched Tazia.

"Wait," the thin Vampire by his dad said, pointing down at Sy. "I think she might be related to my cousin."

"Which one of you put the image of Kappa Tau on your hive?" a female Goblin said near the door.

Three Vampires held up their weapons.

"Did any of you know," the Goblin continued, "this dude named –"

"Wait!" a rotund young Goblin closer to Jackson yelled. "You mean this war is all because some stupid woman left Grotto?"

"I heard she didn't even like Grotto," an older Vampire said. "She said he was a creep. She ended up dumping Chamberlain too."

Jackson could see Chamberlain the Vampire in his head, and he could see the woman too, quite beautiful, but trouble.

"Why didn't you tell us you hated that name 'Goblin' so much?" a different Vampire asked. Several Vampires nodded.

Multiple Goblins answered at once, with one saying, "We did! Wait, didn't we?"

Buck-Bill – or rather Ferdinand – yelled out, "Gargoyles! You could have called us gargoyles. That's way better than Goblins."

"That was just Michael," a different elderly Vampire said, his body armor hanging off his haggard frame. "He made up nicknames for everyone. It was a joke. I mean, he called me Balloon Ball." He looked around the silent room. "Don't ask."

One of the Goblins laughed, then another. A Vampire next to the elderly one laughed too, punching him on the shoulder. Soon the entire church echoed with laughter.

"Kill them!" Tazia screamed.

Silence fell, but no one moved.

"I liked you better dead," Jackson said.

The laughter returned.

"Fools! All of you!" Tazia ran toward the side door. Goblins and Vampires alike cleared a path for her, and she charged out into the raging storm.

Two seconds later, blinding light flashed from the doorways and windows as a massive "Hawumph!" noise shook the church. Then silence. Sunlight from a clear blue sky streamed in through the stained-glass windows.

The Vampires and Goblins looked at one another. Some sheathed their weapons, while others sat on the floor.

"Can you untie us now?" Jackson asked.

Mandy the Blue Loon removed his bonds while the slick Vampire and a stocky black Vampire untied the others. He had fought them earlier, but that was a memory of strangers. These people he now *knew*.

"Looks like we have some talking to do," Buck-Bill said as he walked over to help the Vampires with untying the others. He would never be "Ferdinand" to Jackson — that was just wrong.

Jackson stood and stretched his legs. He patted his chest. His blood-soaked shirt was riddled with holes and tears, but most of the pain was gone.

"Pretty cool, huh?" the black Vampire said, walking over to check on him. Jackson reached out his hand, and the Vampire shook it, his hand engulfing Jackson's like a bun around a hot dog. Jackson now knew his name was Bronson.

"What I miss?" boomed a voice in the back of the church. The mountainous Goblin that Jackson had felled with the maces staggered into the room from the stairway to the caverns. He dragged his polearms behind him. He looked up, his eyes distant. "Wait, I see Vampires! Is Brutus a Vampire now?"

Noise burst from the doors at the front of the church, behind the racks of equipment. Pounding boots approached.

Jackson felt their hostility.

"Blockers!" he yelled. "Shields up! We fight!" He leapt to his feet, the blood rage reviving him.

The air filled with the hum of deflection fields as the bubbles shot outward, the different color shields overlapping. The sound of automatic weapon fire echoed off the stone walls and stained-glass windows from an approaching assault force.

Tovacs.

Vampires and Goblins shrieked and threw themselves onto the attackers. As one.

CHAPTER 84: HANGIN' WITH GRANDMA

"Sunspots," Jackson said as he sat with his arm around Sy on her couch. "That's what they said today on the news about the storm the other day. Sunspot activity interacting with high levels of magnetic particulate matter in the upper atmosphere, along with ash from the volcanic eruptions in the Pacific."

"That's bull," Victor said from the loveseat, pieces of Sy's Parmesan Tempura fried chicken flying out of his mouth as he spoke and gestured with a thighbone. "It was those damn scientists again."

"I don't know what's better," Jackson said. "The storms being over or the fact that we don't have to go into the Zone again."

"I still think the storms ended because we stopped fighting," Abner said. He looked around, but no one even nodded. "Anyway, there's nothing wrong with the Tovac Zone, especially now that we've thinned out their security a bit." Leaning against the mantle, he took a bite of meat off of a chicken leg, then shook the bone toward the femur on the sword rack. "No offense."

Sy said, "Mr. Krol, what do you think happened to Anastazia?"

Victor leaned forward, threw the remains of his chicken thigh onto a pile of bones on his plate, and wiped his greasy hand on his shirt. "I think the sky tried to swallow her and the damn thing choked."

"She's gone," Jackson said. He couldn't feel her any more at all. He would know if she were still around. Maybe the sky had actually taken her as it had so many others.

"Hey," Chester said, wedged on the couch between Sy and Mandy. "Mandy and I have to go in a minute. I promised her I'd show her how to play School Rampage. I just hope it's not too violent for her."

Everyone else burst out laughing.

"What?" he asked. "What's so funny?"

ABOUT THE AUTHOR

Matt Usey likes to write. He also likes to eat, but we're not here to talk about that. His wife and two daughters grew tired of him laughing at his own jokes and banished him to the study where, in desperation, he wrote a few novels, giggling as he typed.